MIDNIGHT MADNESS

"You are a poor chaperone." Lord Wentworth's finger tilted her chin toward him. "For her and for you."

"For me? I have no need of a chaperone."

His arm slipped around Emily's waist. "For the first time, you are mistaken."

Before she could reply, he tightened his arm around her. His fingers curled around her nape, sending tendrils of luscious warmth along her. Gently, he tipped her face closer. The brush of his lips against hers was scintillating, but he drew away with only that brief touch.

This was not the type of kiss she had thought would satisfy a man who had earned the name Demon. He seemed the kind of man who wanted so much more.

"You need not fear for your reputation. After all, you have done nothing which would tarnish it."

"I let you kiss me."

"Kiss you?" He laughed as he grasped her elbows again and drew her back to him. "That was no more than a chaste salute."

His mouth, this time, was anything but gentle as it claimed hers. She wanted this kiss from the man. It might be madness, but she had been practical for too long.

Also by Jo Ann Ferguson from Zebra Books

RHYME AND REASON

Jo Ann Ferguson

Zebra Books
Kensington Publishing Corp.

http://www.zebrabooks.com

ZEBRA BOOKS are published by

Kensington Publishing Corp.
850 Third Avenue
New York, NY 10022

First Printing: February, 1998
10 9 8 7 6 5 4 3 2 1

Printed in the United States of America

For Edie and Andy Anderson,
who are the definition of Southern hospitality—
Thanks for the warm welcome to your mountain

Chapter One

Snoring was unquestionably not her sister Miriam's finest trait, but Emily Talcott ignored the low rumble as she paced from the wide door to the window at the front of the cozy sitting room. She did not push aside the gold drapes. Too often during the long night, she had peered out of the window overlooking the shadowed heart of Hanover Square. The hour now was so far toward dawn that not a carriage would be moving on the street. 'Twas too late for most revelers to be about and too early for the peddlers.

She should be accustomed to waiting. And waiting. And waiting. Yet, she could not sit still. She kept walking back and forth past her slumbering sister in the white satin wing chair. Her ears strained for the sound of the clatter of wheels upon the cobbles as a hired cab slowed in front of the house. All she heard were her sister's snores, for the night was undisturbed. Going back to the chair in the middle of the dimly lit room, she pulled a coverlet over Miriam, whose hair was the same rich gold as the carpet and the striped silk on the walls.

Dear Miriam! Her sister should have been abed hours before, but she had not been able to sleep as she relished retelling all that she had experienced this evening. Even though Emily had been at her side through most of the gathering, Miriam liked to relive every conversation and bit of scan-mag she had heard among the guests.

As a bell from the mantel clock chimed four times, its sound melancholy in the depths of the night, Emily sighed again. She had been an air-dreamer to hope Papa would be home before they returned from Miss Prine's coming-out. The ball had been lovely, and Miriam had stood up with three different men who had not concealed their interest in calling during the at home the Talcotts held weekly.

Emily pulled the lacy collar of her mauve dressing gown more tightly to her chin as she continued her anxious journey from the window to the door opening onto the foyer and back. She should be delighting in what had happened this evening. The party had been an undeniable success for Miriam. Two of the men, who had been intrigued with Miriam, were not the best choice, in Emily's opinion, for her younger sister, but Lord Reiss came from an excellent family. Although his meandering conversation always dulled Emily's mind with ennui, she thought Miriam had enjoyed his attentions.

Miriam's first Season was sure to end with a successful marriage. Her sister's golden curls—which contrasted with Emily's smoky tresses—as well as her merry blue eyes and warm smile made her the center of attention at any party, but Miriam had shown no particular interest in any of the suitors last night.

With a sigh, Emily knew she could not explain to either Miriam or Papa why she was so eager to see her sister wed. Neither of them suspected the fragile state of their household, for she had taken great pains to keep the truth hidden. Only Kilmartin might know about their precarious finances, because Emily had chanced upon her abigail perusing the accounting books that usually were locked in the drawer of Emily's writing desk. Emily was not worried, though. Kilmartin had been with the family for enough years to keep her tongue in her head. Miriam had not seemed to notice Kilmartin's tongue clicking in dread whenever Miriam spoke of the need for a new gown. Papa never noticed anything beyond his cards.

Cards! Dash the soul who had invented the devil's books! If it were not for such sport, the family would not be in such trouble.

The amount of money Emily had set aside for her sister's nuptials was being depleted by Papa's gambling, and she was uncertain when she would be able to replenish it. She had been able to get nothing definite from Mr. Homsby the last time she had visited his bookshop. Nothing but complaints that his new patron wanted to review the business and its accounts before embarking on any new projects. That was understandable, but it left Emily—and her family—in shaky circumstances.

Forcing herself to sit, she stared at the door. Worrying about the bookseller did no good. Mr. Homsby had promised to send her a message as soon as he had answers for her. In spite of his penurious ways, she doubted if he would forget his vow to her.

Where was Papa? So many evenings he had stayed out late, but seldom this late. She tried to shake from her head the images of pickpockets and land-pirates setting upon her father. Going to the window, she looked out.

You are letting your rambunctious imagination control you. One of these days, it will betray you.

How often Papa had repeated those words to her! And he was right. She wished she could be more like her prosaic father and her sister. Neither of them imagined anything more interesting than the entertainments available during the Season. Miriam delighted in every conversation, even if the topic was the same one she had heard discussed over and over.

Emily was too easily bored by the same music, people and wine. Instead of waiting for some young man to ask her to stand up with him, she found herself captured by the sights and sounds and people she passed each day and . . . imagining . . .

How the faint moonlight sparkling in the center of the square looked like milk that had been splattered across the cobbles and how . . .

Her thoughts were interrupted by the welcome sound of carriage wheels. Brazenly, she pulled the drapes farther aside. She smiled when she saw a closed carriage slowing to a stop in front of the door.

At last! Emily breathed a sigh of relief, then took another deep breath to calm the exasperation boiling within her. Dash it! If only Papa thought of something other than the cards in front of him. He could have sent word to Hanover Square that he would be late; then she would not have worried. Or not as much.

Pausing only long enough to discover if Miriam was awake, and seeing she was not, although she had shifted and no longer snored, Emily tiptoed out into the hallway. She hurried to the stairs and rushed down to the foyer which was the glory of the house. The white marble floor was cool through her thin slippers. Overhead, a crystal chandelier sprayed light onto the painted friezes climbing the simple stairs of darkest mahogany.

Johnson nodded to her as he reached for the door. She stood by the base of the stairs and watched the short, round butler lift the latch. Wishing her father had hired a more mature man for this important job, Emily could hear Mrs. Hazlet, the housekeeper, complaining about the young man's inability to handle his important position. Emily had listened without comment, although she shared the housekeeper's concerns about Johnson's competence.

The dank smell of dew flooded the entry when the door opened. Johnson held up a lamp to light the steps.

Emily said, "Papa, I was beginning to—" Her hands

clutched the throat of her dressing gown when she realized her father was not alone.

Beside Charles Talcott stood an imposing man. In fact, the tall man was supporting him. He helped her father lift his foot up over the top step, then guided him into the circle of light. The stranger's hair was a gleaming black beneath his stylish beaver. Although her father's cravat was loosened and his black evening coat falling haphazardly from one shoulder, the other man looked as if he had stepped from a fashion-plate. His black breeches and gold waistcoat were unblemished, and not a hint of dust detracted from the perfection of his navy coat. The buckles on his shoes flashed silver as he entered the foyer, her father's arm draped over his shoulder.

Emily put out her hands as her father swayed, but faltered when the stranger regarded her with a cold, gray stare. Heat climbed her cheeks when that gaze roamed along her *déshabille*. Knowing she looked no better than a demi-rep with her black hair streaming down her wrapper, she raised her chin. This was her home. She had expected no one other than Papa.

"I trust," said the stranger in a warm tenor voice that did not match his austere expression, "Mr. Talcott's man can be called with all due haste to assist him to bed."

Emily signaled to the butler. Johnson nodded and stepped back, but not before she saw his covert smile. She tried to disregard his impertinent behavior—Why did he always have to forget his place when her father was late?—as he hurried to call for Bollings, Papa's valet.

"Thank you for escorting my father home, sir," she said quietly to the stranger.

The tall man had the decency to hide his astonishment at her cool words, save for a widening of his eyes. "I had doubts he could find his own way here."

"Would have been fine. Told you that." Papa mumbled something, then swayed.

The stranger said, "He is quite glorious tonight."

Emily could not help smiling at his droll comment. Papa seldom got foxed, but, when he did, he lost his head completely in the attempt to give the bottle a black eye and himself a headache the next day.

She stepped aside as Bollings rushed down the stairs and slipped his shoulder under Papa's other arm.

The tall man eased away, tugging on his gray gloves. "There are quite a few steps ahead of you. Do you want some help?"

"I can manage," the pudgy valet said through clenched teeth as he turned Papa toward the staircase.

"Do help him, Johnson," Emily urged. "Those steps are steep."

The butler nodded, but she saw his indignation at being assigned what, to his mind, was such a demeaning task. Vowing to speak to him later when only his ears would hear her exasperation, she looked back at the man by the door.

"Thank you again, sir, for your kindness."

"You are welcome." The tall man smiled and turned toward the door. When he closed it with himself still within the foyer, she fought to hide her amazement that he would act as if she had invited him to run tame through her father's home when he was a stranger.

But he is no stranger to Papa, she reminded herself. That thought offered little solace when her father, who was as drunk as a piper, was on his way to the land of nod, and she was standing in the foyer with a handsome stranger in the hour before dawn.

Her uneasiness must have been visible because the man said, "I trust I may wait until Mr. Talcott's man returns."

"Of course," she answered, her voice rather faint. She recognized his satisfied tone. It could mean but one thing. *Oh, Papa! How could you gamble all night when the butcher sent a note demanding payment today?* She could not blame this tall man. If Papa had lost heavily to him at the card table, he had every right to expect to collect his winnings.

"Is there somewhere I may wait?" Again he smiled, but she saw little warmth in his expression. "I do not want to keep you from your own sleep, Miss Talcott."

She dampened her lips, then said, "Forgive me, sir. Do come upstairs." Pausing as she put her foot on the first riser, she added, "I must ask you to be quiet, for my sister is asleep in the sitting room."

"You Talcotts choose the oddest places to fall asleep. Your father in the middle of my foyer, your sister in a sitting room. Do you, perchance, prefer a more traditional mode and slumber in a bed?"

For once glad her cheeks did not betray her with a blush as Miriam's porcelain skin often did, Emily said, "We may talk more comfortably in the parlor."

"Upon another subject, I collect."

"Quite rightly."

His chuckle followed her up the stairs, spurring her feet to a more rapid pace. The sound was rich and much warmer than his smile, but she had not stayed up through the night to provide fodder for this man's peculiar sense of humor. Hearing no footfalls behind her, she wondered if he had decided not to follow her.

She turned, and her nose nearly struck his. Knowing her astonishment was mirrored in his silver-gray eyes, she edged back when a slow smile tilted his lips. Unlike his other smiles, this one possessed an obvious warmth which reminded her how unsuitably dressed she was to receive callers, even a most unexpected one.

"Is something amiss, Miss Talcott?" he asked.

"No."

"Then is there a reason why you have stopped so suddenly I almost trod on the hem of your wrapper?"

His hand slid up the bannister, brushing hers. A shock, as abrupt and resonating as a clap of thunder, burst through her. She pulled her hand away and spun to hurry up the stairs, hoping that was not a muffled laugh she heard behind her.

The long lace at the wrists of her dressing gown tickled her palm as she motioned toward the parlor across the hall from where her sister slumbered, unaware of the contretemps in the foyer. She drew the doors of the sitting room closed and leaned against them as she said, "Please make yourself comfortable in the parlor, sir. I believe Johnson left some brandy on the sideboard."

"You are not joining me?"

"I thought to check with Papa's valet."

"Of course, although the man seemed quite capable of handling the situation. I trust his competence does not come from regular practice."

Emily frowned. "Sir, Papa is not himself tonight."

"This morning," he corrected, then smiled and gestured for her to lead the way into the parlor.

She was about to refuse, then silently she admonished herself. He had every right to expect she would act as his hostess. With his steady gaze slicing into her back, she heard no sound but her wrapper's train swishing on the floor and the light sound of his shoes. She hushed the uneasy suspicion that she was prey being stalked by a skilled hunter.

The light-green parlor would be bright in the morning sunshine, but now was lackluster with the dim light from the small lamp set on a table near the marble hearth. She crossed the dark carpet to the cherry sideboard. Picking up the bottle of brandy set there, she asked, "Would you like a glass, sir?"

"If you would join me."

"I find it a bit late for brandy."

"Or a bit early."

Emily wished he would stop funning her, for she did not feel the least like laughing. Saying nothing, she put the bottle back on the sideboard and sat on a settee which was upholstered in pale green muslin. As if he were a frequent guest, the man made himself comfortable on the settee facing her.

Or tried to make himself comfortable, she noted with a stray hint of amusement. The delicate piece of furniture did not welcome his height. He finally stretched his legs beneath the low table set between them. When he regarded her with an abrupt frown, she lost any inclination to smile.

"Since you have not corrected me when I have addressed you," he said into the silence, "I would collect you are Miss Talcott."

"Emily Talcott." Folding her hands in her lap, she tried to keep her voice as even as his. "Did you meet Papa at the card table this evening?"

"We have played before, but no session has gone this long."

"I am certain Papa would have been eager to settle his debts with you if he were more himself," she answered, pleased she could speak past the thickness in her throat. *How much had Papa lost tonight? She hoped the total would be no more than a few guineas.* If it were more— There was no more. "Under these unfortunate circumstances, I pray you do not consider it untoward of me to handle the settlement of his obligations in his stead."

"You need not concern yourself about such matters, Miss Talcott."

"But I do." She wished he would be less polite. Surely it had been simpler to deal with the men who snarled their demands for their winnings with no hint of courtesy. Raising her chin so she could meet his eyes that were above hers even when they sat, she said, "We are a proud family, and our pride comes from always paying our debts, Mr.—?"

He smiled again, and his face was transformed from its stern façade. Although she had seen it on the stairs, his metamorphosis startled her anew, for she saw glints of mirth in his eyes that had been steel cold. "Forgive me, Miss Talcott, for being such a confirmed chucklehead that I failed to introduce myself. May I blame it on the hour? Allow me to redeem my tarnished honor." He stood and, lifting her hand, bowed smoothly over her fingers. "I am Damon Wentworth."

"Wentworth?" She almost choked on the name, but restrained herself enough to ask, "The viscount?"

"One and the same."

Emily was sure her heart had plummeted into her slippers. What a perfect widgeon she was! She should have guessed Papa was fated to meet this rogue sooner or later, for Lord Wentworth's reputation was well known throughout the Polite World. Even she, who disdained the whisper of gossip, could not be unaware of the viscount's hunt for adversaries who were as skilled at cards as he and who had pockets plump enough to keep the stakes high.

Charles Talcott was neither.

"Dare I believe we have met before, Miss Talcott?" he continued when she remained silent. He gave her a warm smile, a smile which she might have deemed charming under other circumstances.

"No, my lord," she managed to say.

"For that, I'm glad."

"Glad?"

He sat again and folded his arms on one knee. "I would consider myself quite the gawney for failing to remember making the acquaintance of such a lovely lady."

Emily ignored his compliment and the peculiar mixture of pleasure and disquiet it sent reeling as wildly as Papa's drunken steps through her. Locking her fingers together in her lap, she said, "My lord, I know you must have much to do elsewhere. I have no wish to delay you, so if you will tell me the amount of my father's losses to you, I shall tend the matter posthaste."

"His debts to me?" He laughed and relaxed back against the settee. "Now I understand why you are wearing such a dreary face. Do not fret, Miss Talcott. There is no need for you to worry about your father's debts, for he often proved the victor at our table."

"Papa won the night?"

"Lady Luck is, at best, a fickle companion and chose this evening to make your father her favorite. You appear astonished, Miss Talcott."

Not wanting to own that she was exactly that, for she could not imagine her father trouncing this glib lord at the board of green cloth, she demurred, "I fear my thoughts are quite unsteady with fatigue."

"I would think so at this hour. You prove your devotion to your father by waiting up for him as if he were a young sprig."

She was able to smile more easily. "My sister and I arrived home not long ago."

"From Miss Prine's coming-out?"

"Yes, but how—?"

He smiled, his eyes crinkling to accent his deep tan. She wondered how he spent much time in the sun if he played cards all night every night. "It was the most heralded event of the evening, if I am to believe her brother who joined us at the table tonight. You must be exhausted from the dancing and conversation."

"Mostly from playing the watch-dog. I find launching my sister on the Season more tiring than I had anticipated."

"*You* are launching your sister?" His gaze swept along her again, and she knew she had been want-witted not to think before she spoke. She fought the urge to chide him for being presumptuous. Whispered rumor warned her words would be wasted on this man who set mamas to quivering with trepidation any time he looked at their daughters. "I must be mistaken. I thought you said you were *Miss* Talcott."

"I am."

"Then, if I may be so bold, may I say you are doing the young misses enjoying the Season a great service by not competing with them for the Tom-a-doodles who wish to buckle themselves to a bride?" He folded his arms across the front of his pristine waistcoat and smiled.

"You are as bold as brass, my lord, to speak of such things on our short acquaintance."

"I prefer to be honest, and I speak of nothing but what any man with a bit of life in him would notice on a single glance."

She started to reply, but turned as approaching footfalls slowed by the door.

Bollings's coat always strained across his stomach. Thick, brown hair belied his many years of service to Charles Talcott, but his wrinkled face was lengthened by fatigue and distress. "Mr. Talcott is asleep, Miss Emily," he said with a wary glance at the viscount.

"Thank you, Bollings." When the valet hesitated, she added, "Please let me know when Mr. Talcott wakes on the morrow."

He nodded, then backed out of the room. He glanced once more into the room before he hurried along the hall. Emily ignored the small voice that urged her to call him back. Instead, she faced the viscount who was setting himself on his feet.

"My lord," she said with the best smile she could affix on her lips, a sorry one she was sure, for every thought was weighed with fatigue, "I thank you again for being sure that my father reached his home and his bed without incident." Rising, she added, "My family is indebted to you for your kindness."

"The debt, as I must remind you, Miss Talcott, remains mine." He started to reach beneath his coat, but halted with a laugh. "I find it impossible to remit your father's winning to you." Clasping his hands behind him, in a motion that tugged at the broad shoulders of his coat, he smiled with the glint of mischief returning to his eyes. "When you are dressed so enticingly in such a flattering shade of silk, Miss Talcott, my mind envisions other scenes in which a man might be placing gold upon a woman's palm."

Emily gasped as his indecorous words created a similar

scene in her fertile imagination. Although she had no idea what the inside of a seraglio might look like, she shuddered. How horrifying to think she resembled a natural while she was speaking with a man who had gained a reputation for being as attentive to the ladies, both of quality and not, as he was to cards! Heat seared her cheeks again at that unseemly thought.

Again happy she did not flush, she answered, "I cannot speak to what you might picture in your mind, my lord."

"No?" He brushed a strand of her hair back from her face. "I had thought you a woman of much more imagination, Miss Talcott."

"Why?"

"You did not slap my face for my impertinent words, so I guessed you worldly enough to speak with honesty."

"If I were worldly enough to envision what you suggested—"

He chuckled. "Which you clearly are, if I am a judge of the righteous indignation in your voice. I did not mean to bring you to cuffs with a demure hit, Miss Taloctt. My words were meant as a compliment." He raised his hands in a pose of surrender when she opened her mouth to retort. "Forgive me, Miss Talcott. When I asked to speak to you here, I meant only to compliment you for being such a devoted daughter and to reassure you that your father has suffered nothing more than too long an acquaintance with a bottle of brandy."

"Thank you," she said, wondering why embarrassment taunted her as if she were the one who had forgotten her manners. "If it discomfits you, my lord, you need have no concerns about me collecting your debts to my father. I shall leave that matter to you and him."

"Wise of you."

"If you are assured that my father is well ..." Emily knew she was being rude, but dawn would be arriving before she could seek her bed.

The viscount nodded, his dark hair dropping across his

forehead. He tossed it aside with an ease that must come from habit. "I am assured of that, and you may assure Mr. Talcott that the accounts between us will be settled to his satisfaction." When he took her hand and bowed over it, his eyes rose to meet hers.

She saw amusement in their gray depths, and she gasped when he held her gaze as he pressed his lips to the back of her hand. That breath became a soft sigh when an explosion of delight careened through her again. His finger stroked her palm, sending tingles along her skin. He drew her a half-step closer and bent toward her hand again. Instead of kissing her hand, he looked up at her and winked.

Shocked, she pulled her hand away. She was completely dicked in the nob to let him treat her like one of his convenients. Raising her chin in her most imperious pose, she said, "I bid you a good evening, my lord."

He set his hat back on his head and, smiling, tipped it in her direction. "And I bid you good morning, Miss Talcott."

Emily had no chance to answer as he strode from the room. She decided that was a good thing, for she had bumbled everything else she had said in his hearing.

Chapter Two

Damon Wentworth whistled a light tune as he climbed into his carriage. His coachee regarded him with bafflement, but Damon did not ease the man's curiosity at his good spirits at this late hour. Talking about Miss Emily Talcott to his servants would be beneath reproach—even for him.

Chuckling, he drew the door closed and slapped the roof. As the carriage was driven around the square and toward his own home on Grosvenor Square, he leaned back and smiled. The night had not been a waste of time, after all. He had been afraid it would be when he saw how Charles Talcott played and how often the man tilted the bottle to his glass.

He closed his eyes, bringing forth the image of Miss Emily Talcott with ease. He had honed the skill of noting the details others might miss, for it served him well when he tried to gauge what others held in their hands as they sat at the board of green cloth. Just now, he had noticed how, while they sat in the parlor, Miss Talcott's hands had been clasped so tightly her knuckles were white with anxiety. She clearly had expected that her father had lost heavily to him, and that fact disturbed her. The woman was more insightful than most he had met. At the same time, she was an enticing combination of sophisticated ennui and girlish naïveté.

A smile tipped his lips as he recalled how her black hair had been as silken as her skin and how her blue eyes had sparked with sharp emotion when he had been bold enough to discover that. High cheekbones and an assertive chin would not label her pretty in some minds, but she had a face that suggested there was more to her than the simpering misses who tried to gain his attention when their chaperones were busy elsewhere.

He chuckled again. Miss Emily Talcott had allowed neither his sullied reputation nor his request to speak to her alone in her parlor to unsettle her. She had not been consumed by a fit of giggles when he caught her gaze. All in all, she was a rare woman of uncommon composure.

The carriage stopped, and he opened the door. The sunrise glittered off the stones on the front of his townhouse and the windows marching in unvarying precision across its front. At the door, his butler stood, his mouth working as he struggled not to yawn.

Damon did not try to hide his smile. Hillis had served in this household since both he and Damon were young, so Damon knew by the butler's squared shoulders that Hillis was distressed about something. Not the late hour of Damon's homecoming, surely for there had been many mornings that had found him at his club still enjoying the company of his fellows and the cards in front of them.

Something struck his foot as he stepped out of the carriage. With a quick motion, he caught the article before it could fall onto the street. A hat! He tilted it, recognizing the silver band above its conservative brim. Talcott's hat. The man had been so foxed, he had not noticed it was not on his head.

Climbing the steps to his front door, Damon said, "Good

morning, Hillis. You look as if your night was as sleepless as mine."

"Cut short, my lord, by the arrival of a messenger." He held out a folded sheet of paper. "The lad said you were to read this the instant you arrived here."

Taking it, he handed Hillis his hat. " 'Twas good I decided not to stop in St. James's first."

"I would have sent it to you posthaste."

Again Damon struggled not to smile. Hillis was so blasted correct! Did the butler think Damon could not recall how they had caused mischief throughout this house and Wentworth Hall in their younger days? Now, looking at the butler's stern demeanor and graying hair, no one would believe Hillis had been the one to suggest they put a frog in the housekeeper's apron pocket or glue the pages of Damon's tutor's chapbook closed. The only one who made heads shake now was Damon Wentworth.

Reading the short note, he lost all temptation to smile. By the elevens, he had thought those he had hired were competent enough to handle such trivial details. He had hoped to leave London for a few days and see how the work was coming on Wentworth Hall. That would be impossible now.

"Tell Roche not to put the carriage away," he said, sighing. "I will need to deal with this immediately."

"Without breakfast?" Hillis's expression suggested only a barbarian would begin the day without a hearty meal to fortify him.

"If Mrs. Foy has some muffins cooked, please bring me one and a cup of coffee while I change into something suitable for reminding these witless chuckleheads why I pay them their wages."

"Yes, my lord." Hillis cleared his throat. "Your hat, my lord?"

"I gave you . . . Oh, this one!" He smiled. " 'Tis not mine. It belongs to Charles Talcott."

Hillis held out his hand. "I would be glad to have it

returned along with your request for your winnings, my lord."

"Winnings?" Shaking his head, he said, "Your faith in me is amazing, Hillis."

"In your skill with cards, my lord."

"I stand corrected." Chuckling, he gave the hat to his butler. As Hillis turned away, he added, "Wait!"

"My lord?"

Damon took Talcott's hat. "I have not decided when this should be returned to Talcott."

"My lord?" This time there was a hint of dismay in the butler's voice as well as bafflement.

"There is no need for this to be a completely intolerable day just for me, is there?"

"I am sorry. I don't understand."

Damon slapped him on the shoulder and laughed. "You will." He began to whistle again as he climbed the stairs to his private rooms.

As the clock in the hallway marked midday, Emily came into the breakfast-parlor to discover her sister perched on a chair and enjoying the sunshine as she read the morning paper. A serving lass was bringing fresh biscuits from the kitchen. With a smile, Emily took one of the steaming biscuits and lathered it with the strawberry jam waiting on the sideboard. She poured a cup of cocoa and carried both to the round maple table.

"Good afternoon, Miriam," she said.

She got a mumbled answer in return, which was what she had expected. Miriam intently searched every column of the newspaper for familiar names and never wished to be interrupted. With her golden hair washing down over the shoulders of her white wrapper, she looked as sweet as a cherub in a church window.

Smiling, Emily sifted through the stack of mail which Johnson had remembered to bring to the breakfast-parlor.

Mayhap the man was learning his job after nearly six months of fumbling through it. She scanned the mail, separating it into three stacks, one for her, one for Miriam, and one for Papa. As always, she slipped the ones she knew were demands for payment into her pile, although they were addressed to Charles Talcott.

"Miriam?"

"Mmmm?"

"You might wish to see these." She handed her sister the trio of what surely were invitations.

Miriam broke the seal on the top one. "Oh, look, Emily! Lady Stoughton is having a hurricane next week, and she would be delighted if I would attend." Her blue eyes glittered with excitement. "Of course, you must attend, too."

"Of course."

"We will go, won't we, Emily?"

"If you have accepted no other invitation for that evening."

Miriam gasped, "Oh, I couldn't have! I must go to Lady Stoughton's party."

"But why?" She set her cup of cocoa down, startled by her sister's vehemence.

"She is Mr. Simpkins's cousin."

"Graham Simpkins?"

She nodded, smiling hesitantly.

Emily's brow furrowed as she tried to recall when she had seen Miriam talking with Mr. Simpkins. He was a most nondescript man, neither tall nor short, neither broad nor thin. He had inherited his mother's black hair and his father's imposing nose. The family, although untitled, was known to be full of juice. Such a match would well provide for Miriam . . . and for Papa.

Leaning her chin on her hand, she sighed. As she glanced at the thick pile of letters still sitting in front of her, she hoped a betrothal would come before all money for Miriam's wedding was depleted to pay for the household expenses that once had come out of Papa's inheri-

tance. That, like most other money they had had, was long
spent, much of it because her father continued to increase
his gambling debts.

"Emily, is something wrong?"

Her sister's concern drew her out of her dismals.
Quickly, to hide her uneasy thoughts, Emily replied, "Of
course not. I was just noticing how rested you look after
your late evening."

"I woke early and took myself upstairs to sleep in a
decent bed." Miriam laughed her musical laugh. "Why
didn't you wake me when Papa came home?"

"It was late," she hedged. If her sister heard of their
unexpected caller, Miriam would pester her with a flurry
of questions Emily was too tired to answer. So few hours
had passed since Lord Wentworth's departure, and she
had found scanty slumber in that time. "You were sleeping
sweetly, and I did not have the heart to disturb you."

"You are so kind." She sampled the scrambled eggs
before adding, "I trust Papa's losses were less than a
disaster."

"What?" Emily was startled by the question, for her
sister seldom bothered herself with mundane details like
household accounts.

Miriam laughed again as she reached for the cream.
"You look quite pleased with yourself this morning."

"I do?" She had thought she would look nothing save
fatigued.

"Yes, and, mornings after Papa has lost at the card table,
you ordinarily wear a worried expression which draws your
lips as tight as an old tough's. Or could it be you are so
pleased with Mr. Colley's attentions that you can think of
little else?"

Chuckling, she shook her head. "You minx! I should
have guessed you would notice that less than charming
fellow dangling after me."

"And why not? You were one of the loveliest ladies

attending the party last night. Mr. Colley may not be the best mannered man, but his pockets are very plump."

"Miriam! Whatever is wrong with you this morning?"

She leaned forward, her gold curls falling onto the table, and whispered with an irrepressible grin, "Lord Reiss asked me to stand up with him twice last night."

"I saw that."

"And did you see that Mr. Simpkins saw us dancing, too?"

"That I did not see."

"You are not as observant as others."

"What others?"

Miriam held up the newspaper. "The ones who write for this."

Emily laughed and snatched the paper from her sister's hands. When she saw the article in the center of the page, her eyes widened. "So even the *Morning Post* noticed the baron's attention to you." She read aloud, " 'Miss Talcott was much the star of the evening. She . . . ' "

Miriam giggled as Emily's voice faded into amazed silence. Rising, Miriam stretched so her finger underlined each word as she read, " 'She was seen often in the company of Mr. Bernard Colley, noted barrister of this city.' It was you they noted. Not me."

"Enough!" Because her voice was sharper than she had meant, Emily hurried to add, "Forgive me, Miriam, but I find the gossip tiresome at best. You would think they would know that—as I have never had a coming-out—I am not looking for any attention."

"But your feelings do nothing to change Mr. Colley's."

She sighed. "He is being a cabbage-head to dangle after me when I have made it quite clear I have no interest in him."

Miriam patted her sister's shoulder. "My dear Emily, I fear you're too gentle to make the truth obvious to that gaby. I heard your attempts to rid yourself of him last night, and you must not let your tender heart keep you from speaking the truth."

"I shall endeavor to be more forthright." She put her hand over her sister's. "Do sit and finish your breakfast."

"No time." She plucked her mail from the table. "I told Madame I would be at her shop before noon, and it is already past that. You know how she gets on the high ropes when anyone is very late." Although she gave an emoted sigh, she could not keep from giggling. Then her smile vanished. "Mayhap this will be the gown to persuade Mr. Simpkins to do more than watch me dance with other men."

Emily wished she could ease her sister's sorrow, but Miriam might be wishing for something that would never happen. Not once in the weeks since Miriam's coming-out had Graham Simpkins asked her to stand up with him. Emily could not recall him saying more than a score of words to Miriam.

Knowing Miriam would detest pity, Emily said only, "While you are out, will you stop by the milliner's and see if my blue bonnet has been repaired?" As an afterthought, she added, as she did each time her sister went to the *couturière*'s shop on New Bond Street, "Be sure you are home before the Bond Street Loungers appear."

"Of course. I know how jobbernowl it is for any young lady to stroll along Old or New Bond streets during the afternoon when the Bond Street Loungers are about." Sighing, she said, "I do wish they would stop their skimble-skamble parading up and down the street."

"How else could they show off their dandy-set clothes?"

"Or create a scene?"

"Just take care."

"I will." Waving, Miriam hurried out, her light voice, as she greeted Johnson, drifting back into the breakfast-parlor.

Emily picked up the newspaper and turned to the front page. There was no need to chastise her sister for being

loud when their father was still abed. Papa would ᴉ
until late into the afternoon, and then Emily was ᴄ
mined to get answers to the questions taunting her: W
had Papa been want-witted enough to play cards with Lord
Wentworth? And how could he have possibly won?

When the front doorbell was twisted, the sibilant sound
resonated through the house. Emily paused on the stairs,
her gardening gloves in her hand and her straw bonnet
pushed back so it hung from her neck by its red grosgrain
ribbons. She glanced at the clock in the upper hall. It was
nearly three. Where had the time gone? This was the hour
for calls, and she still was dressed in an old gown that was
stained with dirt and grass from working in the garden.
Once the unfashionably long dress had been her best, but
time and the rage had relegated it to the garden.

She rushed up the stairs so she could change into her
favorite pale gold tea gown. Its puff sleeves and stiff skirt
that revealed the openwork on her stockings were appropriate for receiving callers.

"Miss Emily?"

Her hand clenched on the bannister. If Johnson had
the wit of a goose, he would know better than to call her
when she had not a chance to change.

"Lord Wentworth, Miss Emily," he continued in a pompous tone.

Emily was about to urge Johnson to take the viscount
into the parlor while she made her escape, but, as she
turned, she stared at Lord Wentworth's smile. He stood
directly behind the butler. His gaze slipped along her, and
she resisted the temptation to apologize for her beau-nasty
dress.

"This is an unexpected pleasure, my lord," she said.

"I had hoped you would think so." He took off his hat
and handed it to Johnson.

Her dismay deepened. Lord Wentworth was perfectly

The gold buttons of his single-breasted, ⋯ere undone to reveal his embroidered ⋯uffled shirt topped by his casually tied ⋯ream-colored trousers strapped beneath ⋯e possessed an elegance that made her ⋯er dishevelment.

"If you would be so good as to wait in the parlor, I will—"

"There is no need for you to scurry off to change on my account, Miss Talcott." He climbed the stairs until his eyes were even with hers. "You look as if you have spent the day in a more productive manner than I have."

"Yes. I mean . . ." She took a steadying breath. If only his eyes did not twinkle with that hint of devilment, words might come with more ease. His smile suggested he was a naughty lad, but she had heard enough of this viscount to know better.

As Johnson returned to his post in the foyer, Emily led the way up the stairs to the parlor. Again, as in the early hours of this morning, she sensed Lord Wentworth's gaze on her. Its feverish caress urged her to face him.

And what then? she asked herself. *Will you stand toe-to-toe with him and demand that he stop looking at you? Do not be absurd! Just find out his business and put a quick end to this call.*

When they entered the parlor, she noted he held his right hand behind his back. She had no time to wonder about what he held, for he said, "Forgive the intrusion, Miss Talcott."

" 'Tis no intrusion. Johnson should have told you that I always am at home on Thursday afternoons."

His smile broadened. "He enlightened me, but, as we have only the slimmest and shortest of acquaintances, I consider myself ill-mannered to arrive uninvited."

"I should ask *you* to forgive *me*, my lord." Untying the ribbons on her bonnet, she said, "I took advantage of this splendid day to work in my garden, and I fear the time slipped away."

"I would very much like to see your garden."

"You would?" She put her fingers to her lips, then lowered them quickly. The childish motion was unsuitable for a woman of five-and-twenty years. "I had not guessed you would be interested in roses."

"Mayhap because you know nothing of me, but what rumor spouts." Lord Wentworth's smile was matched by the mirth in his gray eyes. "Allow me to complete the task that brought me here, then I will ask you to indulge me with a tour of your garden." From behind his back, he pulled out a crumpled hat. "Your father's, I assume. I found it in my carriage this morning."

She took the battered beaver and silenced her groan. This was Papa's newest hat, and it would not be cheap to have this damage repaired. "Thank you for returning it, my lord. You continue to increase my debt to you."

He chuckled. "What a charming turn of events!"

"My lord?"

"To have a lovely brunette in debt to me." He tapped her nose, and she pulled back, aghast, at his outrageous motion. Her astonishment became chagrin when he added, "The splotch of soil right there adds charming color to your face, Miss Talcott."

When she spun to peek into the pier glass over the mantel, she could not keep her eyes from straying from the bit of earth on her nose to the tall man behind her. His smile dared her to chide him for acting like an ill-mannered beef-head. He said nothing, simply handed her a handkerchief.

Dabbing it against her nose and cheek, she murmured, "Thank you."

"Mayhap my small kindness will help mitigate some of your debt to me. I own that I find it most uncomfortable to have you believe that you owe me a duty."

Emily faced him, although she wished she could keep

her back to him. Not that that would help, for his face was reflected in the glass. Making certain that her expression was as serene as his, she said, "Mayhap you should as lief consider it my father who owes you such a debt."

"Excellent idea! It makes an uncomfortable beginning to any friendship to have outstanding obligations." He offered his arm. When she hesitated to put her fingers on it, he said, "If this is an inconvenient time for you for you to give me a tour, Miss Talcott, I can return at another time to visit your garden."

"Of course it is not inconvenient. I would be delighted to show it to you now." She looked away before her face could reveal the truth hidden by her trite words. She found the idea of Lord Wentworth calling again troubling. As troubling as the thought that he wished to be her friend. That he would show any interest in her family beyond her father's skill—or lack of it—at the card table surprised her.

Lord Wentworth drew her fingers within his arm as they walked together down the stairs and out onto the sunswept terrace at the back of the house. Setting her wide-brimmed straw bonnet back onto her head, although she did not have to fear the sun as her blond sister must, she motioned along a brick path to where the roses were bursting into bloom.

"How lovely!" he said.

She glanced at him, startled by the abrupt change in his voice. Gone was the cynical good humor. In its place was a genuine appreciation that amazed her anew. Nothing she had heard suggested Lord Wentworth would be interested in anything that could not be shuffled, dealt, and gambled, save for the light-skirted ladies whose names were so often attached to his. She frowned. Heeding gossip was an invitation to misconception.

He bent to look more closely at the flowers. His intense expression was so different from the ironic smile he had worn this morning.

"My special favorite is the white one," she said quietly.

"I can see why." He tilted the prickly vine toward him so he could better view the velvety petals which were the color of fresh cream. "The lush collection of blossoms on these bushes bespeaks the time you devote to your garden, Miss Talcott."

" 'Tis quiet here." She took a deep breath of the air that was perfumed by the roses. "I find I sometimes need to seek a sanctuary from the hubbub of the Season."

"That I can understand."

She paused as they continued to walk among the flowering shrubs. "You can? Again you surprise me, my lord."

"Why?" His smile vanished, and, as she saw the intensity in his gray eyes, she wondered if she were seeing his true feelings for the first time. "A Season in London is enough to make one all about in one's head. I speak from experience, for I have endured too many."

"Yet you have come to Town for this one."

"Enjoying the flats alone is meager sport. Anyone with an ounce of skill at cards is here now, so I, by necessity, have followed." Bending to examine the purple buds on a row of peonies, which were about to blow, he said, "I can see you have a singular gift for growing flowers, Miss Talcott. I would enjoy speaking with you about—"

"Emily!"

Emily turned. She waved to Miriam who stood in the doorway. Miriam's tawny curls were half hidden beneath her white turban, the beads upon it matching the ones on the bodice of her Clarence-blue cambric gown. With ecru ruffles beneath her chin and at her wrists, she was the perfect picture of a lady ready to welcome her guests. Miriam raised her hand, then froze, her gaze affixed on the man beside Emily.

"Miriam, do come out and join us," Emily said, as if every day she entertained Lord Wentworth in the garden. Her sister took only a single step onto the terrace before halting. Exasperated, Emily added, "Lord Wentworth, if you have not had the opportunity to meet my sister, allow me to introduce her.''

"I have not had the opportunity, so this will be a pleasure.''He glanced once more around the garden, and Emily thought she heard him sigh. He added nothing else as they went to where Miriam stood.

"Lord Wentworth," Miriam said coolly, "I am surprised to see you here.''

"Are you?" he asked.

"He came to return Papa's hat." Emily wondered what was wrong with her sister. Miriam's manners usually offered no cause for complaint.

"How kind of him!"

She flinched at her sister's taut tone. Why was Miriam acting so rag-mannered? Not willing to risk a glance at the viscount, Emily said, "I thought to see you home a while ago, Miriam.''

"I was delayed because I saw this in the window of Mr. Homsby's bookshop, and I guessed you would want a copy as soon as possible.''

Taking the book that was wrapped in plain brown paper, Emily frowned. What book would Miriam guess she wanted with such haste? Mr. Homsby had told her only a few days past that Mr. Cobbett's book on gardening was not yet ready for publication.

Through the door, she saw Mrs. Hazlet taking the tea tray up to the sitting room. Thank goodness the housekeeper was keeping her head about her. Emily was glad one of them had during this call.

"My lord," she said, "we would be delighted if you would join us for tea.''

"How could I say no to the company of two lovely ladies?''

Emily recoiled from his suave tone. It had been missing while they spoke in her garden, and its resurrection was as harsh as the crack of a coachee's whip.

Letting her sister lead the way up the stairs, she tried to

conceal her disquiet. Lord Wentworth was a chameleon, changing his personality before her eyes. Which was the real man—the debonair, pleasure-seeking lord or the man who had expressed such delight in something as simple as a rose? Was he either man? Or had she not met the real Damon Wentworth yet?

Her uneasiness increased when the viscount sat next to her on the settee. Miriam's smile appeared forced as she poured the tea. Handing Lord Wentworth a cup, she held another out to Emily. The wrapped book fell from Emily's lap as she reached for her cup.

"Allow me, Miss Talcott," Lord Wentworth said, retrieving the book from the carpet.

"Thank you." She choked back a gasp when his fingers brushed hers as she took the book. It was as if the sun had followed him into the house and settled in his fingertips. Liquid heat spread out from where his skin had grazed hers, pooling over her thudding heart. She hoped he could not hear its wild beat.

He touched one corner of the package. When she drew back, he frowned. "I only wish to ascertain if the book has been damaged by its fall."

"I shall check." Giving her fingers something to do other than tremble would be wise.

They were clumsy as she undid the string and the brown paper. Her eyes widened when she saw the gold embossed words on the royal-blue cover. *Reflections on a Summer Love* The title was repeated in French beneath the author's name.

"Oh, my goodness!" she breathed.

"When I saw it in the bookshop window, I was sure you would want the marquis's new book," Miriam said with the return of her usual enthusiasm.

"Yes," she murmured as she opened the book to look at the frontispiece. How had this book come to be in the bookstore *now?*

Lord Wentworth tilted the book to look at the spine.

"This is what you were anxious to read? The latest volume of poetry by Marquis de la Cour? I would have guessed a woman of your temperament would find this drivel, Miss Talcott."

"Why? The marquis is lauded as a favorite poet among the *ton*," she answered in a stiff voice. *Remain calm,* she warned herself when Miriam's eyes widened with shock at her unmannerly retort. Neither Miriam nor Lord Wentworth must guess why she found his words insulting.

No one must know the actual author of the poems published in this book. If anyone suspected the truth—that Emily Talcott struggled to write each one behind the locked door of her bedchamber—the scandal would give the élite something to prattle about for weeks. Miriam's reputation would be ruined. If only there had been another way to raise the money to keep the household from bankruptcy and her father out of debtor's prison, Emily never would have invented the passionate Frenchman who wrote of love and desire.

Lord Wentworth smiled as he thumbed through the book. "It is true *Le Beau Monde* lauds him. The incomparable Marquis de la Cour! How often have I heard this frog's poetry venerated as a genius comparable only to Byron?"

"Frog?"

"He is French, isn't he? The poems from his previous opus are still upon the lips of everyone in the Polite World. No doubt, even beyond. I suspect the accommodation houses in Covent Garden probably keep copies of his books for their clients, who find themselves short of praises for the *bona robes* plying their trade there."

"Unlikely, but something I cannot deny."

At her terse answer, he chuckled. "I beg your indulgence with my sense of humor, Miss Talcott." He turned to Miriam who was listening in stunned silence. "And you, Miss Talcott. I own to being amused by the growing interest in this insipid poetry."

"The marquis should be heralded as a poet of Byron's ilk." Miriam looked to Emily to second her words.

"Do you feel the same?" Lord Wentworth asked, also turning to Emily. He opened the book to a page at random, put his hand over his heart, and read, *"Tu es mon coeur, mon âme ma raison d'être."* With a laugh, he asked, "Who would want to be de la Cour's heart, soul, and reason for living?"

Emily held out her hand. When he placed the book on it, she set the thin book on the table by the silver tea service. She lifted her cup to her lips to take a soothing sip before she said something she might rue.

"I have offended you," Lord Wentworth said, but she heard no apology in his voice. "Miss Talcott, I remain surprised, for I would not have counted you among the marquis's myriad mindless admirers."

"May I remind you, as you reminded me, that you know little of me?"

As if he held a wineglass as lief a cup, he raised it in a salute to both her and Miriam. His smile suggested secrets only he was privy to when he said, "I trust that is something that shall be rectified swiftly, for I suspect you and I, Miss Talcott, shall be sharing each other's company very often in the weeks to come."

Chapter Three

"Emily, what do you think Lord Wentworth meant by saying we would be sharing his company often in the weeks to come?"

Emily continued to wander about her light-blue bed-chamber on the second floor. It was not a grand room, but was bright with early afternoon sunshine splashing across her writing table. As she paced the striped rug, she wove a familiar path between the two chairs and the high tester bed.

"Miriam, you are becoming overwrought. Lord Wentworth was simply being polite."

"Having him about would be want-witted."

"Yes." She sat by her writing table. The sound of carriage wheels did not entice her to push aside the white damask curtains. If Lord Wentworth glanced back as he drove from Hanover Square, she did not want him to discover her peeking out like a naughty child.

"Miss Miriam is right, Miss Emily."

Emily leaned her chin on her palm and avoided her abigail's reproving gaze. Kilmartin seldom missed any-

thing, so the gray-haired abigail must know the viscount
had called on the slimmest of excuses and had joined
Emily in the garden.

"I did nothing but what was required of a pleasant hostess," she answered. Not giving either her sister or Kilmartin
a chance to go on about what was now over, she asked,
"Is Papa up yet?"

"I can check with Bollings," the abigail replied, a definite tinge of dismay remaining in her voice.

"Let me," Miriam said as she bounced to her feet.
"Here. Emily, you forgot this downstairs."

She took the slim volume of poetry and forced a smile.
"Thank you."

Her smile vanished as soon as the door closed behind
Miriam. Tapping her fingers against the book's cover, she
fumed. Mr. Homsby had assured her this would not be
available for several weeks. She had hoped that would give
her sister time to make a fine match before Marquis de la
Cour became the focus of conversation again. How could
Mr. Homsby be selling a book without telling its author?

"If you wish to read, Miss Emily, I can pull the curtains
back," Kilmartin said.

"Thank you, but no." She guessed her abigail wanted
to talk about this afternoon's caller as she put Emily's best
gown on the bed in preparation for the evening.

She opened the book and began to read, in spite of her
words to the contrary. As always, she delighted in seeing her
hard-won words in pretty print. How dare Lord Wentworth
mock these poems! It was not Byron, but . . . She sighed.
It was the best *she* could do.

She admired the title page. This was the third book
supposedly penned by the marquis, but she had not
become accustomed to seeing someone else's name on
her poems.

Drivel, came Lord Wentworth's voice from her memory.

She would like to see him do better. Not that he needed
to, for any man who had gained his reputation as a game-

ster must be full of juice. The viscount would not need to create an alter ego who could write books of love poems to keep his household from having to leave the key under the door in shame. Her father depended on her, as did Miriam. This was the only way she could provide for her sister the security Emily once had taken for granted.

You could get married yourself. Emily gave that thought no credence. Save for the odious Mr. Colley, no suitors came calling for her. It was well known and accepted by everyone, save Mr. Colley, that Emily's only interest in marriage was for her sister. Once Miriam was settled happily, then . . .

Emily smiled as she leaned her chin on her hand again. Then she would leave London and do the research for the book that held her heart. She would visit all the grand old gardens of Europe and the exciting new ones in America, and she would pen a book that would be as informative and entertaining as anything Mr. Cobbett might write.

And she probably would continue to write these little volumes for as long as there was interest. Papa showed no signs of giving up the card table, and she was sure his luck would seldom be as good as it had been against Lord Wentworth.

Lord Wentworth! She wished she could banish him from her head, yet she found herself recalling their comfortable conversation in her garden. What a surprise that he had an interest in something other than cards.

The door opened, and Miriam entered. "Papa is still abed."

"Thank you," Emily said, grateful for the interruption.

In a flurry of blue cambric and bright ribbons, Miriam dropped onto the padded bench in the bay window overlooking the street. "Do you think *he* will call here often?" Her voice quivering with awe left no doubt who *he* was.

Emily rose and placed the book on a shelf by her bed. Her fingers lingered lovingly on the three books she had written. Forcing a smile, she faced her sister. "Do not make yourself all about in the head. Lord Wentworth called to return Papa's hat which was left in the viscount's carriage last night."

"Papa was at *his* house?"

"Miriam, it is not our place to select Papa's companions."

" 'Twas not Papa's companionship he wished today. It was yours." She wrapped her arms around herself. "This is most unsettling. How could Papa spend time with that man?"

Emily was tempted to give voice to the truth teasing the tip of her tongue. If Lord Wentworth were as charming at the card table as he had been in the garden, she could understand why anyone would seek out his company.

Instead she glanced at Kilmartin, knowing her abigail was aware, by this time, of the state Papa had been in last night. When she saw the gray-haired woman's lips were pursed with disapproval, Emily said, "I shall call when I'm ready to dress for Lady Bealer's rout."

"Miss Emily—"

"I shall leave time to prepare," she said as if that were the only concern. Certainly her sister would believe that, for Emily often had to scurry to be ready when writing stole her attention from the time.

Kilmartin wore a worried expression as she left. Emily understood that all too well, too, for she could not keep from fretting at the discovery Mr. Homsby was selling her latest book without informing her. Yet, if the book were her main concern, why did her thoughts return to the handsome viscount and his uncommon delight in her roses? He was an enigma, and Emily disliked enigmas. She lived with secrets every day and needed no more.

Sitting in her favorite white wicker chair, she put her hand on her sister's arm. "You are fussing over nothing."

Miriam's blue eyes were dim with anxiety. "You must speak to Papa. He should stay away from Demon Wentworth."

"Miriam!"

"Demon Wentworth is what the *ton* calls him, friend and foe alike."

"So I have heard." She rose and went to the bookcase. Taking down the book again, she said, "However, what *they* do or say need not influence our actions. Lord Wentworth was a gentleman of first respectability by bringing Papa home and returning his hat, especially after Papa bested him at the card table."

Miriam's eyes widened. "Papa won? What a coup! Papa shall dine out for months on the retelling of that story."

"Miriam! Why are you showing such a want for sense today?"

"What is wrong with *you?*" her sister returned. "To be with that man in the garden alone—" She pressed her hands to her abruptly pale face. "Oh, my dear Emily, what if it becomes known that you were alone with *him?*"

Emily was tempted to say her prayers backward, but, in an even tone, of which she was proud, she answered, "Do not be silly. Lord Wentworth was simply returning Papa's hat."

Miriam nodded in reluctant agreement. "That is true."

"I have never turned anyone from our door."

"No one like *him* certainly!"

Silently agreeing, Emily paged through the book. Her eyes were caught by the line Lord Wentworth had read. The words in his deep, warm voice had taken on an ardor she had despaired of attaining. Then he had mocked them. She closed the book with a snap and shoved it back onto the shelf.

"Emily, you shall ruin it."

"If I do, I can get another copy." Blast that man for deriding her hard work! She had strained her imagination to create these poems. Never again did she want to think about lovers on a moonlit night . . . or a moonless one.

"Do not be so certain."

She looked at her sister. "What do you mean?"

"There are not many copies left." Miriam chuckled.

"When Miss Dreyer heard the marquis's new book was for sale, I do believe she was ready to fly out of Madame's in little but her smallclothes."

Emily smiled. The excitement was good news, for that suggested excellent sales. Yet none of this explained why Mr. Homsby had failed to let her know of its publication. He always had alerted her, and she hoped this change did not bode others.

The afternoon was almost over before Emily was called to her father's room. She rapped on the door.

A muffled shout ordered her to enter. She pushed aside the door and smiled. The high bed was covered with discarded clothes. Dresser drawers were open, the contents spilling onto the floor. Both chairs were topped by hastily folded coats, and a pair of boots sat in the very center of the Oriental rug.

As always, her gaze went to the only painting in the room. The small portrait had been created by an artist with no skill, but somehow it captured the glow on the woman's face. Or it might be nothing other than Emily's memory giving it life, for she recalled little of her mother, who had died when Emily was very young. So often she had come to look at this painting. Emily saw her own straight black hair and her eyes, which like Mama's were slightly tilted, although she had inherited their blue color from Papa. The painting had blurred the high cheekbones she shared with her mother's family.

As Emily picked her way through the messy chamber, her father shouted to his valet, "Where is my black waistcoat, Bollings? It always brings me luck."

"Mr. Talcott, you sent it to the tailor after you discovered a rip beneath the left arm," replied the valet.

Emily offered Bollings a sympathetic smile as she asked, "Papa, you wanted to talk to me?"

Charles Talcott peeked around the dressing room door. With a broad smile, he motioned for her to sit.

Papa was still uncommonly handsome, although silver was woven through his hair that was as light as Miriam's. The passage of years had not slowed his step or his wit. Since Miriam's coming-out, Emily had seen how her father could charm any lady—be she young or a dowager. Charles Talcott loved life and all its pleasures, and, for years, life had been benevolent to him and his family.

Then five years ago his second wife had died. Before her death, Papa seldom had gone out. Now he was so infrequently home. Emily wondered if he always had wished to be out, or did he leave every evening for a game of chance because the very sight of Miriam reminded him of his lost love for her mother Marlene? She could not guess, and she refused to ask, not wanting to resurrect the grief he vowed was buried with her stepmother.

Papa tossed another shirt onto the bed and ignored the pained expression on his valet's face. Stopping in front of the glass between the two windows, he began tying his cravat.

When he cursed and undid the mess he had made, Emily rose. "Would you like some help with that, Papa?"

"What would I do without you? Your stepmother always tended to this for me, and I swear I shall never learn a young sprig's tricks. You shall make some lucky buck a fine wife." He smiled as she finished tying his cravat. "You have a pensive expression, *ma chérie*. What is bothering you?"

"Why don't you tell me why you wanted to talk with me?" She sat again. "Or was it for nothing but doing your cravat?"

He collected his boots and dropped into a chair. "I wish to know how your evening passed."

"Miriam danced often."

"With one man?"

"With several."

"Good." He pushed on the boot, then stood to force his heel into it. "I thought she would find her first Season enjoyable." Reaching past her, he picked up a folded newspaper. "However, it appears you were much the center of attention yourself, *ma chérie.*"

Emily tossed the newspaper back onto the bed. "Papa, that is prattle. I spent most of last evening trying to convince Mr. Colley that others would savor his company more than I."

He laughed. "If all is going so well, why do you look so uneasy?"

"Because of Lord Wentworth."

His lips straightened into a taut smile. Turning away to look in the glass, he pulled on his coat.

She tensed. She had not expected the mere mention of the viscount's name to bring the same cold reaction from Papa as it had from Miriam.

"Did you encounter him at Miss Prine's coming-out?" Papa asked. "Not that I would expect such a rakehell to be interested in that tame fare."

"Lord Wentworth brought you home."

For a long minute, she was unsure if he would answer. Then he faced her. For once, his face revealed his years. "The companions I choose for myself are not the same ones I would choose for you and Miriam."

"Miriam is scared of him."

"Good."

"But, Papa, what happened last night?" She stood slowly. "You are no brandy-face, yet you couldn't stand alone, and you left your hat in the viscount's carriage."

He frowned. "So that is where it went to. I must speak to Wentworth about it on the next occasion we meet."

"No need. He returned it."

"*He* is calling here?"

Emily was startled, for she never had heard such acrimony from Papa. "Why won't you tell me what happened last night?"

"Because it's not for your fragile ears." When she gasped, his smile returned, and he patted her shoulder. "Do not look shocked, *ma chérie.* I did no more than spend the evening in the company of friends while I punished my pockets with losses at the card table." Rubbing his forehead, he added, "And in the company of too much fine brandy."

"Losses? But, Papa, the viscount said you were the victor."

He sat on the bed, then, grimacing, motioned for Bollings to clear it. The short man flashed Emily a wry smile. Nothing would change Charles Talcott. She suspected he found a solace at the card table that neither she nor Miriam could provide. Especially Miriam, for so many people spoke of how she was the image of her mother. As Emily was of her mother, but no one in Town knew that, for Papa kept the only portrait of her in this room.

"He was being a gentleman, *ma chérie.*" Standing, he wiggled one foot, then the other, to be sure his toes were securely inside the boots. "Even a man like Wentworth knows the correct way to treat a lady. I trust you will give him his *congé* if he attempts to speak to you or your sister."

"But, why? He has—"

"Called upon you and your sister for the final time." He faced her, a sudden frown on his lips. "You and Miriam shall not receive him here."

"Yes, Papa," she whispered, although she knew it mattered little if she obeyed Papa or not. Lord Wentworth was not a man to be put off by a polite rebuff. She suspected he would be an uncomfortable part of their lives longer than either she or Papa wished.

The tinny bell echoed through the small shop. Because the mullioned windows were shaded by stacks of books, the interior was dusky and cramped. Emily needed little light, for she had patronized this bookshop many times.

Taking a deep breath of the dusty, warm smell from the books stacked on the shelves—each volume waiting for an eager reader—she walked to the low counter. She looked about, not seeing anyone nor expecting to, for Mr. Homsby tore himself from his reading in the back room only when necessary.

She took a moment to survey the selection of books, careful not to let her pink muslin skirt brush them. Mr. Homsby had no interest in cleaning his shop, and his customers seemed indifferent to the dust, for he had, in Emily's opinion, the best bookshop along Old Bond Street. She tilted her bonnet, because she could not see past the bow of brightly striped pink and gold that matched the ribbon laced beneath her bodice.

Pulling off her gloves, she selected a volume. It was an edition of Byron's poetry she had never seen. As she paged through it, she became lost in the sensual flow of words. She sighed as she placed it back on the shelf. How much simpler her life would be if she had been blessed with such a gift for words! She wondered if the great poet had to struggle for each phrase as she did, tossing out more than she kept. Yet it was her ridiculous poetry—or the poetry of Marquis de la Cour, she must be careful to recall—that had brought her here.

"Mr. Homsby?" she called.

The red velvet curtain behind the counter parted. Mr. Homsby, who had the misfortune to resemble an overfed squirrel with his bushy, gray mustache and tiny eyes behind his gold-rimmed glasses, peered out. A smile puffed out his full cheeks as he scurried to the counter and leaned his pudgy hands on its cluttered top.

"Miss Talcott! This is, indeed, a pleasant surprise. When your sister stopped in last week, I was delighted she bought one of the newly arrived books for you." He rubbed his fingers against his mustache as he grinned. "I could hardly contain my amusement when she spoke of how excited you would be to see the marquis's latest collection."

Emily would not let him draw her into a conversation of polite nothings. "Why wasn't I told the book was available for sale? I could hardly contain *my* astonishment when Miriam brought it home."

He flushed nearly to the color of the drape behind him. "Miss Talcott, I told you the book would be printed by midsummer."

"It's barely the beginning of June. Spring is still with us."

"But you must own my words were true, for it's before midsummer."

"I wish you had informed me before you put the book in the window," she said, not willing to concede completely.

He raised his hands in a broad shrug. "How could I do that? If I had sent a note, I was unsure who might intercept it." Pointing past her, he asked, "But can you deny that it looks lovely there?"

Emily went to the window. Rings holding a strip of paisley fabric rattled as she put her hands on the half-height railing. In spite of herself, she smiled when she saw the books glittering in the sunshine. Mr. Homsby's publisher had topped himself with this volume, for the gilt letters gave it an appearance worthy of a marquis.

She sighed. She had been a blind buzzard to start down this path of lies, but she was as sure today as she had been two years ago that her name on the cover would create questions. It was easier to collect her royalties from Mr. Homsby anonymously and slip them into the household accounts to keep her family from ruin. Yet she was growing tired of her double life.

"It is a pretty book," Emily said as she faced Mr. Homsby.

"I shall tell the publisher that."

"I would like to tell him that myself."

The quarto lost his cheerful expression as his mustache drooped. "Miss Talcott, you know that is impossible. The publisher hired me to find him materials suitable for publication and to sell them. He wishes to have nothing to do with the authors, for he has no time to deal with their concerns.''

''But—''

''Miss Talcott, you have been satisfied with your books, haven't you?''

''Yes, but—''

''And haven't you been paid on time?''

''I believe I have you to thank for that.''

Swelling up with pride so broadly that she was afraid he would pop his waistcoat buttons, he said, ''And I thank you for being such a fine author. That is the second shipment of books this week.''

''You still have not given me a reason why I cannot meet with the publisher. Where can I contact him?''

As the bell over the door rang merrily, Mr. Homsby looked past her. Sure she heard him sigh with relief as a grin lit his face, Emily turned. Her eyes widened as she met Lord Wentworth's smile.

As before, the viscount had adonized himself. His nankeen trousers and deep-green fustian coat covered a ruffled shirt and simple waistcoat. On his ebony hair, that was dulled by Mr. Homeby's exuberant curtain, was a top hat with a tilted brim. He carried a walking stick in one hand. When she saw a cicisbeo of the brightest yellow tied to it, she was startled by the affectation she had not suspected he would assume. She chided herself, for she knew no more about the viscount than when they first had met a week ago.

Lord Wentworth came forward, tipping his beaver. ''Seeing you here is an unexpected delight, Miss Talcott.''

''Good morning.'' She was *not* delighted to see him again, for he had been false about the card games he had shared with Papa. He had betwattled her then, but he would not again. Even Mr. Homsby had the decency not to lie outright.

''My lord,'' gushed the bookseller, his smile broadening

so far Emily feared it would escape his face, "I have the book you requested waiting."

"Very good." Lord Wentworth turned back to Emily before she could take her leave. "You are a most pleasant sight in this shop, Miss Talcott. I believe your snapping eyes light up even its darkest corners."

Papa had been right. So had Miriam. This man deserved being called *Demon* Wentworth. After spinning tales which, like a goosecap, she had swallowed wholeheartedly, he had the gall to act as if she would be delighted to see him. She wished to leave, but that was impossible when he stood between her and the door. Pushing past him was unthinkable, yet continuing this conversation when Papa had forbidden her to receive Lord Wentworth was as impossible.

"Miss Talcott," he continued, smiling, "if I may be so bold as to speak the truth, Homsby would be wise to keep such lovely company as you here in his shop to persuade the gentlemen to pause and browse among his books."

"You are bold, and there is no need to lather me with compliments. I appreciate being told the truth."

He laughed. "And I may trust you to speak the truth."

Shame seared her, for she was being anything but truthful when she stood next to her books in the window. But she was not the only one guilty of falsehoods. Lord Wentworth had lied to her about her father's losses and showed no regret.

"Do you come to look," he went on, "or do you have a specific volume in mind?" He ran his gloved finger along the spines and selected one. "If I may offer a suggestion, Miss Talcott, I believe you would find this book on roses interesting."

Emily took it. The book was by Dr. Osborne, who was gaining a fine reputation as an expert on gardening. With a sigh, she replaced it. She did not have money to indulge in the luxury of a book.

"It wasn't to your liking?" Lord Wentworth asked, warning she must guard every reaction, for his eyes were keen.

"Quite to the contrary." She hoped her smile would not falter. "Thank you for pointing it out, my lord."

He nodded and went to the counter. Releasing another sigh, but this one of gratitude that he had not pursued his curiosity further, she glanced at the book on roses. Mayhap she should ask Mr. Homsby to hold it. When her royalties were sufficient to pay for it, he could send it to her.

Emily's happiness vanished into amazement when she saw what Mr. Homsby was handing to Lord Wentworth. It was *her* book.

As if he sensed her thoughts, which she found a discomfiting idea, Lord Wentworth said, "You need not stare at me like a disgruntled schoolmaster, Miss Talcott."

"I find it peculiar you should deride the marquis's poetry upon our last meeting and now purchase a copy." She should remain silent, but she was frustrated with what might be another of his out-and-outers. How many more tales would he tell her before she had the good sense to— To what? Put him from her life? Ridiculous! He was not a part of her life. She was acting as moony as Miriam each time she thought of Graham Simpkins.

"This book is not for me, but a gift, Miss Talcott." His smile was dazzling and urged her to believe him.

"Forgive me. I did not mean to stare."

"But you were, and just like a schoolmaster." He winked at Mr. Homsby who was listening with ill-concealed interest. "A lad would pay much more attention to his lessons if he had a teacher like Miss Talcott. Don't you agree, Homsby?"

"Yes, yes, my lord," the bookseller said so quickly Emily frowned. Mr. Homsby was often obsequious, but this was absurd.

Lord Wentworth set the book on the counter so it could be wrapped. "As I suspect you well know, Miss Talcott, a gift should be selected for the pleasure of the recipient, not for the taste of the giver. I have not changed my opinion of the book or its contents."

"Honesty at last, I believe."

Mr. Homsby interjected, "Miss Talcott, I assure you that Lord Wentworth has a reputation for being honest."

"Thank you for the testimonial," Lord Wentworth said, "but I am curious why Miss Talcott jests with me on this matter." His eyes narrowed as he rested his hand on the counter.

She was not bamblusterated by his nonchalance. It was no more than a pose. As she was not certain how long she could maintain her own pretense of serenity when those incredible eyes were focused on her, sending a swift, sweet pulse resonating through her, she said, "I leave you to your gift buying, my lord. Good day to you." She nodded toward the bookseller. "And to you, Mr. Homsby."

"You have not answered my question," Lord Wentworth said as she started for the door.

"I did not hear you ask one."

He smiled, but it was as cool as Papa's had been. "That is true. I cannot accuse you of dishonesty, can I?"

Heat coursed up her cheeks. Her gaze was caught by Mr. Homsby's, but she looked hastily away. What a widgeon she was! She was wanting for sense to chide Lord Wentworth for being deceitful when Mr. Homsby could denounce her.

She must leave without delay. If she remained, either Mr. Homsby or she might reveal the truth. As she reached for the doorknob, a broad hand covered the latch. She looked over her shoulder, every word she had ever known vanishing from her head as she stared up into Lord Wentworth's gray eyes. Storms she did not want to challenge filled them.

Slowly he drew his hand away, his sleeve brushing her arm in the most chance caress. She knew he had heard her gasp when his smile returned, warm once more as it had been in the garden.

No! She would not give it credence again. He had lied to her about Papa and about . . . She could not be sure what else, and she did not dare to stay to find out

"Good day," she murmured again. She was out the door before he could halt her, although she doubted if Lord Wentworth ever needed force to keep a woman by his side. His charm would garner him a place in any woman's heart. But not in hers. She could not let that happen, not when her whole family's future depended on her and the secrets she held in her heart.

Chapter Four

Emily looked out the window of her carriage as it came to an abrupt stop. The carriage rocked, and her coachman's freckled face appeared in the window.

"What is it, Simon?" she asked, putting down the notebook where she had begun sketching out her next collection of poems. She must not let opportunity pass her by. If this book did as well as Mr. Homsby suggested, she could not delay beginning another.

"Accident, Miss Talcott." He squinted at the pages she held, and she folded them, placing them on the seat. "Looks like a horse stumbled up ahead."

"The passengers?"

Before he could answer, she heard a familiar, slightly too high-pitched voice. Simon opened the door and assisted her to the cobbled street. She rushed to the assistance of her bosom-bow.

Lady Valeria Fanning was, in Emily's opinion, the most beautiful woman in Town, even when she was wringing her hands in distress. With gloriously red hair that curled perfectly about her heart-shaped face, she always dressed with just a hint of the garish. Her bold Kashmir shawl covered a pelisse that was opened to reveal her bright gold silk gown. Tall feathers perched on the top of her muslin poke bonnet and had been dyed to match the fancywork on her stockings. Valeria was not a woman to be ignored, even at the largest assembly.

Beside her stood the man of Miriam's dreams, although Emily could not fathom why. Graham Simpkins was as bland as Valeria was beautiful. True, his hair seemed like spun ebony in the sunshine, and he possessed a strong silhouette. As usual, he hunched into himself as he watched the thrashing horse in the middle of the street.

"Valeria, are you hurt?" Emily asked, hurrying to her friend's side.

"I do not believe so." She nudged Mr. Simpkins with her elbow. "Graham, do recall your manners and say good day to Miss Talcott."

"Miss Talcott?" He squinted into the sunshine. "Which one?"

"Emily, of course, you silly block." Valeria pressed her hand to her bodice. "I swear that lame-hand coachman should never be allowed in the box again."

Drawing her friend away from the center of the street, Emily asked, "Can you find someone to help that poor beast, Simon?"

A voice deeper than her coachee's answered, "I think they are hoping to tend to that distasteful matter after you ladies have left."

Emily whirled. Lord Wentworth! Was he following her, determined to continue their truncated conversation?

Again she had the peculiar uneasiness that he could guess her thoughts, for he smiled. "Traffic is in a tangle all along the street, and my curiosity would not be quelled without seeing the cause for myself." Not giving Emily a chance to answer, he tipped his hat to Valeria. "Good morning, Lady Fanning. And to you, Simpkins."

"I am so glad to see you," Valeria moaned, putting her hand on his arm. "Can you help us?"

"Us?" His brows arched.

Mr. Simpkins murmured, "Damn good horse. What a shame."

"Miss Talcott would certainly offer—" Damon could not keep from smiling as Lady Fanning swooned into his arms. What a to-do! Who would have guessed a simple errand to collect a copy of that book of silly poems would lead to this? Lifting the lady into his arms, he gritted his teeth when her reticule struck his leg and that silly feather tickled his nose.

"Bring her to my carriage, my lord," Miss Talcott said. When she put her hand on his arm to guide him, he was not astonished, even though, at the bookshop, she had acted as skittish as a gamester with creditors on his tail. Emily Talcott had proven she would be a rock in a crisis when he had brought her father home.

He nodded and let her lead the way to the simple carriage. Her coachee leaped forward to open the door, then stepped aside.

When he set the senseless woman on the seat, several sheets of paper fluttered about the carriage. Miss Talcott first smoothed Lady Fanning's dress over her comely ankles, then gathered up the pages which were covered with neat handwriting. Curious as to what she was writing, he bent closer. She folded them closed before he could read a single word. He was treated to a sweet, musky scent he had enjoyed in the bookshop. He did not recognize the cologne, but it was perfect for Emily Talcott.

He handed her into the carriage and asked, "How does she fare?"

"She still is bereft of her senses."

"Do you think we should set fire to that absurd feather in her bonnet to bring her about?"

Miss Talcott stared at him in amazement, then began to laugh. Damon rested his hand on the open doorway and enjoyed the sight. Laughing was something she should do more often, for her eyes sparkled like twin candles.

"I don't think," she said in a prim tone that did not match her smile, "such extraordinary measures will be necessary. She seems to be waking."

Before Damon could answer, another voice, a most annoying one, in his opinion, asked, "How is Valeria? Alas, I should have picked a more experienced coachman."

"That is your carriage, Simpkins?" Damon asked, glancing at the ruined vehicle.

"It was."

He saw Miss Talcott struggling to hide her smile. She should smile, for Graham Simpkins was amusing even at a moment such as this.

Quietly, Damon ordered, "Do be a good man, Simpkins, and get Lady Fanning's things. I am sure Miss Talcott would be glad to see Lady Fanning home."

"That is my honor," Simpkins insisted, squinting at Miss Talcott as if he had just taken note of her.

"And how do you intend to do that? Carry her home in your arms?"

Simpkins puffed up like a cat ready to spit at a dog. His hands clenched at his sides.

Damon folded his arms in front of him. He had no interest in providing more of a public spectacle.

Miss Talcott said, "Hush, the two of you." Her voice softened. "Valeria, open your eyes slowly."

"Dear me," murmured Lady Fanning, "my head aches. Oh, do let us be on our way."

"An excellent idea," Damon seconded. "The morning is nearly over. It would not be wise of you ladies to remain here past midday when the Loungers are about."

Emily nodded. For once, she could agree with Lord Wentworth. She wanted to be gone before Old Bond Street became filled with the bored young men who looked for entertainment with any lady opaque enough to linger.

"Will you be all right?" asked Lord Wentworth as Mr. Simpkins went back to oversee the removal of his carriage.

"Yes, thank you." She drew the door closed. "I know Lady Fanning appreciates your assistance, my lord."

"And do you?"

She had been about to slap the side of the carriage to give Simon the signal to start. As lief, with her hand half raised, she asked, "Pardon me?"

"I merely wished to be certain *you* are fine as well." He reached into the carriage and put his hand on her wrist. With a smile, he said, "You seem calm, for your heartbeat is not racing."

"I am fine, thank you." She pulled her arm away. Again he was plying her with his balms. At his touch, her pulse had jumped like grease on a hot stove.

"I am glad we concur again." As he motioned to her coachee, he tipped his hat toward her. "I trust you will have a much more pleasant afternoon, ladies."

As soon as the carriage was underway, Valeria leaned forward, her eyes wide. "When did you meet Lord Wentworth?" Color returned to her cheeks. "Do tell me *everything*, Emily."

"There is not *everything* to tell. He is Papa's friend."

"And yours, too." Leaning back against the seat, she wafted her hand in front of her face. "Or he would like to be. Be careful, Emily. He is a dangerous man."

"Dangerous?"

"He has been the cause of more heart palpitations within the breasts of young women and their mothers than any one man has a right to be."

Emily chuckled. "He has no interest in calling on me."

"No?" Valeria patted her hand. "Listen to someone more experienced and wiser than you in the ways of men. A rogue does not look at a woman as Demon Wentworth looks at you unless he has something very definite in mind." She raised her chin. "And you can be certain it is not an honorable offer of marriage."

"I do not want to marry him!"

"This is all for the good." Her smile returned. "Now tell me, Emily, what errands brought you to Old Bond Street."

Emily relaxed. Chatting with Valeria was sure to halt her thoughts about the disturbing viscount and her curiosity about who would be the recipient of her book he had bought.

Valeria's house, where she had lived with her late husband, was as gloriously adorned as the lady herself. Lord Fanning had been rich as a nabob, and Valeria had wasted little time spending his money.

Sitting in a sunny room, Emily admired the freshly painted friezes. Once her father's house had been as magnificent, but now she found it difficult to pay for maintenance. London fogs and smoke had little sympathy for paint and paper.

"I do hope your sister can convince Graham to pay more attention to her tonight at the rout." Valeria smiled as she leaned back on a divan. "I am surprised Miriam has failed to convince him of her interest. After all, she is the pattern-card of loveliness."

Emily shrugged and stirred her tea. "Who is to say why Mr. Simpkins ignores her? I assume she shall meet someone else who will intrigue her heart."

"And what of you, dear Emily? Now that Mr. Colley is following you about like a love-smitten puppy, there is talk that you might be making an announcement soon."

"Quell the talk, if you can. My sole interest in the Season is finding a good husband for Miriam."

"And none for yourself?" Valeria gestured broadly. "My dear Albert was as generous before his untimely death as his estate has been since. You should find yourself a man who dotes upon you and gives you your heart's desire. How lovely you would look in the gown I saw in Madame's this morning! All ruffles and lace that you, slight thing that you are, can wear better than someone with my unfortunate figure.''

Emily was accustomed to Valeria's need to be endlessly complimented on her appearance and taste. She spoke the reassuring words without thinking.

Valeria lifted a book from under the rosewood table by the divan. Its bright blue cover told Emily it contained her poetry.

"Have you seen this?'' Valeria asked.

"Miriam purchased me a copy earlier in the week.''

Her mouth became a moue of displeasure at not being the first to discover the new collection of poetry. She pressed the book to her breast as her high spirits returned. "I do love the marquis's poetry. How I wish I could meet him!''

Emily smiled. "Who knows? Now that the war is over, it's possible to travel across the Channel.''

"Yes.'' She sat straighter. "Surely he must know how many people adore his poetry, and he will journey to London. Have you ever imagined what he must be like?''

"Not often.''

She let Valeria prattle while she fought not to laugh. She must not let slip that the marquis was neither tall nor well favored with a manly air. Valeria was as enthralled with the mysterious marquis as with his poetry.

Taking a sip of tea, she quelled a shudder. The marquis would never appear in London. That would destroy Miriam's chances for a first-rate marriage. She sighed. The noose of truth was tightening, but the furor would die down again once something else caught the élite's attention.

"Yes, I like the marquis's poetry,'' Emily said when her friend paused to take a breath, "but I prefer Byron's.''

"Bah! Even Byron doesn't have the romantic magic of this Frenchman.'' Valeria's eyes brightened. "I have just the jolly. I shall host a poetry reading tomorrow evening.'' She clapped her hands with pleasure. "What fun it shall be! We will enjoy the marquis's newest poems and our favorites from Byron. You and Miriam and your dear father will come, won't you?''

''I'm not sure of Papa's plans.'' Emily tried to devise a reason to refuse. The idea of sitting all evening while others lauded the poetry would be nearly as disturbing as Lord Wentworth's insults to her work.

She almost gasped as the viscount's image appeared in her head yet again. Since his call, she had been successful at keeping the handsome man from her thoughts. Her father had remained mute about his encounters with the viscount, and she had not pressed.

''You will come, won't you?'' Valeria asked again.

''Of course.'' Emily's smile grew more sincere as she said with a wryness her friend would not be able to appreciate, ''This may prove to be the most unforgettable party you have ever given.''

Chapter Five

Emily needed have no concerns about her sister's interest in attending the reading. Once Miriam discovered Mr. Simpkins had been invited, she was aglow. Emily could not comprehend her sister's interest a man who seldom spoke to her. Every morning, Miriam scanned the newspaper, searching for any word of Graham Simpkins. If she found his name connected to another woman's, she was bereft.

Emily kept her curiosity about Miriam's heart to herself as they entered the Fanning home. She smiled a greeting to Valeria, who embraced her warmly. Valeria's gown of brilliant blue would challenge a midsummer sky. With gems glittering on her fingers and pearls laced through her hair, which had a tendency to appear orange in this light, she could be found by any of her guests.

"What a lovely gown!" Valeria said, clearly not noticing how Emily's hands clenched her fringed shawl. "Is it one of Madame Girouard's?"

"Yes, I own to being enchanted with the material when I saw it at her shop," Emily answered, her voice as taut as her fingers. Tonight she would as lief think of the color which was not truly pink nor deep enough to be mauve than the idea that soon people would be reading her poetry aloud.

"No one designs as well as Madame Girouard. I am grateful you introduced me to her." A frown ruffled her brow. "She's been asking for you as if you no longer patronized her shop."

"You know how she loves to prattle." She did not want to reveal that she had not visited the *couturière* in months. She had no need to worry, for Valeria's—and Miriam's—attention was taken by the arrival of Graham Simpkins.

His cravat looked as if he needed help with tying it as much as Papa did. With his gaze affixed firmly on his feet, he edged through the crowd.

Emily whispered, "Miriam, do not stare."

"But he is so—" Her retort ended in a low moan as Mr. Simpkins paused in front of Valeria and captured their hostess's hands.

"My dear Valeria," he said, "I should have guessed you would be the first to celebrate the new poetry by Marquis de la Cour! Allow me." Offering his arm, he led her into the parlor.

Miriam gave a half-sob.

"Miriam, I am sure he wishes only to—"

"You need not be kind. He acted as if he did not even see me. It is obvious Mr. Simpkins cares as little for me as you do for Mr. Colley."

"You know Valeria has no interest in him."

Miriam's eyes filled with cobalt tears. "She has him hanging on her every look, and she doesn't want him?" She hurried up the sharply turning stairs to where she could pipe her eyes in a secluded bedroom.

About to follow, Emily halted when she heard, "What a pleasure to see you again so soon, Miss Talcott!"

Emily turned, for she recognized Lord Wentworth's voice. Why had Valeria invited him? Emily had been certain her friend believed Lord Wentworth was beneath her touch.

She glanced toward the stairs, but Miriam needed time to regain control of her ragged emotions. Before going to her sister, she was determined to obtain an explanation why the viscount had lied to her.

"Good evening, my lord," Emily answered as Lord Wentworth motioned for her to precede him into the parlor which was brilliantly lit by the crystal chandelier in the center of the expansive ceiling. "I own a tremendous amazement at seeing you here. Could you have had a change of heart about poetry? Does this drivel bring you something other than ennui?"

He handed her a glass of champagne before selecting one for himself. "You misunderstood. I do not find all poetry drivel. Only the poems penned by Marquis de la Cour. His sickish sentimentality epitomizes the reasons the French lost the war. They believed Napoleon's pap, but hiked off like cowards."

"You fought in the war?" She could not imagine the viscount, who always dressed in high kick, living the low life of a soldier.

His smile became as sly as a fox prowling a chicken coop. "There were many rôles to be played. Mine was not upon the march with the infantry. Yet I pride myself in having some small part in our victory."

His cryptic words suggested he might have been a spy. A fair task for him, for not once had Emily guessed the course of his thoughts. Yet she could not envision him far from this breezy life. Irritation filled her. Was he hoaxing her? These could be the same lies he had fed to her with such success.

Emily said, "If you will excuse me."

"But I won't."

"You won't?" Simply because he was as handsome as a new penny was no reason for him to put aside his manners.

"Miss Talcott," he continued, "I would appreciate an

explanation of why you have treated me, both at the quarto's shop and again now, with the scanty civility you would offer a knight of the road."

"Odd that you should expect an answer, when you have been less than honest with me."

"Again that charge of dishonesty. I recall no lies I have spoken to you."

"No?" She kept her voice low. "The very first words you spoke to me were fabrications, for your tale of what happened at the card table differs from my father's version. I ask you, my lord, whom I should believe."

He set down his glass. Holding out his arm, he gestured toward the French doors leading to a balcony overlooking Valeria's garden. "I think it would be wise if we discussed this in private."

"I have nothing to say which would shame me."

"Nor do I. However, Miss Talcott, your eyes are snapping like two blue-hot embers, and I fear your words shall bring me shame." Taking her hand, he drew it into his arm.

She wanted to argue with this glib viscount, but again failed words failed her. As his fingers settled over hers on his arm, she was suffused with warmth. Warnings careened through her head. This was the man who made mamas swoon with dismay when he spoke to their daughters. Now she understood why. His silver eyes were hooded with secrets she could not resist trying to expose, even at the risk of involving herself with a rakehell.

As that slow, bewitching smile tilted his lips, she forced her gaze away. Was she all about in the head? Even if she were skimble-skamble enough to entangle her life with his, this was the very worst time. She had to deal with the vexing problem of Marquis de la Cour.

Curious gazes followed them through the open doors. Tendrils of fog oozed in the early dusk. The damp aroma of dew was intoxicating, but Emily ignored it. She withdrew her hand from Lord Wentworth's arm and faced him. She tried not to be disconcerted by the fact that her eyes were level with his lips.

Raising them, she asked in her coolest tone, "Why did you lie to me? You told me Papa had won at the card table."

"So he did, on numerous occasions." He smiled as he leaned against a large concrete planter. "I, on the other hand, won on many more. Lady Luck was his companion during the evening, but she turned her favor on me through the night."

"You intentionally misled me!"

"I was honest with you."

"You said there was no need for me to even Papa's accounts with you."

His lips straightened. "No matter what you have heard of me, Miss Talcott, I do not call on pretty brunettes to dun them for their fathers' debts."

"I was offering to pay them."

"Do you do that often?"

She tightened her fringed shawl around her shoulders. The night was not cold, but his voice was. "I manage my father's household. All of its expenses are my concern."

"What a paragon you are!"

"It's a daughter's place to do what I do."

"By the elevens, you are as dutiful as I have heard! Sponsoring your sister, although she can be only a few years your junior, during the Season and watching your father's household as close as wax. What sort of life is that for a young woman?"

"My life is mine to spend as I please."

"Or squander."

"Am I the one squandering my life, my lord?" she returned with heat. "I have my friends and my family and a reputation of which I am proud."

Lord Wentworth suddenly grinned. "Now I understand your loathing of my company. You fear I will taint your sister's chances for a good match. I must assure you, Miss

Talcott, that my reputation, as is the case with most reputations, I have discovered, is based more on fiction than fact.''

"You wish me to believe that you despise playing cards?"

He laughed. "Not in the least, but I enjoy other facets of life as much. I know it is said that I would as lief play cards than eat or—" His chuckle became softer. "Excuse me, Miss Talcott. My crude language proves I've been too long away from the gentle company of a winsome lady.''

Emily looked at the fan tied to her wrist. She found it difficult to believe that "Demon Wentworth" was this man who was as gentle as the amusement twinkling in his eyes. Was either the real Lord Wentworth, or was he trying to baffle her with the sense of humor he had warned her of when he called at Hanover Square?

"Then it would behoove you," she said, "to recall yourself. Lady Fanning expects a certain propriety from her guests.''

"Now you are wondering why Lady Fanning invited me to her home.''

"My lord, I never—"

"No, you would never say that," he interrupted with another chuckle, "but your eyes betray your thoughts.''

Emily decided the only way to salvage her faltering composure was to answer as boldly. "I would have guessed you find such gatherings boring," she said.

"I have little interest in the travesties of the Season, that is true. Riding in the Park is boring. Plying the dowagers and the young misses with court-promises suits me as a saddle suits a sow. Trying to avoid covetous mamas with marriageable daughters is tiresome. I would as lief retire to the card table." He sat on the edge of the planter and smiled. "Do you play cards, Miss Talcott?''

"I leave that to Papa." She started to add more, but her eyes were captured by his that were even with hers for the first time. Hastily, she lowered her eyes. Her heart thumped against her chest as if she had raced from Hanover Square to Hyde Park.

"That is much the pity."

His even voice irritated her, although she was being want-witted. He was not going to apologize for lying to her, so she should put an end to this conversation.

"That is your opinion, my lord. Now I must ask you, again, to excuse me." She folded her hands behind her back. "I must see to Miriam."

"Another of your duties. Which ideal man has your sister chosen to ensnare before the end of the Season?"

"Really, my lord, you ask such inappropriate questions."

He laughed. "And you avoid answering every one. I doff my cap to you, Miss Talcott, and give you warning. You should not play cards, for your countenance betrays every sentimental sentiment within you." He stood. "Mayhap you should try your hand at rewriting the marquis's drivel. Surely you could do no worse."

"I leave poetry to the poets."

He held out his hand, and she was sure her heart had stopped. Her breath caught in her throat, but her thoughts were alive with anticipation of his broad fingers touching her once more. Knowing such fantasies were unseemly, she was unable to dampen them . . . She did not want to dampen them.

She swallowed her gasp as Lord Wentworth reached past her and lifted the sagging branch of an azalea. "Lady Fanning could use your skill with her garden. This is hard to kill, but it appears she has managed that."

Emily blinked. She had been a cabbage-head to think he was intrigued with her. Closing her eyes, she sighed. She was lucky he intended to be a gentleman this evening, for her thoughts were constantly wandering off in a most unladylike direction.

"Valeria tries very diligently to improve her garden," she whispered. When he gave her an odd glance, she added in a more casual tone, "I have offered her what advice I can."

Shaking his head, he looked down into the garden where the plants showed as little life as the stone statues. "If you want my opinion, you should suggest that Lady Fanning leave the gardening to someone with your gentle touch." He squatted and peered under the bush. "The soil here is too dry and tasteless for this plant."

Emily faltered, astonished anew by his obvious interest in plants. When he glanced at her, she hurried to say, "The plants get little light and rain here."

Standing, he wiped his hands to loosen any dirt. "Something we can agree upon. Mayhap there is hope for salvaging our nascent friendship."

"I expect my friends to be honest with me."

He smiled as he offered his arm. There was a challenge in his voice when he said, "As I shall be from now on."

Chapter Six

Emily tried to concentrate on the reading, but Lord Wentworth's words intruded into her thoughts. She could not force them from her mind. Why was he intending to be a part of her life?

Or was it Papa's life he planned to play a part in? She wanted to warn him to stay far from her father, but that would be useless. As she had told Miriam, she had no say in Papa's choice of companions.

She found it impossible to listen to Valeria. Her friend was reading a sonnet Emily particularly disliked, especially when she thought of how many hours she had labored to make the words fit together. She winced as Valeria stumbled on a word. It was not Valeria's fault, but the rhythm of the line.

She was too aware of Lord Wentworth standing at the back of the room, his arms folded over his chest, no expression on his face. He could have been one of the statues in the garden. His assurances that he enjoyed poetry had sounded hollow. Or had she wanted them to sound that way? If she could discount him as nothing more than a gamester, it would be easier to ignore her pleasure when he sought her out.

Silk rustled behind her, and she glanced over her shoulder as a quivering hand grasped her arm. She stared into Miriam's red-ringed eyes.

"Emily, I can't stay here," Miriam whispered. She glanced toward the front of the room where Valeria was accepting the polite applause.

Clapping along with the others, Emily saw Mr. Simpkins was standing behind Valeria. The man never seemed willing to emerge from the shadow of Valeria's beauty. She sighed. This evening was taking a bad turn all around.

"Get your bonnet, Miriam, and I shall make our farewells."

"Thank you."

Wanting to urge her sister to put aside her foolish dreams, Emily knew how silly that was. She had dreams of her own. Being free of the responsibility of her family and being able to write the book on gardens was a future she might savor only in her dreams. Patting her sister's hand, she rose as Miriam went to collect their bonnets.

She eased along the row of chairs and started toward Valeria. When a glass was held out to her, blocking her way, she looked past it to see Lord Wentworth's smile.

"Drink with me to our delight at the cessation of that mewling mess of words," he said.

"If you do not like the poems, you need not have stayed!"

"There is no reason to leave until my companions at the card table do." Chuckling, he added, "Allow me to join you on your journey which seems so incredibly crucial."

"Crucial?"

"You were acting as single-minded as Simpkins when he is in pursuit of Lady Fanning. Your gaze focused on the floor, hands at your sides, and a frown on your face."

Emily could not keep from laughing when he aped Graham Simpkins's mannerisms with ease.

"Much better," he said, straightening and offering her the glass again. "If you do not wish to drink to the end of the readings, then let us drink to something else."

"What would that be?"

"Friendship."

"Ours?" she asked boldly.

His eyes crinkled in his bronzed face. "Why not? Unless you think it would be a waste of good champagne."

"A waste?" She tapped her glass against his. "Anything is possible, my lord."

Taking a sip, he said, "Almost anything. I find it unlikely I will ever be a fan of the marquis's poetry."

Emily fought to keep her smile in place. Why did he have to speak constantly of his distaste for her work? How she wished she could enlighten him, but the momentary pleasure of seeing his shock would come at the cost of her reputation and Miriam's.

"I hope your friend appreciated the book you bought," she said quietly.

"Yes." He held her gaze as he took another drink.

Blast this man! He had a facile gift for words, even when he used a single one, that she longed for.

Raising her own glass, she said, "You need not worry, my lord. I have no interest in prying the name of the recipient from you. I was simply inquiring."

"I am not worried, Miss Talcott." He held out his arm. "If I were to buy a gift for an incognita, it would not be something as chaste as a book of bird-witted poems."

"Chaste? Half the ladies in the room had rising color in their cheeks when Valeria read."

He drew her fingers within his arm. "And most of the men were trying not to chuckle, knowing they had said something as weak-minded to their convenient in order to court her favors."

"You are outrageous!"

"So I have been told on numerous occasions." He bent

toward her as they walked across the room. "And you find it most amusing, Miss Talcott."

"Yes."

When she added nothing more, as he had, Lord Wentworth laughed. "A bittock of my own medicine?"

"I prefer to think of it as honesty."

"That is very important to you, isn't it?"

Emily chided herself. She knew better than to speak out of hand, but she did so over and over in his company. "Of course, honesty is important to me. I—"

"Emily!"

Sure she had never been more pleased to see her friend, Emily turned to take Valeria's out-stretched hands. "A wonderful reading, Valeria."

"Thank you." She flashed a brilliant smile at the viscount. "Are you enjoying the reading, Lord Wentworth?"

"As much as Simpkins, I would say."

Emily had not noted Mr. Simpkins lurking, as he was so often, behind Valeria.

"My dear Emily," Valeria said, giving Mr. Simpkins no chance to respond, "you must read for us now. In French!" Her smile broadened. "She speaks it with rare flair, my lord. Did you know?"

"As Miss Talcott and I are the newest of friends, there is much I do not know of her." Lord Wentworth finished his champagne and put the glass on a nearby table. "I had thought she might be more familiar with Latin."

"Latin?" asked Emily.

"To know the scientific names of your plants."

Glad for the course the conversation was taking, Emily forced the tension from her shoulders. "Fortunately I need not know more than which ones prefer shade and when to water."

"You underestimate your skill."

Valeria, who never could bear to be left out of any conversation, interjected, "But will you read one of the marquis's poems for us in French, Emily?"

"Yes, please do," Lord Wentworth said. "It should be most enjoyable."

Emily shook her head. "I came to tell you that Miriam and I will be taking our leave."

"So early?" Valeria's lips became a perfect pout. "But why?"

She glanced at Mr. Simpkins, who seemed to be intent on the toes of his shoes. Resisting her yearning to scowl at him and ask him why he treated her sister so basely, she faltered. The truth would hurt Miriam; to lie would hurt Valeria. What a bumble-bath!

A footman rushed up to Valeria, who bent to listen to what the servant had to say. Her eyes grew as round as her mouth.

"Impossible!" she gasped.

"What is it?" asked Lord Wentworth.

Valeria flushed, grew pale, then regained her normal color. "Please wait here. I must tend to this without delay."

"Valeria—"

"Emily, please do not leave until I come back." She grasped Emily's arms. "Promise me!"

Unsettled by Valeria's fervor, she nodded. She watched as her friend rushed away in the wake of the footman. The orchestra in the corner of the room began to play.

Lord Wentworth raised a single brow, but said nothing when Mr. Simpkins mumbled something under his breath and scurried away.

Not sure what to do, Emily sipped on her champagne.

"Would you like more?"

She flinched at Lord Wentworth's question. Disquiet hung in the air like the heaviness before a storm. Something was wrong. Something was horribly wrong. Something much more than Miriam's shattered heart, although that was enough to break Emily's own. Looking down at her glass as Lord Wentworth repeated his question, she discovered it was empty.

"No, no more champagne, thank you," she said.

"Miss Talcott, you look as if you could use some fresh air."

"I think that would be a good idea."

"May I?"

This time when he offered his arm, she did not hesitate to put her fingers on it. She seldom got these troubling sensations, but she had learned to listen to them.

Before they had walked more than a few steps, trouble materialized in front of her. Lord Lichton was a pudgy man with an over-inflated sense of his own worth and few manners. She had never seen him wear the same waistcoat twice, so she guessed he was full of enough juice to intimidate much of the Polite World. His hair was thinning to the light brown of his eyes.

"Good evening," he said with a nod toward Lord Wentworth. "May I steal a few moments of Miss Talcott's time from you, Wentworth?"

Sickness cramped Emily's stomach. Only one reason would bring her to the earl's attention. Papa's gambling debts!

"If she wishes. Do you, Emily?"

She stared when Lord Wentworth used her given name. His mouth was drawn into a straight line, and she suspected he shared her distaste for Lord Lichton. If he hoped to spare her the earl's court-promises by suggesting an intimacy between them which allowed such informality, Lord Wentworth was kind, but mistaken. The glitter in Lord Lichton's eyes did not come from adoration, but avarice.

"I would be delighted to speak to Lord Lichton," she said.

"I shall find us some more champagne," Lord Wentworth said. "I think it is time we drank another toast to honesty."

Emily recoiled from his fury. Not that she could fault him when she had reprimanded him for being false. Yet how could she speak of what she was certain were Papa's gambling obligations to Lord Lichton in front of Lord Wentworth?

"Valeria has a small parlor this way," she said, gesturing toward a narrow arch. "We may speak there." She hoped she could pay her father's latest debts. Even a few guineas might bankrupt them now.

Lord Lichton nodded and stepped back to let her lead the way. He was silent until he was seated across from her in the tiny room which was bright with lamplight and the rose-colored upholstery. He folded his arms over his barrel chest and said, "I enjoyed your father's company at His Grace's table last night."

"I am pleased to hear that," she answered, although she was nothing of the sort.

"Your father plays the king's books with fervor."

"But with little luck."

The earl had the decency to blink at her forthright answer, but a smile spread across his full mouth. "You are a unique woman, Miss Talcott. As pretty as a spring morning, but with a wit that rivals a man's."

"Thank you." She clasped her hands. "Then I am sure you won't take offense when I ask you what Papa owes—"

"I thought I might find you here." Lord Wentworth entered the room, grinning. "It is quite bright in here, isn't it? I suspect our hostess does not want to allow an untoward rendezvous to take place."

Lord Lichton stood as the viscount handed Emily the glass he held. "Wentworth, we are speaking of a private matter."

"Emily, I trust it is not too private." A crestfallen expression did not fit well on his face, especially when his eyes, dancing with merriment, warned he was enjoying the chance to fun the earl.

"Of course not." When Lord Wentworth motioned with the tips of his fingers, she whispered, "Of course not, Damon."

Lord Lichton's eyes widened. "I did not know you and Miss Talcott were so well acquainted, Wentworth." Suddenly, he chuckled. "Ah!"

"Ah, what?" asked Lord Wentworth.

"Dare I believe you have your mind on obtaining something other than your winnings from Talcott's elder daughter?"

Lord Wentworth smiled, but Emily saw disgust in his gray eyes. "Lichton, your words prove you are in no danger of losing your reputation as a boor." Holding out his arm, he said, "Emily, you have suffered his company too long."

She let him lead her out of a door at the far side of the room. Even though she was grateful to Lord Wentworth for helping her escape, she knew Lord Lichton would be calling at Hanover Square soon to demand his winnings from Papa. She was certain he would be in a foul mood.

"Are you all right?" Lord Wentworth asked.

"Yes, my lord."

" 'My lord?' " He grimaced. "I had hoped to be in the absurd position of owing Lichton a debt for allowing us to set aside such absurd proprieties." Turning to face her, he took her hands and led her to stand in front of the windowseat and a tall window that patterned starlight across the floor. "Would it upset you too much to continue calling me Damon? Unless you have taken a liking to 'Demon.' Your sister seems to enjoy using that epithet when she thinks I cannot hear her."

"Miriam meant nothing by her words, my—"

"Damon," he said softly.

She nodded, knowing that battling him on such a small matter was futile. "Allow me to apologize for my sister's insult."

"No doubt she believes her words to be the truth, but 'tis not your sister we are speaking of. Would you be too distressed to continue to call me Damon?"

"I—"

"Honestly, Emily."

Again she could not halt her lips from tilting in a smile. "Honestly, it would not upset me too much."

He did not release her hands. When she looked up from where his fingers caressed hers as lightly as a twilight breeze, a smile drifted across his lips. It was provocative, daring her to release the flood of questions dammed within her. She must not, even though she longed to know why he continued to seek her out.

"I believe," she continued, "I owe you another thank you for coming to . . ."

"Rescue you?" He laughed when fire billowed up her cheeks, and she feared the truth had put her to a rare blush. "No need to mince words, Emily. I know Lichton for the irritating block that he is. It was my pleasure to *rescue* you from his company."

"Now I must ask you to excuse me." She drew her hands out of his. "I have left Miriam too long alone."

"You are a poor chaperone." His finger tilted her chin toward him. "For her and for you."

"For me? I have no need of a chaperone."

His arm slipped around her waist. "For the first time, you are mistaken."

Before she could reply, he tightened his arm around her. His fingers curled across her nape, sending tendrils of luscious warmth along her. Gently, he tipped her face closer. The brush of his lips against hers was scintillating, but he drew away with only that brief touch.

This was not the type of kiss she had thought would satisfy a man who had earned the name Demon. He seemed the kind of man who wanted so much more.

Her voice quivered. "Mayhap you are correct. I should have considered I might need rescuing from you."

"Do you truly wish to be rescued from this?" His face lowered toward hers.

Before she could reply, an elbow struck her back. She whirled out of Damon's arms and stared at Graham Simpkins who recoiled.

"Pardon me, miss," he mumbled. Cowering back into himself, he did not raise his gaze above the middle of Damon's waistcoat. "Pardon me, sir."

"Are you lost, Simpkins?" Damon asked, the taint of amusement stealing the warmth from his voice.

"Wentworth?" Mr. Simpkins wrinkled his nose and shook himself like a dog coming in out of the rain. "I thought you had taken your leave."

"Not yet."

Mr. Simpkins turned toward Emily. His eyes grew wide. "Miss Talcott? Here alone with— Well, well." He continued to mutter to himself as he hurried away.

Emily wondered what else could go wrong tonight. She should have listened to her own instincts to stay home this evening.

As if he could hear her thoughts, which was a most uncomfortable idea, Damon said, "No one heeds Simpkins's grumbling. You need not fear for your reputation. After all, you have done nothing which would tarnish it."

"I let you kiss me."

"Kiss you?" He laughed as he grasped her elbows again and drew her back to him. "That was no more than a chaste salute. You would have had to worry far more if Simpkins had witnessed this."

His mouth was anything but gentle as it claimed hers. It demanded that she give as much pleasure as he offered. He pulled her up against his firm chest. Her hands were sliding along his arms before she could halt them. She wanted this kiss from this man. It might be madness, but she had been practical for too long.

His lips coursed along her neck, eliciting a spark on each touch. Delighting in the brush of his hair against her cheek, she swept her fingers through it. Her knees threatened to betray her when his tongue teased the curve of her ear. With his breath burning a tempest through her, she clenched onto his sleeves.

Slowly, his lips rose. Opening her eyes, she saw his face

so close. He smiled, his gaze sending another flush of pleasure through her.

"See, Emily?" he whispered. "That is a kiss that would set every tongue in the Polite World wagging."

She pulled back, horrified.

Damon smiled. "No one saw us, so you need have no worry."

Emily sat on the windowseat, gratified it was so close when she could not trust her knees or her heart that urged her back into his arms. "I hope you are not mistaken."

"I am not. But you are mistaken about many things."

"What do you mean?"

When he sat beside her, he folded her hand between his. "Do not look so shaken by my simple comment, Emily. I meant only that I had hoped you now would understand why only the ladies in the room flushed at the so-called passion in the marquis's poems."

"I don't understand."

He grazed her cheek with his lips. "That is the limit to the passion that frog puts in his poems." Cupping her chin in his palm, he said, "I prefer more."

As he bent toward her, Emily stood. Her breath strained against her bodice, but she fought to keep her voice even. "You have made your preference clear."

"And you disapprove?" he asked, setting himself on his feet.

"No, I mean—you should not have taken such liberties, my—"

"At the very least, I believe our kiss shows we are good enough friends, Emily, so you may continue to use my first name."

"Friends do not kiss on the lips."

His smile returned. "Now that sounds like the voice of experience. You have kissed many friends? Any as you just kissed me?"

"No, I mean—" She clamped her lips closed. A brangle with him would gain her nothing. He was too facile and would twist every word she said. Clasping her hands in front of her, she said, "That is none of your bread-and-butter."

"I believe that is the most honest thing you have said to me this evening."

"I must return to Miriam. She expected we would be leaving posthaste."

"You are right. I have taken too much of your time, but I trust you now see my point about that frog poet."

"You have your opinion, Damon, and I have mine."

He laughed and offered his arm. "Allow me to escort you back to the gathering."

"That would not be a good idea. If we were seen together—"

"You fret far too much. Lichton knows I came to retrieve you from his attempt to dun you."

"But he thinks we are. . ." She lowered her eyes as he chuckled again.

"You do have imagination." His finger under her chin tipped her face up. "I enjoy that virtue in my friends."

"The only virtue you enjoy in your friends?"

Again he laughed. "Now you sound as if you still are listening to your sister who labels me 'Demon Wentworth.' " Again he held out his arm. "While I enjoy your virtues, Emily, allow me to vaunt what you seem to believe is my singular one by gallantly escorting you."

"Why are you belittling yourself?"

He drew her arm within his. "In hopes that something I say might bring your smile back. I had not intended to distress you so."

"You did not."

"Ah, more honesty." He led her along the corridor. "Or I hope it was honesty."

"It was."

Emily waited for his reply, but he said nothing as the music of the orchestra swelled over them. Her trepidation that every eye would turn toward them disappeared when no one seemed to notice them. For that, she should be happy, but why were they being ignored? It was not the way of the *ton* to disregard a potential topic for gossip.

One pair of eyes had been watching for their arrival, she realized when Mr. Colley strode toward them. The handsome man flashed a smile at every woman he passed, but he had none for Emily when he halted in front of her. He gave Damon a curt nod before saying, "This is disturbing, Miss Talcott."

"This?" She wished just one person would make sense tonight.

"What I hear of the time you are spending in Lord Wentworth's company."

Horror struck her anew. "Did Mr. Simpkins—?"

Damon's hand squeezing her arm halted her. Smoothly, he said, "Colley, you should not be berating Miss Talcott."

"I simply question her taste." He raised his nose and sniffed. "You are making calf eyes at both Wentworth *and* Simpkins, are you?"

Emily was not sure whether to give in to laughter or tears. "Mr. Colley, you misunderstand."

"Apparently, for I believed we had an understanding. I bid you good evening and good-bye, Miss Talcott."

Damon chuckled as the affronted man stormed away. "He enjoys making an exit, doesn't he?"

"I am afraid he was beginning to believe what he read in the gossip columns." Emily shook her head. "I should not say this, but thank you."

"For ridding you of Colley?" He gave her a sardonic bow. "My pleasure."

Emily looked about the room. "This is odd."

"I agree."

She glanced at him and saw his smile. That he perceived what she meant was unsettling. Sharply, she told herself that Damon had been a part of the Polite World longer than she, so he could not be unaware of the peculiar lack of interest in their return to the ballroom together.

Scanning the room, she saw her sister in the midst of a conversation with several friends. Miriam must have sensed Emily's gaze, for she turned and waved before hurrying across the ballroom where no one seemed to be interested in the music or the food or the wine.

"Good evening, Miss Talcott," Damon said with a bow. "It is a pleasure to—"

"Emily, have you heard?"

"Please do not interrupt, Miriam," Emily chided.

She bobbed her head toward Damon. "Yes, yes. Forgive me. Good evening, my lord." Turning back to Emily, she could not hide her excitement. "What do you think of this?"

"This what?" When she looked at Damon, he shrugged.

Miriam linked her arm with Emily's and drew her away. "You shan't believe what I just heard."

"About some surprise Valeria has?"

Her smile became a disappointed pout. "Do you know what it is?"

Emily did not answer as she heard excited voices on the other side of the room. As Valeria's guests crowded toward the far doorway, more joining the throng on every breath, she tried to see what the to-do was about. Too many taller people stood between her and their hostess.

When a hand tugged on her arm, she looked up at Damon. "Come this way, Emily. Over by the balcony door, I believe you shall be able to see Lady Fanning's grand entrance with whatever she has devised."

"So you have no idea whom it is?" persisted Miriam.

Emily almost retorted that she had been concerned with things more important than their hostess's attempt to make her party memorable among the many of the Season. She bit back the comment, for Miriam would be scandalized to discover her sister had been in Damon's arms. "Who? Is the surprise a person?"

"That is what I have heard." Excitement filled Miriam's voice. "Look! There he is!"

In the doorway, a man stood next to Valeria, his arm
through hers. She was smiling with satisfaction as she stared
up at the man who was tall and undeniably handsome. He
was dressed in spotless white breeches beneath his red coat
and silver vest, and his ebony hair glistened like his knee-
high boots. A finger-thin mustache accented his full lips.

"Who is that?" asked Emily.

The answer came back at the same time from a half
dozen people. "Marquis de la Cour."

Chapter Seven

This was impossible!

Emily stared at Valeria and the slender man beside her. This could not be happening! He could not be Marquis de la Cour! *She* was the marquis. Coldness sank into her center. She could not say anything. The truth would shame the Talcott family as well as embarrassing Valeria.

The orchestra fell into discordant silence. When a line formed, twisting through the ballroom, so that everyone might have a chance to welcome the marquis to Town, Emily held back. She should take Miriam and leave, but she doubted if her sister would depart now.

"Are you unwell?" asked Damon, his smile becoming a frown of concern. "You have no more color than your sister's gown."

Emily fought to force a weak smile. "I simply am overcome at the thought of coming face-to-face with the author who has written the poetry Miriam enjoys so much."

"And you."

"Yes, and me." She dampened her lips which were as dry as her palms. She stared at the man by Valeria's side.

No question about it, this man perfectly suited anyone's image of a French marquis who spent his time in the pursuit of the exact word to describe the moment when two lovers' gazes met. As he bowed over a woman's hand and kissed it with just the right amount of Gallic fervor that suggested his amorous poetry were reflections of his own *affaires d' amour,* Emily cursed the hour when she had devised this preposterous lie.

Who was he?

"Emily!" cried Miriam. "Isn't this wonderful? Let's go and speak with him!"

"Yes," seconded Damon in a calmer voice, "I think we should do that." He held out both arms, one to her and one to Miriam. "I would not miss escorting the Talcott sisters to meet the incomparable Marquis de la Cour. This should make for a much more intriguing evening than Lady Fanning planned."

Emily wanted to retort. Intriguing was not the word she would have chosen. Horror was closer to what was roiling through her stomach.

When she did not put her hand on his arm, Damon asked, "Why are you delaying? I am sure Lady Fanning cannot wait to introduce her unexpected guest to her best bosom-bow."

"In a moment," she said faintly. Then, noting Damon's curious glance, she added in a normal tone, "We do not want to overmaster him with welcome."

Miriam glanced toward the crowd. "Do come, Emily. By the time we get there, Valeria will sort order out and arrange for all of us to meet the marquis. I own to an incredible eagerness to meet him."

"That is no surprise," Damon said. "Ladies?"

Miriam reached past Damon and grasped Emily's hand. With a tug, she snatched Emily away from him.

"Valeria is motioning to you, Emily," Miriam said without looking at Damon. "Come! You don't want to vex her when she must be half mad with anxiety about the turn this evening has taken." She pulled on Emily's hand again.

Looking from her determined sister to Valeria's strained smile, Emily nodded. Her friend did need her now. And, to own the truth, Miriam's uncivil behavior gave Emily the excuse she needed to dismiss Damon without bringing undue attention on them. She almost laughed. No one was taking note of anything but the bogus marquis.

As Miriam drew her across the room, Emily glanced back at Damon. He was smiling coolly. What he was thinking was hidden behind that polite, slightly arrogant countenance he seemed to prefer when they were with others.

Emily was sucked into the excited crowd. Everyone was atitter with the thrill of speaking to the French poet. She glanced toward the front door. It would be simpler to flee.

"Isn't he just the pick?" cooed one dowager.

"A true clean potato," announced another. "Who would have guessed we would meet *him* tonight?"

"Do you think he dances?"

A scoffing voice chided the young speaker, "He is French, isn't he?"

Emily did not join the eager laughter. If she opened her mouth, she feared she would shame herself by being sick.

A hand on her elbow startled her. She looked up into Damon's eyes which were as chilly as his smile.

When he handed her a glass of champagne, she took a sip and whispered, "Thank you."

"You looked as if you could use some fortifying. I had not thought the chance to meet the marquis would leave you as colorless as a corpse." Before she could answer, he asked, "Do you mind if I join you in greeting this inimitable brother of the quill?"

His contempt strengthened her more than his kindness. "Am I to believe you are interested in meeting him?"

"I am interested," he said quietly, "in discovering why you let your sister drag you away as if I were a demon. Is there something I can say to bring you to your bearings?"

The line moved forward several steps, but his hand her arm held her back to let several others between them and Miriam.

"Damon, I need to stay with Miriam. She is—"

"Pleased to give me my *congé*. Is that your plan as well?" He ran a finger along the smooth skin behind her ear. "You did not seem anxious to rush away earlier."

This evening was whirling completely out of control. She needed to concentrate on what she would say to this fake marquis. She must not think about how wondrous Damon's touch was and how it teased her to think of other ways he might touch her.

"Emily!" Valeria's enthusiastic voice kept her from having to find some excuse. Rushing to where they stood, Valeria wafted a garish fan with pearl spines and glorious purple feathers in front of her face. "I wondered where you might be."

Emily smiled as she took her friend's hand. "I must wait my turn to meet your guest of honor."

Valeria's smile became broader but her eyes narrowed as she looked past Emily. "Lord Wentworth, I am glad you stayed for this surprising turn of events."

He bowed over Valeria's hand. "This evening has been one unexpected pleasure after another."

Again Emily was grateful that she did not suffer Miriam's blushes, for his glance in her direction told her exactly which pleasure he was thinking of now. The same as she was.

Not now. She could not think of his bold kiss now. She had another problem. As she listened to Damon and Valeria trade polite Spanish coin, she appraised with calmer eyes the man who claimed to be Marquis de la Cour.

He was in twig, for his ebony eyes had an exotic tilt that crinkled in his well-tanned face each time he smiled. She watched as he, in turn, gauged each of the guests fawning over him. She wondered if he was gripped with a fear that one of them might denounce him.

As she should.

She silenced that thought when Miriam edged closer. Her sister was gazing at the marquis with the longing of a schoolgirl watching a soirée from the top of the stairs. Even Mr. Simpkins, who came to stand in his customary place in Valeria's shadow, did not draw her attention from this impostor.

Emily resisted seizing Miriam by the shoulders and shaking her. Yes, Marquis de la Cour was present, but . . . she could not be honest.

Valeria herded Emily out of the reception line. When Emily tried to demur, Valeria chuckled and said, "My dear Emily, one of the joys of being a hostess is being able to break a few of Society's canons in order to make my guests happy."

"I would be glad to wait my turn."

"Do not be a goose!"

Hearing Damon's chuckle, Emily silenced her retort. She listened to Miriam's excited giggle as she joined them.

"I cannot wait," Miriam whispered.

"Look out!" Emily gasped as her sister nearly trod on Mr. Simpkins's toes. When he jumped aside, Emily murmured, "Miriam, think about what you are doing."

"I can think of nothing but the chance to meet the marquis."

Emily hoped no one saw her roll her eyes, but she discovered how hopeless that was when they were caught by Damon's gray gaze. He stood to one side, his arms crossed over his chest, as if this were being staged for his amusement. Blast him! And blast herself for creating the marquis in the first place.

"Emily!" Valeria poked her in the side before saying, "Marquis de la Cour, this is my dear bosom-bow Miss Emily Talcott. She, like her sister whom you just met, is much a follower of your work."

Emily could not keep from staring at the man who should be no more than her imagination. Dear God! This could not be happening! She feared every eye in the room was finally aimed at her, not because she had appeared on Lord Wentworth's arm but because she was stricken silent.

The bogus marquis preened as if Valeria's adulation were his rightful due. When he bowed his head toward Emily, she noted he was inspecting her as he had the other guests. She said nothing until he raised his head, although the guests behind her rumbled impatiently.

"I am astonished to meet you, *mon seigneur,*" she said, refusing to let his gaze slide away. In French, she added, "I bid you a warm welcome to our country."

"How sweet your words sound on these ears that hunger for the lush tones of my birth tongue," he answered, but in heavily accented English. "I would answer in kind, but I am endeavoring to learn to speak your language as prettily as you do mine. I fear I shall never achieve that goal."

"Do you intend to write your next volume in English?" she asked, waiting for the opportunity to prove he was a liar without revealing the truth that would damn her.

"Who is to say?" He smiled. "Ah, the muses which whisper inspiration in a man's ear do not serve him. He must serve them. You do understand, do you not, Mademoiselle Talcott?"

Emily flinched. Did he know the truth? How could he? She drew in a deep breath, then released it when she realized he was not speaking to her, but to Miriam.

"I wish I did," Miriam said, her voice lilting like a bird's. "Mayhap Emily would understand. She used to pen little stories."

"Nothing," Emily said hastily, aware of the many ears listening, "that could compare with your poetry, *mon seigneur.*"

"I would hope not," came a low whisper near her ear. "I suspect your youthful efforts showed much more skill."

Emily looked over her shoulder. In the midst of this turmoil, she had forgotten Damon was a witness to this insanity. He was smiling, clearly amused. Well, he should be, for they all were chuckleheads to pay court on an impostor. Not able to retort as she wished, she watched while the marquis drew Valeria into his conversation with Miriam. He utterly ignored Mr. Simpkins.

Valeria was unable to conceal her delight. By the morrow, if not before, all London would be agog at learning Marquis de la Cour was in Town. And everyone would know that Valeria Fanning had been his first hostess.

Emily started to step away. When Damon put his hand on her arm to halt her, she regarded him with astonishment. Again she was thwarted from asking any questions, for Valeria said, "*Mon seigneur*, this is Damon Wentworth."

"Wentworth," the marquis said with a hint of disdain. The two men bowed toward each other, and she realized they were of a height. As he straightened, the marquis smiled at Miriam. "Tell me, Mademoiselle Talcott, which of my poems you love best."

Valeria gushed, "*Mon seigneur*, Lord Wentworth is such an admirer of your work that he left his favorite chair at his club to attend tonight's reading of your work."

"Is that so?" the false marquis asked, turning to look at Damon.

With no sign that he was speaking anything but the truth, Damon answered, "I doubt if you will find another who views your poetry as I do. Isn't that correct, Emily?"

"I have heard you describe the marquis's poetry with words unlike you have used for any other," she said quietly.

"Odd that you should find it so intriguing, Lord Wentworth," the marquis replied. "I write my poetry to appeal to the ears and eyes of our gentler sex."

"Exactly as I mentioned to Emily earlier."

Taking her sister's arm, Emily drew Miriam away from whatever spell the marquis had spun about her. She heard a muffled sound. Damon's face was contorted as if with pain. She knew better. He was struggling to restrain his laughter.

As they walked toward where even the orchestra had abandoned their seats in an effort to meet the marquis, someone called to Miriam. Her sister excused herself before Emily could speak.

Damon laughed as he rested his shoulder against the door leading out to the balcony.

"If you can control yourself," Emily said, "I would ask you not to use me to bait that hapless Frenchman."

"Spoken like a true heroine coming to the rescue of the weak and simple." Taking Emily's champagne glass, he downed what was left in it and set the glass on a nearby table. "However, I was chuckling about your sister. She seems much taken with that frog poet."

She turned away. "She is young."

Damon stepped in front of her. Tipping her face toward him, he said, "Emily, youth is no excuse for being short a sheet. By the elevens, you are no more than a handful of years her senior, but you were not bamblusterated by this marquis."

"What do you mean?" She did not dare to breathe. Could he have guessed the truth? Oh, dear God, she prayed not.

"I can tell you find him as unpalatable as I do." His fingertip brushed her cheek. "Why are you treating me so icily when but an hour ago we spoke of friendship?"

"Can we speak of something else?"

"Of what?" His caress urged her to lower her defenses as he whispered, "Do you wish to speak of how we pledged that friendship with a friendly kiss?"

Emily could not ignore the banked embers in his eyes. That sweet flame had urged her to melt to him when he drew her into his arms.

"Emily!" Valeria hurried to them. "The marquis would dearly love to hear you read his poetry in French. Come! Do not make him wait."

"Damon and I—we were talking about—"

"Excuse us, my lord," Valeria said, smiling. "We must not keep the marquis waiting. You understand, don't you?"

"Do I?" he asked, his gaze holding Emily's.

She longed to shut her eyes, to close out the promise glowing in his eyes. With a sigh she could not silence, she said, "I am afraid you must understand."

"Then I must." He stepped back and bowed his head with the same derision he had shown the fake marquis. "Read that Frenchman's poetry with all the fervor it deserves, Emily. I trust I shall hear of your success."

"You are leaving?"

"Lady Luck beckons. As I prefer her *chanson* to any of de la Cour's, I ask you ladies to excuse me. Thank you, Lady Fanning, for a most interesting evening."

When he turned on his heel, the temptation to call him back teased Emily. But what could she tell him? That she delighted in his company, that she wanted his touch, that she yearned to taste the fervor she had sampled on his lips. As he wove his way through the press of Valeria's guests, her gaze followed him, unable to resist admiring the breadth of his shoulders and the easy arrogance of his stride.

"Now that he has taken his leave," Valeria said with a smile, "we can enjoy ourselves."

Emily regarded her with amazement she could not conceal. "Why do you say that? You invited him to this soirée."

"I gave no thought to the idea that he actually would attend." She linked her arm through Emily's. "Come and read for us. The marquis is going to be delighted with you."

Emily looked at the door, but Damon had left. With him was gone the irreverence that had allowed her to laugh away some of her apprehension. What a muddle this was! She had created Marquis de la Cour, but she feared this fantasy had taken on a life of its own and would now consume her.

Chapter Eight

Damon tossed the cards onto the table and leaned back in his chair to glower at the parlor hearth. Playing alone was no sport. Nor was it any way to clear his mind of the thoughts that had stalked him since he left Lady Fanning's house. Tonight should have been amusing. He had hoped to spend some time chatting with Emily Talcott about gardening and, mayhap, to persuade a few of his tie-mates to take their leave early so they might enjoy time at the club.

Instead, he had let himself be lured into playing the hero for Emily when Lichton proved to be a boor. Then he allowed his own curiosity to seduce him into kissing her. His curiosity or her intriguing eyes and the soft curves which had been so inviting in his arms? Adzooks! He would be the ruin of her reputation and his own if anyone discovered a saucy lass with a green thumb had beguiled him.

He muttered a stronger curse as he went to look out the window at the street side of the simple parlor. Dawn was touching the eastern sky, but the day was gray. Heavy clouds clung to the earth, promising a morning of rain. The perfect day to spend working in a garden.

With a yawn, he stretched. He rubbed his chin, which could use a shave. What was wrong with him? He knew what he wanted and how he intended to get it. Nothing had stayed him from that course before Emily Talcott intruded on his thoughts with every breath.

"Something amiss?"

Damon turned and smiled at Gerald Cozie, who was as thin as an anatomy. That fact was emphasized by his open waistcoat and collarless shirt. Gerald never bothered with the tenets of the *ton*, an aspect of his friend's life Damon envied. Cozie lived in obscure gentility beyond the *on dits* of the Polite World. An altogether admirable way in Damon's opinion, and one he wished he could emulate.

"I did not hear you come in, Gerald," he said.

Gerald set a tray on the table by the window where the dim light glittered on his almost bald pate and the glasses perched on the very end of his nose. "You were intent on your cards. Did you win?"

Damon chuckled without humor. "When one plays oneself, it is not hard to win."

"If it were to be bandied about the élite that you sat alone at the card table, it could be the death of your reputation, Demon Wentworth."

"You have been reading the papers again." Sitting on the arm of one of a pair of overstuffed chairs, he laughed. "I thought you had broken yourself of that habit which you considered unbecoming a man of science."

"Even scientific journals pall after a while." Gerald poured two cups of coffee and offered one to Damon. "Also, how otherwise would I keep track of my favorite ex-student?"

"Pray do not sound like a doting mother." He sipped on the coffee, letting its strong flavor awaken every nerve.

"You have been absent from our discussions for the past pair of fortnights."

"Business."

"Good or bad or simply interesting?"

Damon smiled. "If you want to know, read the papers."

"Not all your business is in the papers."

"Thank goodness."

Gerald's smile faded. "So why are you here?"

Taking another drink, he asked, "Can't I give an old friend a look-in without having an ulterior motive?"

"You always had an ulterior motive in the past."

"True."

Gerald sat at the table and stirred sugar into his coffee. Sipping, he said nothing. The silence grew, but without the burdening tension it would have had at his club if Damon had not answered such a blunt question.

Making himself comfortable in the old chair, Damon stared at the wall of books. He guessed Gerald had read every battered volume. The scent of leather bindings made the room the most welcoming in London and increased his longing to return to Wentworth Hall and his own book-room.

"I went to the club earlier," Damon said quietly.

"Then you obviously left."

He nodded. "All the talk was of Marquis de la Cour. I tired of hearing that block lauded as a master."

"Even Shakespeare had his detractors."

"Pray do not compare de la Cour and Shakespeare," he said with an emoted groan.

Gerald smiled as he refilled his cup with the fragrant coffee. "Do not be elitist. Books of romantic poetry sell well."

"True. There will always be a market for those who delight in the maudlin, I suspect."

"Not all the marquis's readers delight in the maudlin. I have read the Frenchman's poetry."

Damon groaned again. "Why did you torture yourself?"

"I was curious." He wagged a finger. "Curiosity is a gift

for those of us who wish to strengthen our minds with new ideas."

"So what did you think?"

"You want my opinion?"

"Haven't I always?" Damon asked as he poured more coffee into his cup. He doubted if Gerald's thick brew had ever tasted as good as it did this morning. "I value your opinion on any topic."

"You mean you suffer me to stick my nose into all your business, both personal and not so personal." He stretched and plucked a book off the shelf. "I have not read de la Cour's newest tome, but I read the previous two books. Some of this poetry is actually quite good."

"I agree."

Gerald raised a single, bushy eyebrow. "You agree?"

"I will deny I said that most vehemently if you repeat my words to anyone."

"Why this façade of distaste for de la Cour? A poet who writes only of love is just what we need to heal the rift left by the war."

"I fear you give de la Cour too much credit."

Resting his elbow on the table, Gerald said, "Mayhap. Mayhap not. However, either way, that does not explain your call at such an early hour."

"I needed a bit of peace and sanity."

"So who is this incomparable who has caught your eye? Who is she?"

"She?"

Gerald chuckled. "I know you well, old fellow. You argue the triviality of French poetry simply so you can ignore what truly troubles you. As you did not beat up my quarters to enjoy a friendly brangle, I have considered the other reasons you might call."

"Did you consider I might enjoy your company?"

"Yes, but you have always been considerate enough to visit during my waking hours." His smile grew wide in his narrow face. "I supposed there must be an extraordinary reason for this call, and my supposition led me to consider the most inconsiderable. Damon Wentworth of demon fame has had his heart, an organ many in London have questioned the existence of, touched by a woman."

His lips twisted. "Mayhap you should be writing silly poetry. You are developing a gift for imagining the most ludicrous things."

"Damon, who is she?"

With a sigh, he drained his cup. He stood and poured himself yet another serving. As the steam rose to curl in front of his tired eyes, he said, "I never could bamboozle you. I have met a charming woman of rare intelligence."

"Who?"

"By the elevens, Gerald, why are you acting like a matchmaking mother this morning?"

He smiled and crossed one leg over the other, a motion Damon knew signaled his friend intended to extract every detail from him. "Curious only."

"Her name is Emily Talcott."

"Charles Talcott's daughter?" He sat straighter. "Now this is interesting."

"How so?"

"When I was young, I often left my nurse behind and took myself down to the docks where I watched one of the Talcott ships sail for America." His smile became sad. "I haven't thought about that for a long, long time. I wonder if they are still sailing."

"Talcott never mentions it. Neither has Emily." Damon sat again. The chair's soft upholstery urged him to remember Emily's pliant curves against him. "Damn."

Gerald laughed. "Take care, Damon, or someone will note that you wear a moony expression whenever the fair lass crosses your mind."

"Don't be ridiculous. This is the wrong time for me to enjoy more than a flirtation."

"When will the right time be for more?"

He shrugged. "I am not certain, but I know now is

wrong. I have too many matters demanding my attention. Wentworth Hall alone could keep a dozen men so busy they have no time to think of a flirtation."

"No man should be so busy he has no time to think of a flirtation." Gerald pulled a pipe from a stand on the bookshelf and lit it, raising a cloud.

"Odd words from a lifelong bachelor."

"I was too busy with my studies and research and teaching."

"So I am to learn what from that?" Damon laughed. "I have never seen anyone happier with life than you, Gerald. You do as you please when you please without answering to anyone, save yourself."

"A fine state for me, but not for you." He pointed the stem of his pipe at Damon. "You need someone to assist you with the resurrection of Wentworth Hall."

"I have Sanders to aid me."

"I speak of a wife, not of a gardener." His smile became an expression of contemplation. "My dear boy, I know it is none of my business, but I do not wish you to end up alone."

"I do not wish to end up alone." Miriam stretched her hand across the settee and gave Emily a smile. "As it is clear Graham Simpkins has no interest in me, what is wrong with me enjoying the company of a man who seems to?"

Emily counted silently to ten in French and then in English. She had not thought last evening could become worse, but she had underestimated how her poetry seemed to captivate the wrong people. The single poem she had read in French had given the fraudulent marquis a chance to seek out Miriam and engage her in conversation.

But the evening and the poetry reading were past. Now was not the time for romantic nothing sayings. This was the time for sense.

Quietly, she said, "Miriam, you know nothing about the marquis."

"I know his heart." Her smile brightened the room that was lost in the shadows of the cloudy day.

"How can you say that? You met the man for the first time last night." *And, with luck, it shall be the final time you meet him.* Surely the impostor would not dare show his face among the Polite World again.

Miriam picked up the book in her lap. Opening it, she touched the page where the make-believe marquis had autographed the title page. "Emily, how can anyone read these poems and not come to know the heart behind the hand that penned them?"

"They are simply poems! Anyone could have written them."

"Really?" She stood. "I don't believe that. I can imagine no one, save the marquis, creating them."

"Miriam, please, you must listen." Emily set herself on her feet and grasped her sister's hands. "There are some things you don't understand."

Miriam kissed her on the cheek. "Dear sister, I know you have been anxious about my infatuation with Mr. Simpkins. I intend to put it behind me, for now I know what it is to have admiration returned. Having tasted the sweetness of wine, why would anyone wish water?"

"Please don't quote the poems to me." She had never imagined her words might come back to haunt her like this.

With a chuckle, she went to the door. "I cannot wait to write about Valeria's rout in my journal."

"Miriam, wait!"

Either her sister did not hear her or chose not to listen, for Miriam vanished up the stairs.

With a deep sigh, Emily dropped back onto the chair. She glowered at the flowers set in front of the fire screen by the hearth. How could this become more of a shocking mull? Not that she could upbraid Miriam for being an air-dreamer about a man! After all, her sister had not been the one to let a reputed rogue steal a kiss from her in a quiet corner of her bosom-bow's house. If Graham Simpkins had bumbled along only a moment later. . . She hid her face in her hands. What a witless block she was!

"Emily!"

She leaped to her feet at her sister's cry. She was halfway up the stairs by the time she realized the sound had been happy.

"What is it?" Emily asked as she topped the stairs to find her sister rocking from one foot to the other with excitement.

"Let me show you!" She threw open Emily's bedchamber door and rushed in. Sitting on the chaise longue, she cried, "Hurry! You shall want to see this. I know you shall."

Emily glanced at the bills piled atop her writing table and wondered if her sister had any idea how she had been avoiding this room and that stack. Turning her back on them, she sat facing her sister.

"What is it?" she asked quietly. "If Papa heard you screaming like that, he—"

"Would think I had seen a mouse." She giggled. "I think you will agree this is much, much better." In her wobbly alto, she sang, "Look what arrived for you just a few minutes ago!" She held out a folded sheet.

"For me?"

"It was unsealed, Emily, so I peeked."

When Emily took the page, she smiled. She recognized its cream color. The letter must be from Mr. Homsby. Mayhap the bookseller had come to his senses. She almost laughed aloud at the preposterous idea, but, she reminded herself, there was a first time for everything . . . like Damon kissing a woman and meaning the passion on his lips.

Her heart thumped against her breast. Oh, how she longed to be back in his arms for those few stolen seconds when nothing had mattered but the caress of his fingers and mouth!

Are you mad? If rumors were to be believed, Demon Wentworth—how she despised that name!—had been as faithless as Georgie, Georgie, Pudding and Pie, kissing all the girls and leaving them to cry.

"Look at it!" urged Miriam.

Emily nodded. Mayhap this was an invitation to come to the shop to discuss the royalties she was due. The money would not be coming too soon, for Bollings had whispered this morning that Papa had returned in a testy mood after an unfortunate evening at the card table. With those debts in addition to what he already owed Lord Lichton, any payment from the quarto would be welcome.

Her hopes died as she read:

You are invited to a special poetry reading by Marquis de la Cour, the French Byron, at the shop of Homsby, Bookseller Old Bond Street on Thursday evening next at exactly 8. We are honored to share the marquis's talent with London.

Miriam twirled about. "We must go, Emily! Think of it. I shall get to see him again."

"I am not sure that is such a good idea."

"Why not? Dear me, I must be certain my very best gown is ready." Miriam bussed Emily on the cheek and grinned. "You will send the *respondez-vous, s'il vous plait* without delay, won't you?" She did not wait for an answer as she hurried out, whirling about like a child with a beloved toy.

Emily stared at the invitation. She had counted on Homsby to be an ally. She pressed the invitation to her breast. She did not know whom she could trust now, because the greatest out-and-outer had become hers the moment she graciously greeted the false marquis. She was part of his deception. She feared where it might lead, because she had no idea how it might end.

Emily stared at the front of Mr. Homsby's bookshop. The thickly mullioned windows were stacked with books of all types, but her gaze settled on the blue books that held her poems.

The poetry that impostor was trying to claim as his own!

The bell over the door rang as she entered the cluttered shadows. The shop was empty. She called a greeting, then her hands clenched as she saw the sway of the curtain. Mr. Homsby must be trying to avoid her.

"Mr. Homsby!" she called, wondering what she would do if he refused to appear.

She clenched her hands by her sides when a gawky man emerged from the back room. Jaspar, Mr. Homsby's assistant, was intolerable on the best of days, which today certainly was not. He did not hide that any woman, especially Miss Emily Talcott, should count herself fortunate to have the chance to share his company. The last time she had encountered him, he had tried to corner her by one of the bookshelves. Her sharp words to Mr. Homsby had kept his assistant away.

Until today.

"My dear Miss Talcott," Jaspar crowed in his deep voice that would have been pleasant if not forthcoming from such an unpleasant fellow. "I am so very, very delighted to see you."

"Where is Mr. Homsby?"

He stretched across the counter to grasp her hand. "Busy. That is lucky for us."

She snatched her hand away. "Busy planning the poetry reading?"

"Are you attending?" He edged around the counter and caught her hand again. "My dear Miss Talcott, can I implore you to sit beside me during the reading so I might bask in your beauty along with the poetry?"

"Release me at once!"

"My dear Miss Talcott—"

Wrestling her hand out of his grip, she scowled when she realized he had her glove.

He held it to his lips and whispered, "I shall treasure this gift from you always."

"I want to speak to Mr. Homsby."

"I told you, my dear. He is busy."

Emily glanced at the curtain. When she saw the fabric move again, she pushed past Jaspar and went around the counter.

"You shouldn't go there!" Jaspar cried.

"And you shouldn't purloin a lady's glove." Ignoring his horrified expression as she plucked her glove out of his hand, she added in the same stern tone, "Mr. Homsby, hiding from your customers bodes poorly for your reputation as an honest businessman."

When the gray-haired man peeked out, Emily found the bookseller's trepidation annoying. After all, he had been audacious enough to have an invitation to the reading by the marquis delivered to her house.

"Miss Talcott!" With a smile she knew was false, he surged forward to greet her. He motioned for Jaspar to return to the back room, which usually would have been a relief, but today her exasperation was focused on the quarto.

"Send him out of the store," Emily said quietly.

"We are very busy, Miss Talcott."

"I wish to speak to you alone."

Mr. Homsby's face became a sickish shade of gray, and she knew he understood the threat she need not speak. "Wait here." He called quick orders to Jaspar.

Only when Emily heard the back door close did she place the folded page on the counter. "I thought I would reply to your invitation in person. Imagine *my* astonishment when I learned Marquis de la Cour would be reading his poetry here."

"Miss Talcott, I—"

"Spare me from your bounces! How dare you send these invitations? You know that man cannot be Marquis de la Cour."

"Everyone believes he is."

"I do not believe that. Nor do you."

"After his triumph at Lady Fanning's soirée last night, the whole of London does."

Her eyes narrowed as she saw his smile. "You know of that? Did you send him there? Is this masquerade your idea?"

He raised his hands. "You wound me, Miss Talcott. I had no idea who he was when he came in yesterday. He expressed an interest in the book, and I mentioned, as any wise shopkeeper would do, that he should make his purchase without delay. I suspected many customers would want the book in the wake of the reading Lady Fanning was hosting."

"So that allowed him to know where to make his surprise entrance into the élite." She sighed. "No doubt he returned to regale you with how he was the toast of the evening."

"The marquis is delighted with his welcome."

"The marquis is no marquis. If I were to—"

"Think a moment!" he urged, leaning his hands on the counter. "He will enhance sales to such a degree that, even with you giving him half of your royalties—"

"Half? I never agreed to such a cockle-brained scheme."

"It was my idea." He swallowed roughly, the uneasiness returning to his face. "He was hinting there must be a good reason the real marquis had not come to London. If he were to announce now he is a fraud, it surely would be harmful to sales."

She struggled to maintain her composure. "Mr. Homsby, you must inform that man posthaste that your contract with him is invalid, for I did not consent to it."

His gray mustache drooped to match his frown, but she saw little regret in his eyes. Mr. Homsby was certain to profit handsomely from this arrangement. "I cannot cancel the reading when the invitations have already been sent. If you wish to make an announcement at that time—"

"I shall let you know."

She saw his amazement at her cool answer and guessed he had expected her to demur. She had no idea what she would do at the reading, but she would not confide that to a man who already had betrayed her in order to fill his pockets.

Emily opened the door. She gasped as she stared at the man standing on the other side. The fake Marquis de la Cour brushed past her as if she were of the least interest. Her exasperation became anger.

"Mon seigneur, comment allez-vous aujourd'hui?" she called to his back.

He whirled, his self-satisfied smile vanishing. Something flashed through his eyes, but was gone before she could guess what it was. He surged back to her and reached for her hand.

Emily kept her fingers clasped around her bag and her chin high. Past the impostor, she could see Mr. Homsby's face grow greasy with sweat.

The charlatan marquis gushed, "Do not tell me your name, mademoiselle, for I know it well. You are Emily Talcott, who read so beautifully of my poems, while I had the *plaisir* of speaking with your charming sister, the *très belle Mademoiselle Miriam.*"

"Here in England," she replied in her primmest French, "one does not speak so informally of a young woman whom one has just made the acquaintance of."

His swarthy eyes twinkled as he drew off his beaver and tossed it on the counter. "Your French is delightful, Mademoiselle Talcott, but I beg you again to allow me to practice my English."

"You seem much its master."

He pressed one hand over his pristine white waistcoat. "I hope one day to be. Can I believe you have come to this *librairie* to purchase one of my books?"

"No."

"Then allow me." He reached over into the window

and lifted out one of the slim blue volumes. Pressing it into her hand, he said, "Please accept this as a gift from me. *Avec ma gratitude, mademoiselle.*"

"No thank you." She set the book back into the window display. "Mr. Homsby, I believe it is time we spoke of—"

The door burst open into her back, propelling her into the marquis. Jaspar rushed into the shop as she extricated herself from the marquis's embrace. Stepping away from the marquis as he grinned at her as if she were no better than a cyprian, she waved aside Jaspar's hands which seemed to number at least a dozen.

"I am fine," she assured them. It was another lie. Her stomach ached, and her head throbbed, and she wished she never had discovered that words could rhyme.

"Are you certain?" asked the marquis.

"Yes. Good day." Emily grasped the door and threw it open again.

"Miss Talcott! Don't go!" Jaspar called.

She ignored him as she stepped out into the dim sunshine. Hearing a soft groan behind her, she glanced over her shoulder. Jaspar was clutching onto the door, a fearful expression widening his eyes. A hand settled on her arm.

With a gasp, she pulled away. She stared at the strange man, who was grinning broadly. Dismay cramped her stomach as she saw two other men standing between her and her carriage. Another slipped behind her to shove Jaspar back into the shop.

The man by the bookshop door smiled. "Good afternoon, pretty lady. Have you come to talk with us?" He took her hand and raised it to his lips. "Will you entertain us in other ways?"

Emily recoiled. The man had the manners of a sow's baby, although he and his companions were dressed in the varmentish style of the frippery set. Bond Street Loungers! How could she have been so witless? She should have taken note of the time.

With cool disdain, she answered, "I have neither the time for nor the interest in a conversation with you."

"But you talk so pretty, pretty lady."

When she turned toward the carriage, her coachee, Simon, started to climb down from the box. The young man froze when one of the men shouted, "Stay where you are, lame-hand."

"See here—"

The Bond Street Loungers growled.

Emily glanced along the street, but the gaudily dressed young men were the only ones abroad.

A man tugged at the feather on her bonnet. "Strange color for a bird," he said as his cronies chuckled. "Never have seen a lavender bird."

"Excuse me." She tried to step away, but the men refused to move aside.

Fear clawed at her. These nick-ninnies were intent on causing her trouble. Seeing the glint of malevolent amusement in the men's eyes, she feared they would not let her escape.

Chapter Nine

"Ah, here you are, darling! I pray you are not angry at me for being late."

Emily whirled as she heard a familiar voice. Damon! She longed to throw herself into his arms, which were sure to protect her from these boors. As she took a step toward him, a Bond Street Lounger intercepted her again. She edged back, not wanting to let this cad touch her.

"Do tell me you will forgive me, darling," Damon said as he walked toward her. Only the slightest narrowing of his eyes warned that his good humor was only a pose. "Tell me now before my heart breaks."

"Damon—"

"Tell me *now*, if you will find it in your heart to forgive me."

She understood him. To thwart the Loungers at their own game, she must play her part in the masquerade he had devised with a few words. Pasting on a pout, she said, "I thought you had forgotten me."

"Forget you? Impossible!"

The Loungers edged aside as he walked to her as if he had taken no note of anyone but her.

"My darling," he gushed, "I would as soon forget to breathe."

For a moment, she thought the most ill-bred of the Loungers would refuse to move away, but Damon did not slow. She suspected Damon would have trod right over the sad vulgar if the Lounger had not back-pedaled. Taking her hand, he raised it to his lips exactly the same as the Lounger had.

Yet it was not the same, for she was caught by the glow in his eyes which suggested he longed to enfold her to him. The warmth of his lips seared through her glove, threatening to leave her so weak she would have no choice but to fling her arms around him if she wished to remain on her feet. His gaze enthralled her when he lifted his head.

"Damon," she whispered, delighting in the sensation of his name on her lips but wanting his mouth upon them.

Again his eyes slitted as he looked past her. He squeezed her fingers in a silent order to remember their charade.

"Do not be so late next time," she said loud enough so every Lounger would hear. "You know how I hate to wait."

"As I do, darling." His drawl sent a heated shiver through her as she abruptly wondered where the line was between their masquerade and the truth.

A slow smile tilted his lips, and she tried to guess how he would accept such a scold that was not a jest. Not well, she suspected.

As he raised her hand to his lips again, she drew away before his touch ignited that bewitching fire anew. "Then let us be on our way before we are late again," she said.

Damon chuckled and said, as if he were noticing the Bond Street Loungers for the first time, "Take care, my friends, not to give your heart to a woman who watches the clock."

He offered Emily his arm. Putting her fingers on it, she let him lead her to her carriage.

She began, "Thank—"

"Shh," he warned. Raising his voice, he added, "Go along, my good man. I shall see her home."

"Miss Talcott?" Simon asked, his eyes wide with dismay.

Against her ear, Damon murmured, "Do not put a pox on this now. If you try to leave alone, they will halt your carriage."

"But Simon could be hurt if—"

He interrupted her in the same tense whisper, "They have no wish to abuse him. They seek their prey in women who are want-witted enough to be alone here at this hour."

Emily nodded, taking no umbrage at the demure hit. She deserved a scold. Looking up at the coachee, she said, "Simon, please take the carriage home, and let Miriam and Papa know I will be there in odd-come-shortlies."

"Yes, Miss Talcott." The coachman tipped his hat to her, gave the Loungers a scowl that brought a few half-hearted chuckles, then whipped up the horses.

Because Damon said nothing more, Emily remained silent. The Loungers fired some remarks in his direction, but Damon acted as if the boors had vanished from the street. She did the same. It was easy to be courageous now that she was no longer alone. The Loungers wandered away, looking for other quarry for their hard-faced roasts.

She walked by Damon's side, no faster than an egg-trot, and tried to relax. "Thank you."

"For rescuing you again?"

"I needed rescuing today."

He stopped before a handsome white phaeton with red wheels. As he handed her in, he winced as her reticule struck him. "What do you have in there? One of Homsby's volumes?"

"Just a small notebook." She could not own the truth that her fear of the Bond Street Loungers discovering the book with the first drafts of several poems frightened her as much as their salacious comments. "Mayhap I should have used it to teach those blocks a lesson or two."

"Just as well that you did not. They do not appreciate being shown for the dolts that they are." He took the reins that had been lashed around a lamp post. "Are you unhurt?"

"Save for my dignity."

"You should know better than to come here now."

"I know that."

His voice became less hard when hers quivered. "Surely your errand could have waited."

Staring at her clasped hands, she shook her head. "It was quite urgent."

"So urgent that you let yourself be the victim of the Loungers? If I had not come along, they would have insulted you nineteen to the dozen." He put his hand over her clenched fingers. "Emily, I was sure that you, of all your family, would think before you jumped recklessly into something."

"I should have thought first, I realize, but I had to get out of there before I strangled that man."

"Homsby?"

"No. Marquis de la Cour."

Damon glanced at her, surprise wiping away his irritation at the Bond Street Loungers. "He was at the bookshop?"

"Yes."

"That is most interesting."

"If—"

"One moment. Let me get us away from this dray which seems determined to run us down." Damon drove with the cool confidence of a man undaunted by the crush of the traffic, but he looked at her as he said, "I can understand why you took your leave from de la Cour, but you still have not explained what was so important that you could not delay until an hour when it was safe for you."

"I wanted to discuss the reading with Mr. Homeby."

"Reading?"

Reaching into her bag, she pulled out the invitation.

"I recognize it," Damon said, "for I have its twin waiting on my breakfast table, although I have not opened it. What is it?"

"An invitation to a poetry reading by Marquis de la Cour."

Emily was taken aback when he let loose a laugh that caused heads to turn in all the vehicles around them.

"To be sure," he said, "I would hazard Lady Fanning was generous enough to provide our peerless parleyvoo marquis with the names and addresses of her guests who were awed by his magnificence."

She replaced the invitation in her reticule, resisting the yearning to shred it. "That does not explain why *you* received one."

He laughed. "Nor does it explain why you decided to call upon Homsby this afternoon. I cannot believe it is because you cannot wait to hear Marquis de la Cour read his poetry."

"When I was at his shop last, I forgot to ask Mr. Homsby to hold for me that book on roses you pointed out." That much was the truth.

"What does that have to do with de la Cour?"

"Nothing."

"Then what does it have to do with your sister and how she monopolized the frog's attention last night?"

"How—?"

"*On dits* are most efficient, darling."

"Don't call me that."

He smiled. "I was just trying to tease you out of the doldrums."

"You could do that by not repeating poker-talk about my sister."

"I was speaking of de la Cour, I believe."

"Miriam likes his poetry. Nothing more."

"Are you certain?"

"Most certain." The banger was acidic on her tongue.

As they turned onto Picadilly Street, she frowned. "This is not the way to Hanover Square."

"That is true, although I am uncertain how much else you have told me is."

"Where are we going?"

"Do you still fear for your reputation with me?"

"Should I?"

"Do you always answer a question with a question?"

"Do you?" she fired back.

"*Touché.*"

"That is not an answer." She fought to keep the alarm from her voice. "Damon, where are we going?"

She got her answer when he turned into Green Park and drew back on the reins to slow them to a walk. Other carriages drove past as a fine rain began to fall.

"Damon, we should not be here like this." Riding with him without a duenna would bring about her ruin as completely as having the Polite World discover she was the true Marquis de la Cour.

"I had thought we might walk about and enjoy the flowers, but the weather is not favorable. This may be for the best. No one is taking note of us as we take the long way back to Hanover Square."

"How can you say that when people noticed Miriam and the marquis last night?" She put her fingers to her lips. "Oh!"

He chuckled. "I thought that was just poker-talk."

"Damon, please take me home."

"I am, so do not fuss." He smiled and rested his arm along the back of the seat as he steered the phaeton through the mist. "Even if I am not lauded as a hero for saving you from those blind buzzards, my reputation will protect yours. Nobody would imagine the feminine occupant of 'Demon' Wentworth's carriage at this hour could be of quality."

"You are outrageous!"

His smile broadened. "Outrageous, but honest. Can I believe you might consider being as honest with me?"

"The truth is, I am pleased you chanced along." Folding her hands in her lap, she smiled. "I hope your gallantry has not kept you from your own errands."

"It was not critical that I complete my tasks this afternoon."

Emily bit back her next question. She was curious what business had brought him to Old Bond Street. He might have been on his way to visit Mr. Homsby's shop, too. To buy another copy of her book?

Do not be absurd! But she could not keep from wondering who had been the recipient of the book he had bought. A book was not a gift a man took to his convenient. Or did he? She knew nothing of such things.

Realizing she must say something, she asked, "Do you often have critical business?"

"By Jove!"

When she looked at him, sure he was furious with her prying, she saw he was grinning. Hastily, she turned away before he could see her confusion. He never acted as she expected. She gasped when his finger beneath her chin brought her face back toward him.

"Emily," he said softly with his lips only a whisper away from hers, "I am beginning to understand why we get along so well. You play the rôle of a dutiful daughter and kindly sister, but there is a bit of wanton mischief within you."

"I have never done anything wanton."

"But your eyes suggest you might." He laughed as he put his shining boot on the dash. "Your eyes glitter with devilment, inviting a man to savor thoughts that would earn him a slap across the face if you were privy to them."

"I have never slapped anyone."

"Of course not, for that would ruin the perfection of your guise." His finger tapped her cheek. "Yet, despite the dressing-down I am sure your sister has given you because you have not given me my *congé,* I am flattered you have continued to treat me as a friend.''

"Sometimes I wonder why," she returned with a laugh she hoped would conceal the pleasure that flew through her at his touch.

"You shouldn't." He stared out at the rain as he turned the phaeton toward Hanover Square. "I had planned to give you a look-in today or tomorrow."

"Why?" When her voice rose to a squeak on the single word, she hastily looked away. She did not want to own that Papa had forbidden her from receiving Damon.

"I have to leave in a few days for Wentworth Hall."

"Oh."

"Is that the extent of your regret at my leavetaking?"

"I trust you shall be returning for the rest of the Season." She despised the trite words, but they kept her from revealing how her heart cramped at the idea of not seeing him again. She should be pleased, for that would keep Papa happy. She was not.

"Undoubtedly."

She smiled. His answer contained the dread of a schoolboy told the next session was about to begin. "Why are you going there now?"

"Obligations. Traditions die slowly in the north, and Wentworth Hall's master has duties to his tenants." His gray eyes twinkled as he smiled. "I have just the jolly, Emily. Why don't you join me?"

"At Wentworth Hall?" She faltered, sure he was jesting. When his smile did not waver, she gasped, "Damon, I could not do that."

"Don't say no so quickly. I plan to invite a large group to travel with me. You are simply the first I have asked."

"But why are you taking the *ton* with you when you have said more than once that it bores you?"

"I cannot play cards alone."

Emily laughed. "You are inviting the wrong person. I detest the card table."

" 'Twas not to play cards with you that I asked you to travel with me. I think you shall find a few parts of Wentworth Hall very much to your liking."

"Which ones?"

"Dare I say its lord?" With a laugh, as she stared in amazement at his bold question, he added, "I wish to keep some things a surprise for you. So will you and your family join me?"

"I shall ask them."

"Do that."

When he did not press her as he drove back out into the day's traffic, she wondered if he had heard her despair. Taking Papa away from the temptations of London would be a grand idea, but she knew how much he could lose to someone with Damon's reputation as a card-player. She needed to devise an excuse to turn down this invitation and not let her heart tease her into agreeing to what could be a disaster for her family.

Damon waited for Emily to speak, but she remained silent. What had he said now to unsettle her? He could not understand this woman. Other women had always been easy to comprehend. Some wanted the title of Lady Wentworth. Others were willing to forego the title for some of his blunt and a place in his fine townhouse and his bed. Emily Talcott seemed to want nothing of him. Instead, she challenged him with her wit and won his admiration with her devotion to her garden and her family. He could not understand her at all.

He was shocked when she put her hand over his on the reins. The caress of her fingers tempted him to toss aside caution and pull her back into his arms. What a gull he had been to kiss her! His attempt to tease her had become a craving to savor those sweet lips once more. No, not once more. He wanted to kiss them again and again until his thirst for them was sated.

"Damon," she whispered.

Even though he feared he would not be able to perceive

a single word she spoke past the thunder pulsing through him, he asked, "Yes?" He paused. "I like the sound of that word. Can I hope you will say the same thing to my invitation to visit Wentworth Hall?"

"I am not sure."

His breath caught as he saw grief in her eyes. Not only grief, he realized, as those closely banked fires came to life again when his fingertip grazed her jaw.

"Do you have something else that would keep you here in Town?" he asked. "Some secret admirer who adores you from afar?"

She met his gaze steadily. "You are suggesting my life is much more interesting than it is. I would guess you have many more secrets than I."

Damn, she was too insightful! If he had the sense God gave a goose, he would use this as an excuse to put an end to their friendship.

"How so?" he asked.

"You do not seem to be a demon, in spite of your name."

"I am afraid, Emily, you are wrong." He laughed, relieved to speak the truth. "I gained that name many years ago when I proved I had more than the devil's own share of luck at the card table."

She looked hastily away. This did not surprise him, for two topics seemed to make her as uncomfortable as a sinner facing the minister. Marquis de la Cour and playing cards. The latter he understood, for Lichton's ill manners last night had confirmed what he had heard whispered. Charles Talcott wagered more than he could afford to lose at the board of green cloth, yet, somehow, he continued to play, as he left his daughter to handle that despicable task of paying his debts for him.

As for her repulsion for Marquis de la Cour, he had to applaud her excellent taste, but he could not ignore his curiosity to discover why she drew within herself whenever the frog poet's name was spoken.

"Emily, if I have distressed you, I am sorry."

"You need not tease me endlessly." She raised her gaze to his again, her eyes luminous even in the gray light.

"Need?" he whispered. "You have no idea what my needs are."

Unable to resist the invitation of her lips, he brought them beneath his own. Her soft sigh warmed the interior of his mouth as his hand slipped behind her nape to tilt her head back, so he could delight in each taste waiting for him. Her moan brushed his ear as he bent to let his mouth caress her neck. Each touch, each moist nibble, each brush of her body against his added to the escalating need to relish more rapture.

She pushed him away. "Please do not do that!"

"You don't like my touch?" he whispered.

"I do like your touch, but I will do anything I must to prevent any scandal from being attached to the Talcott name."

"That is no surprise."

"Then you must understand why even considering your invitation is so wrong." Her fingers tightened on his. "I know I must have taken a knock in my cradle to be on Old Bond Street this afternoon, and I appreciate you interrupting the Loungers' troublemaking more than you can guess, but . . ." Her voice faded into a sigh.

Damon wanted to break the silence, but to speak now would entice him into bringing her to him again. He was a complete block! Avowing one thing to his friend and then doing another on the first opportunity—that was the mark of an addle cove.

He drove through the rain, which was striking the top of the phaeton like a tattoo. When he turned the carriage onto the street leading to Hanover Square, he asked, as if it were of the least importance, "So are you going to de la Cour's poetry reading?"

"Miriam will not want to miss it."

"I would be honored to escort both of you there."

Emily was riveted with amazement. *"You* are going? Why?"

"For the same reason I gave you last night. I cannot play cards when my adversaries are elsewhere. Mayhap if I attend the reading, I can convince them to be sensible and leave." His fingers curled around hers. "You did not answer my question."

"I—that is, I—" She wished, just once, she could speak the truth with ease, but she must guard her tongue when his touch beseeched her to fling caution aside.

"What is it?" he asked. "If you do not wish me to escort you, you need only say that."

"No, it is not that."

"That I am pleased to hear, but what makes you hesitate?"

"Damon, the truth is not pleasant."

"It seldom is."

She rested back against the seat as water splattered up from other carriages. "Miriam does not like you."

"So my invitation to drive you to Homsby's shop would send her up to the boughs? Not an easy place to escort a lady from, I must own."

Emily laughed. "I should not find my sister so amusing."

"Why not? I find *her* sister very amusing."

She stared at him, then, discerning what he meant, she lowered her eyes as pleasure flooded her. She was glad he continued speaking, for she did not trust her voice.

"I had hoped," he said as they entered Hanover Square, "that today we might view the day lilies I heard were planted by the Temple of Concord."

"Day lilies? In Green Park?" She was astonished. Had he really intended them to wander about the park enjoying the flowers without a watch-dog?

"Unlikely I know, for the flowers there have been much neglected. All of these beautiful homes were built here in Mayfair without the thought of space for flowers and trees.'' He chuckled. "Mayhap someday someone will build a city entirely of flowers and topiary.''

"Wouldn't that be wondrous?'' she asked, glad he had turned the conversation to gardening.

"You really enjoy flowers, don't you?''

"You have seen my garden.''

"Only for a few moments.'' He smiled. "I would be delighted to explore it more.''

"In this rain?''

"I assure you that I am not made of sugar, Emily, and neither are you.''

"Are you this charming to all the ladies?''

"Only to my friends.'' He smiled, and she was sure her heart would drown beneath a wave of happiness. "However, in deference to the pretty feather in your hat, I shall postpone our tour until you are not about to suffer from vapors from your confrontation with the Bond Street Loungers.''

"I would not succumb to vapors!''

He laughed as he stopped the phaeton in front of her house. "You may be right. I cannot imagine you swooning.''

Emily could as she glanced from him to the house. Her head suddenly seemed so light that it would be squashed beneath a single raindrop. Why had she not thought about this dilemma when Damon said he was bringing her back to Hanover Square? If Papa saw her arriving with Damon after she had been instructed not to be at home to him here, there would be perdition to pay.

She offered her hand. "Thank you for bringing me home.''

"My pleasure.'' He did not take her hand. Instead, he jumped down from the phaeton and came around to help her out.

Hunching her shoulders against the rain, she said, "Again, let me thank you.''

"It is raining, if you have not noticed, Emily.''

"I know." She took a step back toward the house. "I will not delay you."

"You aren't." He grasped her hand and settled it within his arm. Walking her to the door, he opened it.

How could she tell him that Papa had ordered her not to welcome Damon into the house?

"We can talk inside where it is dry," he continued.

Emily tossed aside the idea of arguing when rain slid down her back. If she let him speak his mind, mayhap he would take his leave before anyone was the wiser.

As Johnson rushed forward, clearly once again lax about his post, she had no chance to speak, for Damon ordered, "I wish to speak to Mr. Talcott."

"My lord, he—"

"Now!"

Emily stared in incredulity at Damon while Johnson scurried up the stairs. Once again, Damon had transformed into the arrogant lord who commanded those about him as if they had no minds of their own. As he drew off his driving gloves, he removed his hat and dropped them in. He tossed his hat onto a table by the door.

"What is wrong?" she asked.

"Nothing. I wish to speak with your father," he said in the same cool tone.

When he looked past her, she turned to see Papa coming down the stairs. Papa pulled his dressing gown closed around him, and she guessed he had been roused from his bed. He gaped at Emily, then at Damon.

"Talcott," Damon said with the coldness Emily had heard when he spoke with Lord Lichton. No wonder, she thought with a shiver, they called him *demon*. His eyes were as frigid as the devil's empty heart.

"Wentworth." Papa touched the damp lace on Emily's sleeve, then stared at the wet shoulders of Damon's coat. His lips twisted in a scowl. "Emily, am I to believe you have been out alone with this man?"

Damon answered before she could. "You are chiding her for the wrong misdeed, Talcott."

"You mean there are others that—"

"I mean you should teach your daughter the folly of tending to her errands on Old Bond Street at this hour."

Papa's face flushed as red as Miriam's could, but in fury. "Emily, I thought you were wiser than that."

How dare Damon scold her like a child! Emily swallowed her back-answer when he tilted his head and closed one eye in a lazy wink. He was hoaxing her father as he had the Bond Street Loungers. Was he this dishonest with her?

She replied, "I understand, Papa. Good day, Damon, and thank you."

He bowed toward her. "I should thank you, Emily."

Papa sputtered at Damon's familiarity before saying, "Wentworth, I know Emily will be glad to excuse us while we speak man to man."

"Papa—"

"You are excused, Emily."

She looked at Damon, but his face was as tightly closed as Papa's lips. This anger was not feigned. She could not guess what had sparked his anger. Then she glanced at Papa and saw an answering ire on his face. Dear God! Papa thought she had allowed Damon to compromise her.

"Papa—"

"I will speak with *you* later, Emily. Go to your room!"

She did not want to agree, but to stay would make matters worse. Backing away, she hurried up the stairs and away from Papa's silent accusation.

When Emily heard a familiar knock on her bedroom door an hour later, she stood and squared her shoulders. "Come in, Papa."

He strode into the room, rocking his walking stick in his hand. Dressed in his best, he looked every bit the Pink of the *ton*. Even his cravat was perfectly tied. She wondered who had helped him.

He said with obvious uneasiness, "Wentworth assures me that nothing untoward took place between you this afternoon, and Simon confirmed the viscount's story."

"You asked Simon?" she gasped. "Why don't you trust me?"

"I don't trust Wentworth." He walked to the window and stared out. "I am disappointed in you, *ma chérie*. I thought you had been raised to know the dangers that await you here in Town. Men like Wentworth embody most of them."

She took a step toward him, then paused. "If Damon had not come along, I might not have escaped the Bond Street Loungers as readily as I did."

"True, true." He cleared his throat again. "Very true."

Emily guessed he was waiting for her to add something else, but she had nothing more to say. How could she tell Papa about her crackish behavior in Green Park? After all her efforts to write those wretched poems and hide her identity to protect Papa and Miriam, she had ridden alone with Damon in such a public place.

"I wanted," he continued when she remained silent, "to be certain you were well before I went out."

"Where are you going, Papa?"

"To my club."

"Your club?"

He smiled. "Did I fail to mention I have been honored a membership at Brooks's? Lord Lichton sponsored me."

"Papa, the membership fee for such a club can be dear."

He patted her cheek as he had when she was a child. "You worry too much about money, *ma chérie*. My good friend Lichton was kind enough to stake me for the membership fee."

"How generous of him!"

"Not really." He laughed. "He shall take a share of my

winnings until I have repaid him. Of course, I have the whole year to reimburse him.''

Despair returned doubly strong. ''And if you cannot?''

Looking into her glass, he adjusted his cravat. ''You have little faith in your father's abilities at the card table.

As he told her to have a pleasant evening and left, Emily owned that her father was wrong. She did not have only a little faith in his abilities at the card table. She had none at all.

Chapter Ten

"We are going with *him?*" Miriam threw her ivory fan on the pillow and crossed her arms in front of her, her wounded dignity like a battle shield. Her petulant expression did not match the dainty gown she wore, for its silk was a sunny yellow. Her hair was piled high *à la* Sappho with only a single curl dropping along the creamy length of her neck.

Emily did not look at the glass. Not that she appeared less than presentable, for she was wearing her favorite white silk. Yet, in any company, her golden-haired sister caught the gentlemen's eyes in a way her smoky tresses could not. She longed to take her sister by the shoulders and shake some sense into her head.

"Emily," Miriam went on, "you must be knocked in the cradle to think I would let Demon Wentworth escort me."

"Enough!"

Miriam stared at Emily. "What do you mean?"

Taking her bonnet from Kilmartin who wore an anxious expression, Emily settled it on her hair that refused to stay in curls around her face. "I thought you could set aside your distaste of Damon's company when he was kind enough to offer to escort us to Mr. Homsby's shop.''

"Why do we need him? We can take the carriage—''

"Papa used it to go to his club." She almost had to spit out the words. *His club!* In the past week, Papa had not come home once before dawn. When she had hinted she was interested in how much he had won or lost, he had merely patted her cheek and told her to let him worry about such things. That was like telling her not to think about Damon. Impossible.

Miriam picked up her fan and slapped it against her palm, threatening the thin ivory spines. "I do not understand why the delivery of the carriage you ordered to replace Papa's phaeton is taking so long."

"It has not been very long."

"More than three months!"

Emily sighed as they walked, with the abigail following, down to the foyer. She had hoped that Miriam would not take note of how long it had been since Papa had come nearly to disaster when he crashed the phaeton in an accident he refused to discuss. There would be no new carriage, because Emily had not ordered one. The household accounts did not contain the money to pay for it.

"Be patient, Miriam," she said when her sister continued to grouse.

"I am trying." She looked toward the door Johnson was opening.

Emily wondered if everyone could hear the way her heart beat when her gaze met Damon's. The elegant cut of his coat complemented his white breeches. When he took off his black top hat, his hair glistened in the day's last light.

She rushed forward to halt him, aware of Kilmartin's gasp as he was about to enter the house. "We are ready to leave now."

Puzzlement ruffled his brow. "Emily, what is amiss?"

She motioned for Miriam and the abigail to follow down

the steps. Turning, she saw Damon still standing on the topmost one. "We do not want to be late."

"Late?" he asked, resting his hand on the iron railing. "We could drive around half of London and still arrive before the reading begins." A smile curved his lips when he came down the steps toward where his elegant, closed carriage waited by the walkway. "Although I must say that is not a bad idea. I shall be the envy of every man— gentleman or no—who views me in the company of such exquisitely beautiful ladies."

"Miriam and I are pleased with your generosity this evening." Emily flashed an encouraging smile at her sister.

"Yes," Miriam said with all the enthusiasm of a convicted conveyancer facing the deadly nevergreens in Tyburn.

"Are you pleased enough," Damon asked, "so you will explain why you are hurrying me away from your door as if I were a hell-born hound coming to take you to the old gentleman in black?"

Emily began, "I told you—"

"I know." He drew her hand within his arm as he led her toward where Miriam and Kilmartin had already climbed into the coach with the tiger's assistance. "But I had hoped for honesty."

"I never know when you are being honest and when you are not." The words slipped out before she could silence them.

He turned her to face him. His hands on her shoulders were caressing, but the intensity in his voice lashed her like a flogger. "If we were not here in view of everyone on the square, I would be glad to show you how honest I can be when I say I want to kiss you so deeply your reputation would be damned forever."

"You should not say that."

"Why are you abruptly afraid of the truth?" He brushed one of her recalcitrant curls back from her face. "Or is it abruptly, Emily? I suspect you are less than honest at times,

We'd Like to Invite You to Subscribe to Zebra's Regency Romance Book Club and Give You a Gift of 4 Free Books as Your Introduction! *(Worth $19.96!)*

If you're a Regency lover, imagine the joy of getting 4 FREE Zebra Regency Romances and then the chance to have these lovely stories delivered to your home each month at the lowest prices available! Well, that's our offer to you and here's how you benefit by becoming a Zebra Home Subscription Service subscriber:

- 4 FREE Introductory Regency Romances are delivered to your doorstep

- 4 BRAND NEW Regencies are then delivered each month (usually before they're available in bookstores)

- Subscribers save almost $4.00 every month

- Home delivery is always FREE

- You also receive a FREE monthly newsletter, *Zebra/ Pinnacle Romance News* which features author profiles, contests, subscriber benefits, book previews and more

- No risks or obligations...in other words you can cancel whenever you wish with no questions asked

Join the thousands of readers who enjoy the savings and convenience offered to Regency Romance subscribers. After your initial introductory shipment, you receive 4 brand-new Zebra Regency Romances each month to examine for 10 days. Then, if you decide to keep the books, you'll pay the preferred subscriber's price of just $4.00 per title. That's only $16.00 for all 4 books and there's never an extra charge for shipping and handling.

It's a no-lose proposition, so return the FREE BOOK CERTIFICATE today!

FREE BOOK CERTIFICATE

YES! Please rush me 4 Zebra Regency Romances without cost or obligation. I understand that each month thereafter I will be able to preview 4 brand-new Regency Romances FREE for 10 days. Then, if I should decide to keep them, I will pay the money-saving preferred subscriber's price of just $16.00 for all 4...that's a savings of almost $4 off the publisher's price with no additional charge for shipping and handling. I may return any shipment within 10 days and owe nothing, and I may cancel this subscription at any time. My 4 FREE books will be mine to keep in any case.

Name _____

Address _____ Apt. _____

City _____ State _____ Zip _____

Telephone ( ) _____

Signature _____ RF0298
(If under 18, parent or guardian must sign.)

Terms and prices subject to change. Orders subject to acceptance by Zebra Home Subscription Service, Inc.

AFFIX
STAMP
HERE

ZEBRA HOME SUBSCRIPTION SERVICE, INC.

120 BRIGHTON ROAD

P.O. BOX 5214

CLIFTON, NEW JERSEY 07015-5214

and I am beginning to wonder what you are trying to hide.''

"Nothing!" She cursed the panic in her voice when his eyes became silvery slits.

"Then why are you acting so oddly?"

"I am worried about this evening."

"Your sister and the marquis?"

She nodded.

"But why? Simply because he lathered her at Lady Fanning's is no reason to suspect he will do so tonight. From what little I saw of de la Cour, and that sample was more than enough, I must own, he will not confine himself to one woman. He will wish to woo them all." He smiled ironically. "He is French, after all."

"Is he?" she asked under her breath.

"What did you say?"

"I do not want to be late, for I intend to have a seat right next to Miriam tonight." She must be careful not to betray her suspicions about the marquis, because they could divulge her own secret.

Emily was not able to ignore the tension in Damon's arm as he walked her to the carriage. Nor could she dismiss how his fingers lingered against her while he assisted her in to sit on the scarlet seat across from her sister and Kilmartin. When he sat beside her and reached up to tap the roof, she was overmastered by his strength so close to her.

"Isn't this a lovely carriage, Miriam?" she asked, hoping again to draw her sister into the conversation.

She failed. Miriam nodded if Emily spoke to her, but ignored Damon. Emily had no idea what he thought of her sister's want of manners, because his face was without expression. Even when they reached Old Bond Street, Miriam's disapproving silence did not lessen. Kilmartin seemed as unwilling to speak. Emily wondered why she had ever agreed to come to this blasted reading.

The walkway before Mr. Homsby's shop overflowed with

people, although the reading was not to begin for nearly an hour. Disconcerted, Emily stood by the carriage as Damon handed her sister out.

"Wentworth!"

He grimaced. "If you ladies will pardon me for a moment, I shall see what Newsome wants." Bowing to them, he added, "Unless you would like to speak with him, too."

Emily glanced at the pudgy earl and shook her head. Lord Newsome had been the only man more obnoxious than Lord Lichton about collecting her father's debts. "We shall gladly excuse you."

Damon shot her another glance which warned her simple words had roused his curiosity, but said nothing as he went to where the earl was holding court on the walkway and calling to more of his acquaintances to join him.

"I had no idea the marquis had so many admirers." Miriam smiled when Kilmartin adjusted the paisley shawl over her shoulders.

"Nor did I," Emily answered glumly. Reminding herself she must be especially cautious tonight or she could shatter everything she had labored to create for her family, she forced a smile. Someone bumped into her. Turning, she stared into Mr. Homsby's face, which was awash with a storm of emotions of dismay, then amusement, then a return of anxiety. He mumbled and pushed past her to speak to his other guests.

"How peculiar!" Miriam said. "I never have seen Mr. Homsby in such a dither that he forgot his manners. He may be surprised by the response to this reading."

"Why should he be? He sent the invitations."

"I shall go and find seats for the three of us, Miss Emily," Kilmartin interjected.

"Four," she corrected gently.

The abigail's face lengthened with her frown. "Forgive me, Miss Emily. I did not mean to exclude Lord Wentworth."

Emily flinched as Kilmartin pushed through the crowd. She had not broken her pledge to Papa. She had not received Damon at home, although arguably the front steps still were part of the house.

"Oh, my!"

At Miriam's soft gasp, Emily followed her sister's gaze toward a carriage stopping behind Damon's. The bright orange door announced it belonged to the Fanning family. The door opened to reveal Graham Simpkins. He held up his hand to assist Valeria, who was resplendent in purple and gold.

Tears blossomed in Miriam's eyes. No matter what Miriam professed, she still must have a *tendre* for Mr. Simpkins.

"Let us go and greet them," Emily said, prodding her sister with her elbow.

"He— I mean, they are coming this way." Miriam choked back a sob as Mr. Simpkins looked directly at her and away.

Valeria waved her fan, but let Mr. Simpkins lead her into the shop. Emily put her arm around her sister's shoulders.

Miriam shrugged them off. "Don't pity me, Emily!"

"Why would anyone pity such a *très belle* creature?" came an unmistakable French accent behind them.

Emily groaned. Why hadn't she hurried Miriam inside so they could have found seats far from this fraud? Now was the worst time to have to speak to the marquis, but it seemed she had as little choice in the matter as her sister did in the state of Mr. Simpkins's heart.

"Mademoiselle Talcott!" Marquis de la Cour grinned. He wore an elegant coat of navy-blue velvet and breeches as silver as Damon's eyes. Gold glittered on his fingers beneath the fall of lace at his wrists. "And Mademoiselle Talcott. May I express my great delight in seeing both of you here? I had hoped you would attend, for I know you to be lovers of poetry." He grasped Miriam's hand and bowed over it as he murmured, "It takes a special person to see beauty in words."

Emily was startled when her sister laughed. "How sweet of you to take note of us!" Miriam said, too loudly in Emily's opinion, when the marquis pressed her sister's hand to his lips.

"Only a *chien*—How do you say?—a cur would be indifferent to a glorious creature like you, Mademoiselle Talcott." When she flushed, he added, "I hope I have said nothing wrong, for it would be a shame if I must depend on a poorly chosen word to bring such captivating color to your face."

When Miriam glanced to her right, toward where Valeria was standing at the bookshop door with Mr. Simpkins, Emily wanted to groan. No, it could not be. Miriam must be hoping to make Mr. Simpkins jealous of the attention the marquis was showing her.

He is not the real Marquis de la Cour, she wanted to shout. This was simply too bizarre.

If Valeria would look this way, mayhap Emily could motion for her to join them and bring Mr. Simpkins with her. Valeria was focused on Lady Murrow, who had made no secret of her dismay that Valeria had been the first to host the marquis. The bald-ribbed dowager's hands flew about, warning her distress had not diminished.

"Do let me sit you near where I shall be reading, mademoiselle." The marquis's request pulled Emily's attention back to him.

Miriam giggled and wafted her fan in front of her face. "I would be delighted, my lord."

"My lord? You don't speak French?"

"Only a word or two." Miriam tapped Emily's arm. "Not like my dear sister."

"Yes, your sister." He looked at Emily, his smile never wavering, but his eyes cold. "You speak French with a unique accent, Mademoiselle Talcott. You did not learn it in Paris, that much is clear. Where did you learn to speak it?"

She hesitated, then squared her shoulders. Although

too many ears might be listening, she must be honest, for Miriam might, however innocently, dispute any tale she told. "In America, *mon seigneur.*"

"America?" He ran his finger beneath his mustache, spiking out the thin hairs. "I had no idea you were so well traveled, Mademoiselle Talcott."

"My father's business took us there."

"How intriguing! And what does Mr. Talcott do?"

"The Talcott family has been involved in the shipping business for generations."

"Is that so?" She was unsure what he meant and had no chance to ask, for he added, "No matter where you learned it, you speak it so well."

"Emily does many things well," came a deeper voice, "as you shall discover, de la Cour, if you remain long in Town."

Why had she thought this could not become more higgledy-piggledy? As Damon came to stand beside her, she bit her lower lip. Anything she could say right now was certain to cause more trouble.

"Lord Wentworth, isn't it?" The marquis's sneer wrinkled his nose.

"Yes."

"I thought I recalled you from Lady Fanning's soirée." He scowled. "You left early."

Damon's smile was as cold as Emily's hands. "I regret not hearing Emily's reading, for I am sure her voice could have but enhanced the poetry."

"True, but—" He clamped his lips closed.

Wondering why the impostor took insult at Damon's words when *she* had written the poems, Emily wanted to remind both of them how many ears were heeding this conversation. Slipping her arm through Miriam's, she said, "Let us go in and find a seat."

"*Oui,* let us." The marquis's voice was smooth once more. He took Miriam's hand and placed it on his arm.

A single arched brow dared Emily to try to pull her sister away from him.

As she watched Miriam walk to the door with de la Cour, Emily tried to ignore the dread descending on her. This fake poet was something she was going to have to deal with . . . somehow.

Before it was too late.

"*Merci. Merci beaucoup.* "The marquis bowed his head toward his applauding audience.

"Isn't he wonderful?" cooed Miriam. "Have you ever seen anything like him?"

Emily almost laughed as she said with sincerity, "Never."

The poetry reading had been going on for more than an hour in the increasingly stuffy shop. In a hard chair near where de la Cour stood by the counter, she could find no comfortable way to sit. Any way she might move would bring her in contact with an elbow or a knee or a fluttering fan, for the attendees were packed in as close as a court plaster.

"For my final poem this evening," the marquis intoned in his self-satisfied voice, "I would like to read my favorite. It is so personal, I hesitate to share it like this." His gaze focused on Miriam. "But it seems somehow appropriate tonight when I am surrounded by so much *amitié.*"

Miriam half hid her face with her fan. "Isn't he just grand, Emily?"

"He is—"

"Hush! Listen!"

Emily was tempted to say she had listened too long already. Despite requests from his devotees, the marquis refused to read in French. That solidified her suspicions. The fraud was not even French!

"Before I read this final selection," de la Cour said with a broad smile, "I wish to thank Mr. Homsby for his generosity in allowing me to use his shop tonight. He and my publisher, Old Gooseberry Press, have—''

Emily gasped. Old Gooseberry Press? She never had heard that name mentioned. In the books, the only listing below the title and her pseudonym was the name and address of Mr. Homsby's bookshop.

When she looked at the quarto, Mr. Homsby was staring at the marquis with fury. Mr. Homsby's hands opened and closed at his side as if he already had his fingers at de la Cour's throat. What else had he told the impostor? An icy laugh battered the back of her throat. Mr. Homsby should have taken a page from his own book and been guided more by reticence than greed.

A motion at the back of the shop caught her eye. When her gaze locked with Damon's, she saw no emotion on his face. He must be disturbed by something as well; otherwise, he would be jesting with the fellow beside him about the ineptitude of de la Cour's reading. She wanted to see him smiling, to have his irreverence steal the absurdity from this night.

He looked past her as de la Cour opened the book and began to stumble through what had been her favorite poem, too. She gazed down at her hands folded over her fan. Where was this going to end? She dared not think.

Emily should not have been surprised when Lady Murrow invited all the attendees at the reading to an informal gathering at her townhouse on Berkeley Square. She considered using the excuse of her headache not to attend, but Miriam accepted the invitation before Emily could speak.

''I am sure Lord Wentworth will be delighted to escort us there,'' Miriam gushed as if she had never shown anything but affection for Damon.

''Miriam!'' Emily whispered, aghast.

Her sister turned, and Emily saw her eyes were too bright.

With more tears or with excitement? "Dear Emily, Lord Wentworth must plan to take us home. Why not take us home by way of Lady Murrow's supper?"

"Then 'tis all settled," the rotund dowager said before she rushed off to invite the rest of the attendees.

Miriam preened as she ran her finger through the feathers on her fan. "She was very, very anxious for us to attend, wasn't she?" With a giggle, she squeezed Emily's hand. "I never knew it could be like this."

"Like what?" she asked, although she shuddered at what she feared the answer would be. She was not disappointed.

"Others have noticed how André is so attentive to me."

"André?"

"The marquis, of course." Pretty color splashed across her cheeks. "He asked me to call him that."

Emily put her hand over her stomach. She feared she would be ill right here. The marquis should not have a first name, because she had never given him one.

When broad fingers settled on her arm, she looked up at Damon's smile. It faded into concern. She longed for his arms around her to hold back the insanity. So easily, within that sturdy sanctuary, she could pour out the secrets pillaging her heart. She would rest her head against his chest in the moment before his fingers tipped her lips toward his. Then the madness would be as sweet and dangerous as the flame of his passion.

"Emily?" he asked softly, but his voice resonated deep within her.

Before she could answer, Miriam said, "Lord Wentworth, I hope I was not too presumptuous when I told Lady Murrow you would be escorting us to her supper."

Damon glanced from Emily's ashen face to her sister's high color. No one could doubt that Miriam was aglow with sharing the admiration heaped on de la Cour. That might explain Emily's apprehension.

When he folded her hand between his, he was astounded that her fingers were icy. Her eyes avoided his, and he knew something beyond her sister's enthusiasm distressed her.

"I would be delighted to escort you," he said, "if that is Emily's wish as well."

He almost recoiled when Emily jerked her hand away. The scathing glare she fired at him would have daunted him, if he had not known how her fingers trembled. He had no chance to ask her to explain because her sister pleaded with her to go to Lady Murrow's townhouse.

That Emily agreed was what he had anticipated, for she seemed unable to deny her sister's wishes, but he had not thought she would say nothing else during the short ride to Berkeley Square. Not that the carriage was quiet. Miriam prattled, nonstop, about how well de la Cour had read before his adoring audience.

Damon had heard little, for he had had the good fortune to be at the back of the shop where he could peruse a book on water gardens. What he had heard convinced him the only thing more irritating than de la Cour's poetry was enduring the sound of the Frenchman reading those poems in English. Mayhap it would not have been so atrocious if the marquis had read in French, but his faltering ruined the cadence.

As he handed Emily out of the carriage in front of the townhouse that was bright with lamps, he said, "If you wish to take our leave at any time, you need only to say so."

Emily shoved aside the blue devils that had been taunting her. "Thank you, Damon." She sighed as Miriam hurried up the steps to the front door with Kilmartin in tow. "I am very worried about her."

"I had thought your sister to have better sense than to come under de la Cour's spell."

"She is just pretending," she said as they followed her sister at more decorous pace.

"Pretending?" He paused on the step. "About what?"

"Her calf love for the marquis." She lowered her voice. "She wants to make Mr. Simpkins jealous."

"Graham Simpkins?" He snorted. "Why?"

"She has had a *tendre* for him since the Season began."

"Are you sure?"

Emily gave the footman in his perfect black livery a smile as he took Damon's hat. She ignored the prick of envy when she wished Johnson would be even half as skilled. "She has spoken of little else."

"But are you sure about that *now?*"

She followed his glance up the stairs to where Miriam was standing in the reception line on the marquis's left. Her sister had her arm through his and was gazing at him with all the fervor of infatuation.

"Is she such a good actress?" Damon continued. "Or is she succumbing to de la Cour's froggish charm?"

Chapter Eleven

Emily hoped Damon was wrong. Miriam had pined for Graham Simpkins for so long. Surely she could not turn her back on him simply because a false marquis was turning her head with *bon mots*.

But Miriam did not know the man was an impostor!

"Miriam," Emily said, drawing her sister away from the marquis, who was exulting in his legions of admirers pouring through the door and up the stairs.

"What is it? André asked me to remain by his side in case he needed help understanding someone's English."

"I think he can manage quite well on his own." She flinched as she heard the French phrases he sprinkled more liberally through his conversation when he seemed intent on impressing a person. He need waste them on her no more. She suspected he was as much a Frenchman as he was a marquis. If only she could think of a way to denounce him without divulging the truth . . .

"He is superb, isn't he?" Miriam's face took on a dreamy expression that added to the tightness in Emily's stomach.

"Miriam, you know so little about him."

"You keep repeating that." She fluttered her eyelashes when the marquis blew a kiss in her direction. "I have never been this happy."

Damon's chuckle silenced Emily's retort as he held out a glass of wine. "I thought you might enjoy something to wash away the disagreeable taste of de la Cour's poetry. He— Look out!"

A man, his head down, his hands locked behind his back, almost bumped into Emily, but halted when Damon put out his hands. The dark-haired man looked up, and Emily was startled to meet Mr. Simpkins's wide eyes. Next to her, Miriam stiffened.

"Why don't you keep your eyes on where you are going, Simpkins?" Damon demanded. "You have an intolerable habit of running folks down."

"Forgive me." He squinted at Emily and said, "Excuse me, Miss Talcott."

Emily waited for her sister to speak, but Miriam stared at him, not uttering a sound. Exasperation gnawed at Emily.

Mr. Simpkins took a step back. "Good evening, Miss Talcott, my lord, Miss Talcott." He bobbed at each of them and rushed away.

"Terse fellow," Damon said under his breath.

Emily turned to her sister. "Miriam, I—"

"Say nothing," Miriam whispered. "Anything you say will just persuade me more of how I have been a clod-pate to wish that Mr. Simpkins would speak to me. He must think me a gawney for being unable to speak even a word to him."

"He said little more than you," Damon said. "He may be shy, too."

"Shy?" Miriam cried. "He seeks out Valeria on every occasion. He must be bored with my silliness."

"You can never win his heart if you flee," Emily said. "However, if you wish, we can leave now."

"That would be a shame, for then I would not have the

chance to ask you to stand up with me, Miriam," came the marquis's voice.

"Stand up with you?" Miriam gasped, her smile returning.

"That is the proper phrase, is it not?" He motioned toward the dance floor. "Will you dance with me?"

"Oh, yes!"

"Miriam?" Emily put her hand on her sister's arm and fought the yearning to throw her arms around her sister to keep her from walking out onto the dance floor with the fake marquis.

As the marquis looked at her with a slight smile, she feared once more that he knew the truth she hid. Again she reminded herself he could not guess she was Marquis de la Cour. If he had, he would not be seeking out her sister.

"Yes?" Miriam asked.

Faintly, she said, "Enjoy the music."

As did everyone else in the room, she watched her sister walk away on the marquis's arm. Even Mr. Simpkins, who was standing, as ever, next to Valeria, had frozen with his glass of wine halfway to his mouth. No one moved but the marquis and Miriam, who laughed at some sally Emily could not hear.

She blinked as a waistcoat blocked her view. Raising her eyes, she met Damon's amused ones.

"She is an excellent actress," Damon said quietly. "I doff my *chapeau* to her on her conquest of our frog poet."

"Cut line!"

"Emily!" he called, but she did not slow or look back as she walked across the ballroom.

Miriam floated through the evening, for the marquis seldom left her side. Nor did Emily, who noted the expressions of envy in other female eyes as they watched her sister. She noticed as well that her sister did not waste a glance in Mr. Simpkins's direction. Emily's single attempt to mention that was brushed aside as unimportant, and she wondered how Miriam's heart could be so fickle.

Wandering out into Lady Murrow's garden, Emily sighed. She would find no comfort in this sterile place. She despised its attempt to ape a natural landscape, for the miniature hills and clumps of trees were out of place in Town.

Shadows chased the lamplight along the path of crushed seashells and into the shrubs. The odors from the river drifted toward her, but she paid them no mind. Hearing light voices and a feminine giggle in an arbor near the gate leading to the stables, she turned in the opposite direction. She did not begrudge anyone happiness, but it seemed ironic anyone could be so happy when she was so miserable.

A stone bench was still warm with the day's heat. Emily sank to it and leaned her elbows on her knees as she stared at the pattern her toe traced in the stones. What was she going to do? If she spoke the truth about who had written the poems, Miriam would never make the good marriage necessary to save the household from penury. If she was not honest, that bounder might seduce her sister into believing his lies and giving him her heart. That would be just as disastrous.

"I thought I might find you here in this sorry excuse for a garden."

"Damon!" she whispered, looking up to see his enticing silhouette against the lamps sprinkled through the garden.

"May I?" he asked, pointing at the bench.

Emily nodded. "Of course."

"You are right to be worried."

She smiled, glad he did not lather her with useless assurances.

Her smile disappeared when he went on, "I suspected de la Cour would seek out a willing victim for his charm, although I had guessed your sister to be wiser than this."

"A few dances do not make a match."

"You sound like one of the dowagers, Emily, but you cannot bamboozle me. You are worried."

"I know too little about that man."

He folded his arms over his chest and flashed her a challenging grin. "You are not the only one curious about our Frenchy friend. I cornered Homsby in his shop tonight and put a few questions to him. I was determined to learn more about our infamous Marquis de la Cour."

Emily was sure the world had tipped on its side, for her head was suddenly light. Mr. Homsby would not have told Damon the truth, would he?

Calm yourself. Homsby would want the truth revealed no more than she did. The Polite World would never again patronize his shop if they learned he had hoaxed them.

Taking a deep breath, she asked, "And what did you learn?"

"That de la Cour is a French poet who has gained a ridiculously large following here in Town. That is it. Are you disappointed? Did you hope to discover that the marquis is keeping a secret from the *élite de l'élite?* A wife kept in a dungeon in a castle on the Loire perchance? Or perhaps a mistress living in grandeur in that same *château?*" His voice dropped to a conspiratorial whisper. "Could it be you hoped the quarto was privy to something even more detrimental to de la Cour's reputation?"

"Enough!" She started to open her fan, then placed it in her lap again. The motion would not keep Damon from guessing her thoughts. "I wish to keep Miriam from breaking her heart anew."

"Odd."

"What is odd?"

He smiled. "I never thought to hear you speak such jobbernowl words."

"What is jobbernowl about wanting to protect my sister?"

"Not that. I commend you for your sisterly affection, but she is old enough to find her own way."

Emily glanced back at the ballroom just as her sister and de la Cour danced past. Her sister's face glowed with happiness. When the marquis bent forward, Miriam smiled at whatever he said.

Loosening her clenched hands, for her fingers had been pressed so tightly to her palms that she could feel the prick of her fingernails through her gloves, Emily fought despair. Damon's broader hand eased over hers, and she gasped as a pulse of delight coursed along her arm. So easily she could imagine these fingers tending a fragile seedling in the gardens Damon enjoyed visiting, but she was finding it harder and harder to envision them arrogantly holding a handful of cards. Her gaze slipped up his black fustian sleeve to the high collar edging his square jaw. Higher, until it met his.

"Let us speak of other things," he said in a low voice that urged her closer.

She resisted, for she found her mind drifting from his hands to how easy it would be to place her head on his shoulder. "Yes, let us."

"Of our trip to Wentworth Hall? Have you given my invitation some thought?"

"Yes."

When he smiled, she realized her swift answer was revealing too much.

"Or we could speak of how your eyes change color like the sky with every different mood," he murmured as he slipped his arm along the back of the bench. His hand curved around her shoulder, tilting her toward him.

"Damon, I think—"

"Do not think. Just feel." His palm cupped her chin, his fingers splaying across her cheek. "Just feel this."

His mouth captured hers as his arms enfolded her to him. Straining for breath, she gasped when he traced her lips with moist flames. His kiss deepened when her fingers slid beneath his collar to find the soft hairs at his nape.

When he raised his mouth from hers, she wanted more. More of the danger and more of the rapture. She traced the curve of his lips with her fingertip. He smiled, and she was sure something luscious was melting within her, sending its sweetness to her very toes.

"Better?" he murmured.

"Yes."

"Good, for I came to tell you I must take my leave. I forgot another obligation I have tonight."

"Now? I thought you were going to take Miriam and me home." Emily lowered her eyes. "I am being presumptuous. I should have realized we were keeping you from the card table."

He laced his fingers through hers. "Emily—"

"Emily!" echoed an outraged voice.

She pulled away to stare at her father who was walking toward them. His face was as stern as his voice.

Rising, she swallowed roughly. "Good evening, Papa. I did not know you were attending Lady Murrow's supper."

"Obviously not." His furious footsteps threatened to crush the stones in the path to dust. "Where is Kilmartin?"

"Inside with Miriam." She was so aware of Damon sitting in silence while her father scolded her as he had when she was a child.

Papa scowled. "I thought it was understood that you were to serve as watch-dog for your sister, and that Kilmartin was to play duenna for you, if necessary."

"Papa—"

"Come with me. Right now!"

Emily was too ashamed to meet Damon's eyes as she whispered, "Excuse me."

"I think not," Damon answered as quietly. Turning to her father, he said, "Talcott, you are creating a spectacle."

"Me?" Papa's frown rutted his forehead. "You are here alone with my daughter in the garden."

"We are in the garden, but hardly alone. I suspect you shall find a half dozen others among Lady Murrow's sad collection of bushes."

Papa turned to her, the frustration on his face filtering into his voice. "I am waiting for an explanation, Emily, why you have risked your sister's reputation and yours like this."

Chapter Twelve

When Emily faltered before her father's wrath, Damon answered, "Talcott, the explanation should be mine, because I sought her out."

"I thought even you were more of a gentleman than this."

"You are misconstruing my intent."

"It seems clear when I see you sitting so close to my daughter as you whisper together in this bower."

"I sought her out so I might speak to her of an invitation."

"An invitation? What type of invitation are you offering my daughter?"

Damon silenced his rage. This was no time to lose his composure. Talcott's cavalier behavior was vexing, but he was more irritated at Emily. She did not retort like the intelligent woman she was. As lief she submitted to her father without a thought for her own desires or Damon's, for he found it difficult to think of anything but feasting on her lips again.

"The invitation is for you and your family to join me

on a visit to Wentworth Hall," he answered, satisfied with his calm tone. "I need to return there for several days at the end of the week, and I plan to invite a few friends. I thought Emily and her sister along with the other ladies joining us would enjoy a visit to a local fair while we men lure Lady Luck's smile upon us."

Talcott's frown eased into a sly smile. "A fascinating idea, I must say. Who else would be joining us?"

As he listed the gamesters who would be willing to travel as far as Wentworth Hall to study the history of four kings with Demon Wentworth, he watched Talcott. The man was fairly salivating to begin the play. This, all in all, he had to own with a smile was easier than he had expected.

When he looked at Emily, he was astonished to see anger glittering in her eyes that sparked like faceted sapphires. She was furious. Why? She should be grateful, for he had spared her from her father's dressing-down.

"It could be entertaining," Talcott said as he rubbed his chin.

"My thoughts exactly."

Talcott smiled. "Mayhap I have misjudged you, Wentworth. We accept your gracious invitation." To Emily, he added, "You may prepare the household for the visit."

"Yes, Papa."

Annoyed further by her servility, Damon asked, "I trust that, now that we have cleared the air, I may continue to speak with your daughter about this."

"Of course, but inside." He gave his daughter a quick kiss on the cheek and said, "While you handle the arrangements with Wentworth, *ma chérie,* I will find your sister. I hear she has made the conquest of a marquis tonight."

Talcott strode away, whistling a tune whose words would have brought a blush to his daughter's face.

Offering his arm to Emily, Damon waited until her father was out of earshot before asking, "Why are you giving me a scowl that would curse a witch? I had thought you wanted to join me on the journey."

Unhappiness threaded her forehead, and his fingers longed to soothe the lines away. "If we are friends, as you assert, Damon, I beg a favor of you." As he started to answer, she raised her hand and said in a broken voice, "Please listen before you say something you may regret. I would ask that you take this vow only if you propose to keep it."

"I make no promises lightly," he said, then swore as his terse response brought tears into her lustrous eyes.

"Please do not play cards with my father during our visit to Wentworth Hall."

"Why?"

She raised her chin, and he admired her gentle courage. "Just tell me that you will agree to this small favor."

"Or you will refuse to come with me?"

She closed her eyes and shook her head. "Papa wishes to go."

"So, dutiful daughter that you are, you will agree." When she did not answer, he relented. "Very well, Emily, I vow to you that I shall not play cards with your father either at Wentworth Hall or during our journey to and from it. I vow that, if you will explain something to me."

"I will try."

"Why do you act like a child before your father?"

"I do not!"

"No? What have I heard you say in his presence but 'Yes, Papa' and 'No, Papa?' Why do you submerge your will to him?"

"He is my father." When his brow arched at her trite answer, she added, "Damon, don't try to change me."

He put his hands on her shoulders. "I have no wish to change you. Just to free you from obligations you should not have taken on."

Emily blinked back her astonishment. She should not be astonished, for she had already discovered how Damon saw things others overlooked. "If I had not, who would have?"

He sighed and nodded. "I understand, for each of us has onerous tasks, even Demon Wentworth."

She turned away before the passion in his eyes beguiled her again. "I realize I am keeping you from your club."

"You aren't."

"I thought . . ."

He brought her to face him. "In spite of what you think of me, I do not spend every moment at the board of green cloth. Even that adventure pales with time, so I look for other challenges."

"In your business matters?"

"Now you are sounding like a mama interested in ferreting out every facet of a man's standing." He kissed the tip of her nose.

She stepped back before he could sweep her into his arms and against his firm chest. "I should check on Miriam."

"Your father is doing that."

"I should—"

"What are you afraid of?" His hands glided down her arms to take her fingers.

She drew away. "I am afraid of you."

"I vow to you, Emily, I am not the demon *on dits* label me."

"I know, but . . ." Closing her eyes, she took a deep breath. It could not steady her heart that beat against her breastbone like a drum signaling a quick march.

"Emily?"

She gazed up at him, longing to touch his face, his hair, to let his breath mingle with hers in a soul-tapping kiss. The lamplight burnished his hair with blue-hot fire, but she knew the slightest brush of his mouth on hers would be even more smoldering.

"If Papa had seen me kissing you," she whispered, "he would not have been so willing to forgive you."

Damon twirled a lock of her hair around his finger as he chuckled. "He would be arranging, even now, for the banns to be read in the closest church. In short order, we would be wed."

"Order? My life," she said, toying with a withering blossom on a spindly stalk, so he could not see how his teasing had sent a trill of delight through her, "had order until you came into it, Damon."

"Mayhap it needed to be a bit less orderly." His eyes twinkled with mischief. "That may be why you have not closed your door to me. You like that I upset the order in your life. Mayhap you need a few friends who tantalize you to set aside your obligations and assumptions."

"Mayhap."

He chuckled. "You sound uncertain."

"I am. So much has happened."

"You cannot fault me for the to-do de la Cour is causing."

Hoping her face was not awash with lamplight, she forced a smile. "True, but you have upset my life in many other ways. I had thought it would remain much as it had."

"Shaking up one's assumptions is never a bad thing."

Her smile became sincere. "I loathe having to own that you are right. I often find myself questioning things."

"Questions such as why Lady Murrow is so proud of this desert she calls a garden?"

"Exactly." She laughed. "I wonder if she has her gardener at her country estate trying to coerce the plants there into appearing as if they are growing in Town."

The chiming of a clock from near the door brought a sigh from Damon. "It is even later than I thought."

"I am sorry if my babblings will make you late."

"Late? That does not matter." A slow smile eased across his lips. Holding out his hand, he said, "Come with me, Emily."

"With you? Where?"

"To a place you shall enjoy far more than here."

"I cannot!"

"Bring your abigail."

"But, Miriam—"

"Your father," he said with a grin, "is watching over her. Come with me, Emily."

She knew she should say no. She could think of a dozen reasons why she should say no. And she could think of only one why she should say yes. As she gazed up into his shadowed eyes, she raised her fingers to place them in his hand.

"Yes," she whispered, "I will come with you."

"You will not regret this, I promise you."

That was one promise he would not be able to keep, for she already was having second thoughts. Yet, for one night, with Kilmartin keeping a close eye on her, she wanted to throw aside her obligations to her family and be the one who risked everything on the chance to share one more kiss.

While they drove from Berkeley Square, Damon sat beside Emily in the carriage, his hat on his knee, a smile tipping one corner of his lips, and answered each of her questions with, "You shall see where we are going when we arrive."

Kilmartin was even more silent, but the tapping of her fingers on the window and the parade of glowers aimed at Damon signaled her disapproval.

Emily sighed. Tonight she had escaped her obligations. She wanted to enjoy herself wherever they were going.

When the carriage stopped at one corner of Soho Square, Emily looked out. There was nothing remarkable about the plain house on the other side of the walkway, and she had no clue who might reside within it.

"We are going here?" she asked.

"Why so surprised?"

"I am not surprised, just curious."

Damon leaned forward and winked boldly at Kilmartin.

"She does not want to own that she thought I would lure her to a school of Venus where I would besmirch her reputation."

Kilmartin gasped, "My lord, you should not say such things, even in jest."

"I was not jesting. You thought that, didn't you, Emily?"

Emily laughed. "Do not tease Kilmartin."

As the footman opened the carriage door, Damon stepped out and held up his hand. "Then I shall tease you with a gathering which you will find infinitely more fascinating than that mind-numbing assembly we left behind."

He did not release her hand as she stepped to the walkway. Warmth suffused her. She looked from his gloved hand to the shadowed secrets of his eyes. How many other women had gazed into them before her and found nothing but amusement there? But she could sense something else in that heated glow, something that did not belong to the rakish lord he portrayed with such verve.

A poke in her back was a reminder from Kilmartin. Quickly, Emily withdrew her fingers from Damon's. When he motioned for her to precede him up the steps to the house, she glanced back only long enough to be sure that the footman was assisting Kilmartin from the carriage.

Suddenly she was glad her abigail was with her. The flood of pleasure at Damon's touch was alarming, for it urged her to toss aside all caution.

A small antechamber waited beyond the door. Three servants stood there, although only one wore livery. They took Damon's hat and Emily's bonnet. Kilmartin held her shawl tightly, pursing her lips as she made it clear she expected to leave posthaste.

"Is she always so glum?" Damon murmured.

Emily smiled, but did not answer. Kilmartin sniffed in derision as they climbed the stairs to a large room that opened from the expansive hallway. Tables and chairs were scattered about, but no one was seated at them with some refreshments or a pack of flats and coins to gamble away the evening. The room was not full, for she guessed no more than a score of men stood within it. Dismay pricked her when she realized that, save for her and Kilmartin, there were no women.

"What is this?" she asked.

"Have patience, Emily."

"I thought I had."

"Then trust me."

No quick quip came to her lips. His jest did not hint at what he was asking of her. *Trust him?* Her dismay deepened as she realized she did. Dear God, she might more than trust him. She might be falling in love with this mercurial man who wore even more guises than she did. How could she be in love with a man who might be the demon his tie-mates called him instead of the tender lover who filled her dreams?

Damon did not slow as he guided her among the chairs. He smiled, but did not speak to any of the men who paused in their conversations to watch their passage.

Emily's eyes widened when he paused before a small table where an elderly man sat. Gout thickened his limbs, but his eyes were as bright as a lad's. Tugging at his coat which was decorated with a star that denoted he was a knight, he asked in a creaking voice, "Who is this fair creature you have brought with you, Damon?"

"Sir Joseph Banks, Miss Emily Talcott," he replied with a respectful dip of his head.

"Didn't you sail with Captain Cook on the *Endeavor* to explore Australia and the South Pacific?" she gasped.

The old man did not rise, but smiled. "Miss Talcott, I am delighted that you recall my youthful adventures. It is regrettably seldom that we are able to entice members of your fair sex here."

"But what is this?" she blurted, then flushed.

Banks laughed, the sound as wiry as his whiskers. "One might call it a *conversazione*, although, I must own you will find it different from those so-called intellectual evenings put on by the misguided matrons of the Polite World. This is a place where people can come to talk. Not converse, my dear, but talk. If my good friend Damon brought you here, I trust you have a brain behind your pretty eyes." He waved a vein-lined hand at them. "Do take her about, Damon, and see if she can betwattle one of our number with her opinions."

"Shall we?" he asked.

With a smile for Sir Joseph, Emily put her hand on Damon's arm and let him lead her deeper into the high-ceilinged room. Now that she understood the purpose of this gathering, she was eager to learn more about what drew Damon here. She had been so certain he was bound for his club and nothing more straining to the mind than the odds of his next hand being a winner.

Kilmartin followed like a disapproving shadow, but Emily forgot her as she listened to the wisps of conversation floating around her. No one spoke of *modistes* or trysts or marriages. Instead, the men discussed the latest advancements in natural science and fine art.

When she overheard a discussion of poetry, she was tempted to linger. No one mentioned Marquis de la Cour or even Byron. They spoke of medieval poets and the constraints of sonnets on modern work.

Damon grinned at her and gave a tug on her arm. "I have had too much of rhymes tonight," he said. "Let me introduce you to someone who should be as delighted to meet you as you shall be to meet him."

"Who?"

"Patience, Emily."

"I am beginning to abhor the sound of those two words together."

He chuckled as they left the trio of men to argue over one section of *The Canterbury Tales*.

Emily gazed in amazement at the scientific journals scattered across the tables. She had never guessed there could be so many and on so many erudite subjects. Hearing the debate between two animated gentlemen, one with an accent that was decidedly American, on a new variety of animal discovered in Africa, she glanced across the room to discover another man who was dressed in an alien costume that labeled him a Persian. His turban and flowing robes went otherwise unnoted among the guests.

"Damon," a deep voice said behind her, "you have been absent much of late from our gatherings. I thought perhaps Pipkin had driven you away with his ludicrous arguments."

She turned to see a skinny man who wore thick glasses. His clothes were as wrinkled as if he had donned them before retiring the night before. When his bushy eyebrows raised almost to the sparse hair on his balding head, she saw her own amazement mirrored in his eyes.

"Ah, here you are, Gerald," Damon said. "I had hoped you would be lurking about tonight. Miss Emily Talcott, allow me to introduce Dr. Gerald Cozie. Gerald, despite his want-witted prattling, is a respected fellow of the Royal Society."

Dr. Cozie bowed his head, then straightened, pushing his heavy blinkers back into place. "Miss Talcott? *The* Miss Talcott?"

"I suppose I must be." Once again, Emily was glad she did not blush. Dr. Cozie's words suggested this was not the first time Damon had mentioned her name in his presence. She was not sure if she should be pleased or shocked that Damon had spoken of her.

While Damon had the good grace to appear discomfited, Dr. Cozie gushed, "I was talking with Damon recently about my boyhood fantasy of sailing away on one of the ships of the Talcott line."

She struggled to keep her smile in place. Ships? There had not been more than one ship afloat under the Talcott name during her lifetime, although she had heard tales of when the line enjoyed its heyday. When that final ship had been sunk by a Caribbean hurricane within a fortnight of her stepmother's death, she had feared for Papa's mind. He had recovered. Or had he? If she had not had the good fortune to get her small books of poetry published, the Talcotts would have been all to pieces last year.

"Now I understand what has occupied you while we noted your absence, Damon," the doctor continued.

"You need not show your usual lack of polish," Damon returned with a laugh. "Emily is no blind buzzard concerned only with assemblies and routs. You shall find she shares our interest in the study of the natural world. I suspect, if you had the good fortune to view the garden she has carved out of the most unforgiving conditions here in Town, you would be impatient to hear her opinions on growing roses."

Astounded at the compliment, Emily hurried to say, "Damon is being too kind. My studies have gone no farther than my own garden, Dr. Cozie."

"Which is why I brought her here." Damon smiled. "She should not have to waste her mind on the bibble-babble of the *ton.*"

Dr. Cozie laughed. "For one who counts himself among that species, you have an unending contempt for them."

"I cannot change the facts of my birth, Gerald, only of my life. Now tell Emily what you have discovered about grafting roses."

As Damon drew her into the conversation, treating her as if she were an equal to a fellow of the Royal Society, Emily was thrilled. She had no time to savor her happiness, for she was caught up in an intense discussion where no quarter was given for uncertainty.

Emily guessed her head was choke-full of new ideas when, three hours later, Damon walked her to her door. Kilmartin went in, leaving the door open so there would be no question of indiscretion. The blending of light from the foyer and the carriage lamp created a glowing bubble in the fog.

Damon rested his shoulder against the doorframe. "I trust by your smile that you enjoyed yourself tonight."

"Thank you for taking me there." She rocked from her heels to her toes like a child about to erupt into a dance. So many new and exciting ideas roamed through her brain that she could not be still. "I had a wonderful time."

"I did as well, not in the least because you gave Pipkin a bit of his own sour medicine when you corrected him about Mr. Cobbett's latest thesis."

"He was a bit disconcerted by my visit."

"He was furious because he was shown to be a pompous ass by one of the very sex he ridicules on every possible occasion."

She tilted her head, so she could see him more easily past the wide brim of her bonnet. "I find such posturing distasteful."

"And I found his humiliation delightful." Laughing lowly, so their conversation would not reach anyone within, he said, "I thought you would be diverted by an evening filled with conversation of things other than the drivel penned by that Frenchmen."

Emily fought to keep her smile. Why did Damon have to bring up that blasted poetry now? As he lifted her fingers to his mouth for a chaste kiss, she told herself his inadvertent insults might be a blessing, for they kept her from edging into his arms. Even as she thought that, a mesmerizing smile tilted his lips, and she wondered when she had begun lying to herself, too.

Her heart had filled with joy in Lady Murrow's garden when Damon mentioned marriage, even in jest. But falling in love with Damon would lead to heartbreak. Hadn't she learned from watching her sister? If Damon had a *tendre* for her to match hers for him, that made everything more tragic. Then she would be dooming both of them to grief, for she could not involve him in her life and the secret that was buried even more deeply in her heart than the truth about Marquis de la Cour. The secret the *ton* would find appalling. The secret even Miriam did not know.

The secret that must never, never be revealed.

Chapter Thirteen

"Miriam, be reasonable." Emily guessed she had repeated those words five times in as many minutes.

But Miriam refused to listen as she prowled about the garden. "How could you be so oblivious to my feelings and agree to this jobbernowl idea of going to Wentworth Hall?"

"I thought you would enjoy a sojourn in daisyville."

Miriam rolled her eyes in disgust before stamping to the door leading into the house. "Why would I wish to leave Town in the midst of the Season?" She whirled to face Emily, revealing that tears now glittered in her eyes as brightly as the sunshine on the freshly painted arbor. "Why do you never think of *me*, Emily?"

"I think often of you." She swallowed the truth that would create even more problems. Miriam would be in an even greater huff if she were to suspect how often Emily thought of her sister while composing those poems she now wished had never been penned.

"You did not think of me when you agreed to go with that *man* to that godforsaken wilderness."

Emily smiled. "Lincolnshire is no wilderness. It is not so far from London, and many families of eminence have country seats there."

"Including *his* family?" She sat on the garden bench.

"Damon was generous to invite us to Wentworth Hall."

"Invite you!"

"And Papa and you."

Miriam shook her head. "I do not wish to go. Why don't you and Papa go without me?"

"Miriam, you know you cannot stay here alone. You must be reasonable."

"Why should I?" She jumped up, a swirl of white muslin flowing about her. "I know why Papa agreed to this. He is so determined to win back what he lost to Demon Wentworth—"

"Please do not call him that."

The tears flooded from her eyes. "You would agree to almost anything to keep Papa happy, even if it means you will be destroying my life."

"Miriam, be . . ." She did not finish, for her sister clearly would not be reasonable now. "I thought you would enjoy this chance to travel. It shall be fun."

"Impossible!" Wringing her hands, she whispered, "How could you choose Papa's happiness over mine?"

Emily grasped her sister's hand and drew her down to sit on the bench again. Wiping the tears from Miriam's face, she said softly, "I would never do anything that I thought would hurt you, Miriam. You must know that."

"Yet you agreed for me to leave London just now when I have never been happier."

"Never been happier? You cannot mean—?" She could not even speak the name which once had been amusing.

"Of course. André asked if he might escort me to the next reading he is giving." Standing again, she scowled at Emily. Tears fell in a rapid shower along her face as her voice broke. "Now I shall not be able to go to his reading because you are dragging me away from Town to that dashed viscount's dirty acres. You care nothing for me. Nothing at all."

"Miriam, you know that is not so."

"I swear I shall never speak to you again! You have ruined my life!"

Before Emily could speak, her sister fled into the house. She stared about her garden. Once this had been sanctuary, but now her troubles buzzed about her like bees among her flowers.

"Emily, *ma chérie?*"

She affixed a smile on her face as she looked at Papa, who stood in the doorway. He was wearing a saucy grin that suggested he was well pleased with himself. "I trust you are dealing with everything so we might leave for Wentworth Hall as planned."

"Yes, Papa." She almost winced as she spoke the words Damon had chided her for.

"Good." He settled his hat on his light hair and smiled. "I knew I could depend on you."

"Papa?"

"Yes?"

"Miriam is—um—" She was not sure how to explain, for she did not want to distress Papa over what might be no more than calf love.

He patted her arm. "I know Miriam regrets missing the duchess's party, but she will come around."

"I am not so sure of that." Her stomach cramped, for she understood why Miriam was doubly distressed. Miriam had been hoping for an invitation to that gathering for the past month.

"Do not fret, *ma chérie.* You always manage to work things out." He kissed her on the cheek. "Smile, for you do not want to etch frown lines into your face, do you?"

"No, Papa."

"Are you unwell?"

She knew her wince must have been visible. How could

she tell Papa what Damon had said? Such words were certain to wound him.

"I am fine, Papa."

"Good," he said again.

She followed him into the parlor. Untying her bonnet, she said, "Papa, we must talk."

"Of what?" He gave her no chance to answer. "Bollings, where's my walking stick? I cannot call on His Grace without proper accoutrements."

His harried valet rushed up the stairs.

"Papa," Emily tried again, "I need a few minutes of your time before you go out."

"Drat! Where did I put my *cartes de visite?*" He looked at her and smiled. "Be a good girl, *ma chérie,* and tell Bollings I need my calling cards, will you?"

Emily took one step toward the stairs, then faltered. She squared her shoulders and motioned to a serving lass.

"Caroline," she whispered, "please have Bollings bring Mr. Talcott's calling cards." As the girl went up the stairs, Emily added, softly, "Papa, what I have to say to you will take only a few minutes."

"That is good, for I have but a moment before I must leave." He brushed a speck of dust from his gray gloves. "What is putting that uncomely frown on your face?"

Again she hesitated and wondered why she could be candid with Damon, but not her father. "Papa, we need to speak of the household accounts."

"I trust you to run the household. You are like your mother." He smiled sadly as he did every time he mentioned his first wife. "She could squeeze another penny out of an empty purse, although I swear she never bothered me with tiresome details. Do be a sweet child and stop worrying yourself nigh to sickness. Come, Emily, and smile. You need to put more joy in your life."

"But, Papa—"

"Life is short, *ma chérie.* We must enjoy it while we may."

"We shall not enjoy it if we are as poor as Job's turkey."

His grin vanished. Pulling at his cravat, he said in an irritated voice, "Nonsense! I shall hear no more of this."

"You must listen."

At her rare vehemence, he returned, "Have our debts been paid this month?"

"Yes, except for—"

"Then why are you bothering me with your anxieties?" He smiled as he took his walking stick and calling cards from Bollings. "Egad, Emily, you shall end up with wrinkles before we can find you a husband." As she opened her mouth to retort, he added, "Concern yourself with getting a new gown and mayhap a new hat, so that you can look your best when you go to the next rout."

Emily considered arguing, but it was useless. If she told her father she doubted there was enough money left to buy a new hat, let alone a feather or a ribbon, he would pooh-pooh her again. She saw the understanding in Bollings's eyes, but said in a near whisper, "Yes, Papa."

"I shall see you on the morrow. If you need anything from me, I shall be at the club." He smiled broadly and strode away.

As his lighthearted whistle drifted back to her, Emily closed her eyes and sighed. She prayed *this* was not the day when Papa succeeded in bringing them to ruin. Papa was right. He could depend on her, and he did.

But as they traveled to Wentworth Hall, she must depend on Damon to keep his promise that he would not play cards with Papa. She had not been dependent on anyone for longer than she could recall. She did not like it. Not at all.

The carriage rolled to a stop in front of an inn. Dusk wove through the thatch roof and cloaked the stone walls. A barn behind the inn was edged by a yard where a single, swaybacked horse and a pair of goats grazed among the chickens.

Emily shifted on the seat which had become uncomfortable with the passage of the miles from London. Another long day of riding awaited them tomorrow, and she hoped she would sleep well tonight. She was the only one within the carriage who had not succumbed to slumber.

On one side, her father snored as softly as Miriam did on the other. Shaking his shoulder to rouse him, she grimaced as she readjusted herself on the seat while Papa, grumbling something she could not understand, stretched.

Muscles protested as she turned to wake her sister. The exasperation that had been seething inside her all day threatened to boil out. Damon had abandoned them after only an hour to take to the saddle.

Half a dozen other vehicles pulled to a stop behind them in the inn's yard. The Talcott carriage, which was top-heavy with their bags, carried Kilmartin and Bollings. Three additional carriages held Damon's other guests. More wagons followed. Emily was sure none of the pleasures the *ton* enjoyed in Town had been left behind.

She picked up her small bag from the floor. In it, she carried the journal which contained the poems for her next book. Her fingers tightened on it. Why was she continuing to labor over these little rhymes when that blasted impostor would take credit for her work again? She sighed. Nothing had changed. Miriam needed money to wed, and, since Papa had joined that club, his gambling debts were doomed to increase.

The carriage door opened to flood the interior with heavy scents from the barnyard. Papa leaned forward to peer out.

"I thought we had given up this rough life when we returned to England," he grumbled as he stepped down and held up his hand to assist Emily.

" 'Tis only one night," she answered, trying to keep her yawn imprisoned behind her teeth. "By tomorrow, we shall be luxuriating in Wentworth Hall."

"Be careful what you assume," Damon said as he offered

his hand up to help Miriam out. "Did I fail to mention Wentworth Hall will never be confused with Hampton Court?"

Emily smiled. "Is that the secret you have promised to divulge upon our arrival?"

"That secret is yet to be told." His brows arched when as soon as her feet touched the ground, Miriam backed away from him and hurried into the inn with Papa. "No one would doubt your sister's opinion of this journey."

"Please forgive Miriam's lack of courtesy."

"I admire her honesty at not being afraid to reveal she is furious with me."

"Not with you." Emily's smile grew sad. "With me."

"Why?"

She walked with him toward the inn where his guests milled in relief at being done with the long hours of riding. Lowering her voice, so it would not reach their ears, she said, "Miriam is convinced the whole of this was planned to keep her from spending more time with the marquis."

"Egad! She should be grateful as lief angry."

"She believes he is sincere in his interest in her."

"Which you don't?"

"Why are you making it a question? I doubt if that man has ever been sincere about anything."

"You have distrusted him from the first. I wonder why."

Her steps faltered. Would she never learn to guard her tongue when Damon was about? He seemed to perceive other meanings beneath her trite words.

Because he knew the truth?

No! She would not believe that. If Damon suspected the truth, he would have spoken to her of it. He would not chance divulging the secret to another by accident without telling her his suspicions first.

Wouldn't he?

"Emily?"

She prayed her laugh did not sound as brittle in his ears

as it did in hers. "I had hoped to leave chit-chat about the marquis behind us in Town."

"Agreed." His voice took on the husky warmth which delighted her, urging her to lower the barriers she had spent so many years erecting. Warmth twirled within her like a country reel as he murmured, "I would enjoy a comfortable coze while we speak of how the prettiest roses in your garden are almost as lovely as the roses in your cheeks."

"I pray you do not mean the yellow ones."

He chuckled. "I should know better than to try to compliment a woman who uses words with more skill than our frog poet."

"Damon!"

"I know. I promised no more gab about that gaby while we are away from London."

Emily did not move as he took a step toward the inn's porch. When he turned to face her, she said, "I want you to know that I am very grateful for your invitation. Mayhap some time in the fresh country air will bring good sense back to Miriam."

"You are grateful?" His hand settled on her waist. His ride in the sunlight had added another layer of bronze to his skin, and his hair was brushed back by the day's breeze. He leaned toward her until his forehead touched the brim of her bonnet. With a lecherous grin, he asked, "How grateful?"

Her heart struggled as if it were trying to flee from within her. With her gaze held by the silver fire in his eyes, she fought her arms which longed to sweep up to his shoulders. The aromas of sunshine and dust from his ride were as sweet as the scent of her favorite roses and as enticing. She wanted his lips on hers, the potent caress of his mouth luring her to lose all of herself to his alluring touch.

Edging away a step, she forced a jaunty tone. "You truly are a demon, my lord, to speak so."

"You are not answering my question."

"I am very grateful." She linked her arm through his. "As grateful about that as I am about your promise not to play the flats with Papa."

"You will unquestionably owe me a duty or two."

Better a duty than a debt of mint she could not repay, she told herself as they walked up onto the porch to be surrounded by the others traveling to Wentworth Hall. To no one, not even herself, did she want to own how few guineas the Talcott family had left before her father publicly was deemed a gentleman of three inns.

In debt and with no way out.

Emily had been pleased to discover that, inside, the inn was as neat as the yard. As she descended the stairs to the dining room, she admired a row of plates set on a shelf near the ceiling that was stained with smoke and dust. Whitewashed walls were bright in the glow of the candles. As she crossed the stone floor to where a bearded man wearing a long apron over his breeches and full-sleeved shirt came toward her, she smiled.

"I be yer host Mr. Dengler," he said in a heavy country accent. "Wanted to inquire if yer room is comfortable, miss."

"It is very nice." The room she was sharing with Miriam was cozy, and she had been tempted to drop onto the iron bed and let sleep sweep away her cares. Instead, she had washed the dust from her face and hands with the water in the ewer and bowl set atop the chest of drawers that was nicked and scratched as if a vindictive cat had attacked it.

When his full chest swelled with pride, he said, "My missus thought ye ladies would want a room far from the stables. My missus, she said that be right. Wouldn't be suiting for fine ladies to sniff the droppings in the yard."

Emily thanked the innkeeper and walked into the dining room. She wondered if Damon had ordered every candle in the shire put to use here. A trio of tables were empty save several bottles of wine, and she sighed. She was hungry and tired and ready for the day to come to an end. Mayhap if Miriam fell to sleep swiftly, there might be time to work on that troublesome line with the new poem.

L'amour . . . la chanson d'amour . . . à coeur joie . . . She sighed. Heart's content? Mayhap once she might have believed a heart could be content, but not now, not when her heart longed to flee her breast and find a place next to Damon's. She clenched her hands at her side. The secret that pumped through her with every beat of her heart would ostracize her from the purists of the *ton* swiftly.

Hearing footfalls, Emily turned. She could not keep from smiling as she saw Damon framed by the doorway. Wearing more casual clothes than he donned in Town, for trousers dropped over his boots, he had chosen a green coat and a brown striped waistcoat. He raised a single eyebrow as he came toward her, but she already knew her cream-colored frock was too fancy for the country inn. She did not have the luxury of one wardrobe for London and another for the country.

"Miriam will be down in a moment." She glanced about the room. "I had thought Papa would be here."

"The gentlemen are enjoying a few glasses in another room." His nose wrinkled. "It is stuffy in here."

"Mayhap because of all the candles."

"Dengler is going out of his way to help me impress my guests. I wonder what I have done to invoke his beneficence." He held out his arm. "Would you enjoy a taste of fresh air before we find ourselves confined to this room with our fellow travelers and the joint which should be nearly done roasting?"

Emily let Damon's gentle humor steal away her fatigue as they strolled into the early-summer darkness. Along a path from the back door, stones led through a shadowed garden. Lush fragrances stirred on the breath of a breeze which also brought the sound of voices from the inn, warning her of the many eyes that might take note of this walk.

She stopped to admire the flowers amid the blooming hedges that edged the small garden, but her gaze refused to remain on the blossoms. Her eyes were drawn again and again to Damon as he wandered about with the ease of a man who had no cares. As if he had peeled off an abhorrent skin, Damon had left behind the coolly wry, cavalier behavior he wore in Town. He could not hide his fascination with each plant and how it was planted.

"You truly love gardens, don't you?" Emily asked.

He faced her, wiping his hands of the dirt he had been poking in beneath a bushy rhododendron. Smiling, he said, "I didn't think you would need to ask that after you were a witness to my brangle with Cozie at the *conversazione* about forcing roses to blow out of season."

"But you don't have a garden in Town, do you?"

"No."

"Why not?"

"Time is an unfortunate factor. I am too busy in London to have the time to tend properly to a garden."

Regret pinched her. She had thought he enjoyed gardens more than playing cards. Had she misread him so thoroughly? Mayhap he was no more than the *demon* Miriam called him. No, she could not believe that. The man who had argued with Dr. Cozie so vehemently and with such knowledge could not be satisfied to squander his life away at the card table.

"Why are you wearing such a dolorous expression?" Damon asked as he peered under another rhododendron. "You are not the one who must tend to duties of business instead of the pleasures of a garden. I—" He cursed and took a step backward as a shadowed form burst from behind an arbor.

A young woman with a thick, brown braid dipped in a curtsey. "Pardon me, yer lordship."

"Pardon us," he said with a graciousness he did not

often use with titled ladies in Town. "We have intruded on your quiet. Do you tend this garden?"

"Yes, yer lordship." She gave him a tentative, gapped-tooth smile.

"Your excellent husbandry shows. Do you have only flowers, or have you planted herbs as well?"

"Both, yer lordship."

He grimaced at repetitious answer. "We shall be leaving shortly after dawn, but I trust we may visit your garden in the sunlight."

A call from the inn halted her answer. The young woman giggled and scurried away.

Damon shook his head. "By the elevens, I never have understood how an otherwise sane woman can titter as if she were still a child."

"She was overmastered by your questions," Emily said.

"Unlike her master who is charging twice his usual fare for the food he should have had ready upon our arrival."

Emily smiled and sampled the luxuriant scent of a rose. Looking over her shoulder to where Damon was bending to examine a yew, she said, "I thought you would leave your cynicism in Town. Are you the same man who vowed he found the honesty of the country refreshing?"

He sat on a broad boulder by the wall. Arching one ebony brow, he returned, "I did not realize that you would recall what I say with such clarity. Can I believe you find me unforgettable?"

"Before you lather yourself with pride, recall that an irritating itch is also unforgettable."

Instead of laughing as she had expected, he reached out to take her hand in his. She found herself looking down into his eyes, a decidedly odd and undeniably pleasurable experience, for the emotions alight in them urged her to step closer.

"Do you find me so irksome?" he asked with the rare gentleness that always set her heart to pulsing rapidly. "I would prefer that you think of me in other ways, Emily."

"How?" she whispered, wishing he would stop prattling and kiss her. For the moment, she did not care how many eyes witnessed their pleasure.

"As someone you can turn to, someone you can be honest with." His gaze drilled into her, holding her prisoner as he said quietly, "I know that you have been concerned about your father's habits and losses to more than Lichton and me, and I know as well, for I have made subtle queries, that your sister does not seem to share your anxiety."

"You asked questions like that about us?"

"About your father, primarily, and his business interests in England."

"How dare you!"

He set himself on his feet and grasped her hand before she could storm away. "Blame yourself, Emily, for you must own that it was most unusual that you would request that I not join your father in a game of the king's books."

"But that did not offer you carte blanche to ask about my father's business dealings."

"You are being generous, Emily."

"Generous?" She scowled at him. "I can assure you that my thoughts are anything but generous at the moment."

"I meant about deeming any of your father's dealings *business*. All his transactions seem to take place at the board of green cloth." He gently stroked her fingers.

"Our family has long been involved in enterprises beyond England. During our time in America, Papa—" She pulled her hand out of his. "This is none of your bread-and-butter, Damon."

"True, but I wanted you to know that I will keep my vow. Your father must find his own entertainment while I show you Wentworth Hall." His eyes began to twinkle. "If all goes as I hope, you shall enjoy the surprise I have waiting for you."

Emily knew she should leave him here to stew in his own juices. She should be appalled that he had inquired into Papa's affairs, but she could not force her feet to take her back into the dining room. Even though he was the most vexing man she had ever met, she did not want to lose a moment she could share with him.

"Why won't you tell me what this secret is?" she asked, lowering her chin from its defiant pose.

He laughed. "See? I am not the only curious cat here. Your curiosity, my dear Emily, shall add to my enjoyment of this trip. Shall we go in and discover if Dengler has readied our meal before it is time for breakfast?"

When he drew her hand into his arm, Emily was sure she had never been so happy. Unlike Mr. Colley, who had made himself bothersome with his puppyish attentions, Damon always gave her the chance to be herself with him. She was uncertain if she could say the same for him. Then she realized, as she should have from the beginning, that the many facets of his personality were all part of the man.

Within the dining room, the tables were set with scratched pewter. Emily wondered what was delaying Papa and Miriam and the others, but smiled when Damon led her to a small table that would sit no more than six.

"I brought an extra horse in case mine went lame," Damon said as he drew out a chair for her. "Will you ride with me tomorrow instead of being cramped in that rolling coffin?"

"What a pretty invitation!"

He laughed. "I thought you appreciated my plain words."

"I have had no choice, for you speak little else."

As she sat, his hands lingered on her chair, brushing her skin above the back of her gown's gently scooped neckline. She silenced her gasp when her skin came alive with the powerful sensation she suffered—no, not suffered, for it was a sweetness like nothing else she had experienced—each time he touched her. When he bent forward, she closed her eyes to relish the pleasure as his words grazed her ear.

"Would you have me laud your bewitching blue eyes or the indescribable glory of your ebony hair? I could speak of the enticing lilt of your laugh and the rapier-sharp edge of your wit, but I would as lief treat you with the gentle disrespect I offer all my friends."

"Which I prefer," she answered, surprised to discover that her quick answer was the truth. She did not want Damon serenading her with *billets-doux*. She had seen enough of that with Miriam's silliness in the marquis's company.

When his fingers slid along her face to wander up her cheek, she guided his lips toward her. Let the *ton* and its strictures rot in perdition! She wanted this kiss. Wanting to touch him far more intimately, her fingers clenched in the thick wool of his coat when his mouth gently brushed hers. He drew back, and she whispered a protest.

He put his finger over her lips and shook his head. When he walked around the table, she watched his cool smile return. She understood why when she heard voices past the rush of her pulse.

Damon greeted Miriam and Papa as they walked into the dining room. He urged them to seat themselves while he let their host know that they were growing ever more eager to partake of his handiwork.

"Where have you been?" Miriam asked, selecting the chair next to Emily's. "I was here less than five minutes ago, and I saw no sign of you. Mr. Dengler was little help." She pressed her hand over her heart. "I feared for you in this bleak place."

Emily's joy was startled away. The inn, despite its slow service, was clean and sufficient for a night's lodging.

Her surprise became aggravation when her sister continued, "I should have known *he* would pick such an out-of-the-way spot. No doubt few inns will accept his gold in exchange for being tarnished by his patronage."

"Miriam! That is a horrible thing to say." She smiled

coldly. "I think I prefer you not speaking to me than having to listen to such demure hits."

"I am only being honest." She stared at the door behind Emily. Her eyes grew wide as her frown softened into a smile.

Emily watched, bafflement ruffling her forehead, as Miriam slowly rose. Shifting in her seat, she turned so she could see what had caught Miriam's eye. She could not silence her groan. She should have known the moment she saw Miriam's reaction.

"*Mes amis,* we are well met," called Marquis de la Cour as, with a swirl of his gold cape, he entered the dining room. "I could not remain behind and miss all the fun. That would be, as you say, want-witted, no?"

Chapter Fourteen

"André!" Miriam rushed to greet the man who dared to claim the name Marquis de la Cour. "You came!"

The marquis caught her hand and pressed it to his lips. *"Mais oui, ma chérie."*

Emily gripped the edge of the table as she heard him speak the name that had been so precious between her and Papa. Would he leave her nothing?

He hooked his arm through Miriam's before leading her toward where Emily sat with Papa, who was wide-eyed at his younger daughter's forward behavior. The inn's servants stared, openmouthed, as the marquis took off his tall beaver. He whipped off his cloak. With an easy flick, he sent it and his hat in the direction of Mr. Dengler.

André— She found it more comfortable to think of him like that instead of as the marquis—smiled broadly. He bowed toward Papa, then to Emily, but lifted Miriam's hand again to his lips. Emily tensed as her sister tittered with nervous delight. Looking at Papa, she saw he was watching André, but without emotion.

Emily's fingers clenched in her lap as André's natter

about his journey was accompanied by eager questions from Miriam. It was the greatest irony that the fiction she had designed to protect Miriam and Papa might now be the very thing to endanger them.

"This is a surprise," interrupted a deeper voice.

Emily wanted to beg Damon to free her from this addled situation. As lief, she stood. Taking Miriam's hand, she urged her sister to sit between her and Papa. Emily was not sure if her scowl or André's laugh silenced her sister.

"*Mon Seigneur* Wentworth," gushed the fake poet, "I beg your indulgence, but I could not remain in Town when my dear friends were gone." His syrupy smile was aimed at Miriam.

She flushed but said, "Do let him join us, Damon."

Emily swallowed her gasp as Damon's brows rose at her sister's suddenly friendly demeanor. "I doubt if it would be good form to exclude anyone in such a public place."

"I had hoped . . ."

"Nor will I send him back to London, *Miriam.* He may join us at Wentworth Hall."

Emily wondered if she was the only one to note the layer of sarcasm in Damon's voice. When her gaze was caught by André's, she knew he had heard it as well. He looked away as he began to ply her sister with compliments. The blasted encroaching mushroom! If he thought to cement his status with the *ton* by wooing her sister . . . Emily did not know what she could do to halt him.

Fingers covered her tight fists. Meeting Damon's stern gaze, she tried to smile. He patted her hand as he took the chair beside her. That left André the choice of sitting next to Damon or next to Papa. Wisely, he chose the latter.

"Allow me," Damon said as he poured the wine. "Dengler assures me 'tis the best in his cellars."

André sniffed the glass and winced, as if its simple bouquet were too primitive for his palate. "Can there be no decent burgundy on this island?"

Damon smiled, but his eyes remained cold. "I had

thought, de la Cour, you would have a traveler's charity toward his host and be anxious to sample things beyond what you are accustomed to.''

"On other things, but this.'' He sighed with a martyr's grace and took another sip. "Ah, it seems there are many things we French excel at.'' Flashing a smile at Miriam, he tilted his goblet in her direction.

Miriam flushed and lowered her eyes. Emily promised herself she would talk with her sister about her want-witted admiration as soon as they retired.

Into the silence, Damon said, "After seeing examples of fine art from France, I accede that is one arena where the French outshine the English.''

"You possess a great deal of knowledge of the French,'' returned André. "Have you visited my homeland?''

"On several occasions.'' His smile became secretive. "On errands whose discussion you might, being a loyal *paysan,* find discomfiting.''

Miriam gasped, "You were there during the war!''

"On several occasions,'' he repeated. "I have had no opportunity to return since peace was declared after Napoleon's final banishment. It would be interesting to see Paris as something other than a city readying for a siege.''

Softly, Emily said, "Let us speak of the present. There's little interesting in what has come and gone.''

"True,'' seconded Papa. "We can do nothing to change what has been.'' Hearing regret in his voice, Emily reached across the table. He drew his fingers away, and she recoiled as if he had struck her.

André chuckled, proving he was unaware of anything but himself. "Mademoiselle Talcott, if our two nations had sent you lovely ladies to deal with political matters, I believe there would have been no *guerre.*''

"But then I would never have had the chance,'' Damon said smoothly, "to enjoy that small café in the village near Château Rivedoux on the Loire. You must know of it, de la Cour, as you have told me you grew up in the *château's* shadow. The owner was a burly chap named Marlon, and his daughter who worked there . . ." He let his voice trail off with a laugh that bespoke pleasant memories.

"Of course I know of it," André answered quickly. "I spent many a delightful hour there."

"Did you escape unscathed from that mad rooster who considered the whole yard his private domain?"

He rubbed his arm. "No one escapes unscathed, *mon seigneur.*"

Emily watched as they continued to reminisce. Something was not right. Damon sat back and rocked his goblet of wine, and she almost gasped when her gaze met his. Instead of the bonhomie of the light conversation, deep satisfaction glinted in the gray depths of his eyes. He was pleased with something, and, as his gaze returned to André, she was certain he shared her suspicions about the impostor.

Her fingers tightened on her glass. If Damon had guessed André was a fraud, he was certain to be anxious to unmask him to discover the "real" marquis. She wondered how she could have hoped this journey would be an escape from her troubles.

Ignoring the dust that coated her navy-blue riding jacket with a fine fuzz, Emily reined in her horse as Damon slowed his along the country road. She glanced over her shoulder, but the carriages and wagons were nowhere in sight. A smile tugged at her lips.

How glad she was that Damon had invited her to enjoy this glorious day! Inside the carriage, she could not have savored the song of the lark coming from the hedgerow or seen the scurrying of a rabbit back beneath it. And inside the carriage she would have had to bear André's boasting as she watched Miriam become enthralled with his bangers. She feared she would not be able to hold her tongue much longer.

"There!" Damon pointed across the rolling hills that
were growing a darker green with the end of the day.
Laughing as he flung out his hand, he said, "Behold the
ancestral hall of the Wentworths."

Emily stared, as awestruck as her friends had been when
they had met the marquis, for it was not a house. It was a
castle. Crenellations topped the wall that hid the house
beyond it. Easily she could imagine archers fighting off
some foe. The tame green fields, the glorious blossoms in
the orchards surrounding the estate, and the quiet village
separated from it by a quaint stone bridge over a meandering river could not gentle its massive strength.

"You live here?" she managed to choke out.

"Not within the chambers inside the wall, thank goodness." He motioned with his head for her to follow. "The
Wentworths no longer need to be prepared to withstand
an attack. We have grown more civilized through the centuries."

"Or you have simply disposed of all your mortal ene-
mies."

Laughing as they rode side-by-side, he replied, "If it
were only so easy. I must own there are times when I pine
for the days when the lord of the manor could dispose of
his foes with a strong force of men as lief a barrage of
barristers." He caught her reins and edged closer to her
horse. "And times when I consider the privileges offered
as *le droit de seigneur.*"

"We have grown more civilized."

"Have we?"

She knew she should not let the husky warmth in his
voice entrap her, but resisting the impulse to look into his
enigmatic eyes was impossible. As he drew both horses to
a walk beneath the shadow of the wall that was encrusted
with moss and vines, he leaned toward her. Boldly, her
hand glided up to his shoulder as his mouth slanted across
hers. His arm around her waist tilted her even closer to

him as he probed within her mouth, setting each slick surface alight with rapture.

Sudden brightness struck Emily's face, and she drew back to discover they had ridden through the gate and into the glow of the late-afternoon sun. "Oh, my!"

"I had hoped for a more enthusiastic response to our kiss than simply 'Oh, my!' " Damon said with a laugh.

She stared at what lay within the ancient wall. Her assumption that it was intact had been an illusion, she discovered, for only the one section remained standing. The austere tower, which once encompassed the keep, now was the centerpiece of a trio of wings that must be several hundred years old. Arched windows and deep sills were a reminder that this once had been a fortress. An avenue of trees invited them to explore as they rode past the broad lawns leading to the house and the smaller outbuildings that were set like courtiers around the grand dame.

"I had no idea," she whispered, "Wentworth Hall would look like this. How do you keep from becoming lost within that maze of wings?"

"It was the perfect place for a lad who was eager to find a hiding place to avoid his tutor." Setting his horse to a walk again, he said, "You must explore while you are here."

"And if I become disoriented amid all those rooms?"

"Then I shall have to come to your rescue. That is the duty of the lord of the manor, is it not?" He caught her gloved hand in his as the rakish leer returned to his face. "And then, mayhap, I can learn just how grateful you can be."

Wandering through Wentworth Hall that evening, Emily paused to look at the portraits lining the dusky walls. Faces, proud and somber, were edged with long hair and short as well as ruffs and stiff, starched collars. As she stared at the paintings, she could hear within her memory the sound of her grandmother's voice, telling the old tales of her ancestors. *Family and the family's traditions must always be the most important aspect of one's life.*

Here, with every breath Damon took, he was a part of the past. A line unbroken, a line unblemished.

Emily sighed as she turned to walk along the deserted hallway. Purity of bloodlines was something the peerage took pride in. The purity of the bloodlines of their horses, of their hunting dogs, of their heirs.

She examined the niches cut into the stone wall. They were empty, and she was uncertain if they once had held art or sconces. Everything about Wentworth Hall was grand, but tired. When she had ridden over the bridge between the Hall and a small village, she had discovered, on closer view, the large house wore her age like a confident dowager. As Damon had talked of the renovations he planned, she heard an unusual excitement in his voice. It told her he had an affection for the estate that he wasted on little else.

When she left the huge bedchamber suite where Kilmartin was exclaiming about the dressing room that was larger than the parlor on Hanover Square, she had been certain she could find her way to the sitting room where the guests were to meet. Where was everyone? She could be alone in this house, for not a single voice reached her ears. Only the distant resonance of thunder which flowed along the hallway after lightning flashed. She did not want to own to Damon that she had become lost. She could not trust that glitter in his eyes. Nor could she trust her reaction, the yearning to toss aside caution and thrill in the madness of his kisses . . . just once more.

She was addled to think like this. As long as she held her secrets within her heart, she must not dream of his touch. Such thoughts would only risk breaking her heart and ruining everything she had fought so hard to gain for her sister. Her sister, who was throwing her chance at happiness and a good marriage away by throwing herself at that accursed impostor. Dear God, why was everything as mad as a midsummer moon?

And how was she going to find her way to the sitting room?

Emily paused when she saw a door ajar. "Is anyone here?" she asked as she pushed it farther open.

The light of a single lamp cut through the storm's shadows in the large room. Two walls were lined with glass-fronted cases filled with books. Arched windows that had been thrown wide to catch any breath of air glowed when lightning exploded through the sky. Emily flinched as thunder crackled, the sound rumbling against the stones of the round hearth in the far corner of the room.

Walking to the desk set in front of the closest window, she edged no nearer to the glass as another bolt of lightning outlined the whipping branches of the trees beyond the driveway. She wrapped her arms around herself.

Her eyes widened as they were caught by familiar bindings in the largest bookcase. Blue leather and gold ink pressed into it to form the title she had devised. She touched the glass door hesitantly. Although Damon had urged her to run tame through Wentworth Hall, she did not know if she should be intruding in this room.

The door opened as if on invisible fingers. Her own fingers shook when she drew out a copy of the first book of poetry she had written. Amazement froze her as she realized a half dozen copies of the same book were stacked on the shelf. Kneeling, she read the titles of the other books. All of them were printed in the same blue with the gold lettering.

She set the poetry book back on the shelf and picked up another. *A Season in a Sussex Garden* by a Mrs. Charles Lock. Opening it, she carefully turned the crisp pages. Mr. Homsby's bookshop was listed on the title page along with the name Old Gooseberry Press.

Emily frowned as she put it aside and reached for another with the same binding and printing. An identical imprint was set on the cover page. Spurred by curiosity, she opened several others. Each one contained Mr. Homsby's name, although only about half listed Old Gooseberry Press.

"Looking for something interesting to read?"

She recoiled at the question that was as deep as the thunder. She glanced over her shoulder and discovered Damon leaning toward her. "I—I—" Words refused to form on her tongue.

"No need to look like a Tyburn blossom caught in the act of heisting books from my office." His smile broadened as he offered his hand to bring her to her feet.

Standing, she hid her shock at his clothes which better suited a stable than this grand chamber. His boots were scuffed, and the elbows of his black coat were shiny with wear. A loosely tied cravat threatened to escape from his waistcoat, which was missing a button.

Something must have betrayed her thoughts, for Damon chuckled and said, "I trust you will keep my secret."

"Secret? This is what you have teased me with when you have spoken of a secret?"

"This?" He laughed. "No, that special secret is still to be revealed." He poked at his elbow. "I accede to propriety in Town and am the epitome of a man in prime twig. Here, in the country, I set aside every illusion of being *à la modality.*"

"I believe others will take note."

"I shall change before dinner." He leaned back against the heavy oak desk and crossed his arms over his chest. "In fact, I was on my way to do exactly that, but I was curious to discover who was in my office."

"I did not mean—"

He put his finger to her lips, and she fought the craving to take his hand and lead his arm around her. "Emily, why do you always see wickedness in my words?"

"Mayhap because I always see the wickedness in your eyes."

"Not wickedness." His voice softened to a caressing whisper as he took her hand, drawing her toward him. "Just imagination. An imagination which urges me to presume that you are thinking much the same as I."

When he pressed his mouth to the curve of her neck, she slid her arms up his back. His strong muscles moved smoothly beneath her hands as he stood, enfolding her into an inflamed embrace. Her fingers splayed along him as he etched sweet fire across her cheek and onto her lips.

Her breath was no more ragged than his when he drew back. His hands framed her face as he whispered her name. Putting her fingers over his, she steered his mouth back to hers. Each kiss only whetted her desire for another.

Thunder burst through the room, and rain splattered against the window like fine pebbles tossed up behind a speeding carriage. Emily flinched.

With a laugh, Damon tapped her nose. He released her. Going to the windows, he drew them closed and latched them securely. "Afraid of a bit of rain?"

"No, of course not."

"Just jumpy." He drew off his worn coat and folded it over his arm. "Guilt mayhap?"

She raised her chin. "You told me I could explore the house freely."

"True." He bent and picked up one of the books which had fallen, unnoticed, to the floor. "Did you want to read one of these?"

"No. I was simply curious about all the books looking so much like my—like my copy of the marquis's books."

"Mayhap because they all come from Homsby's bookstore."

"You patronize only his store?" she asked, pleased that he had not noticed her slip.

Damon smiled and closed the glass door. "To own the truth, I seldom visit his shop. He arranges to have books delivered to me."

"Even the marquis's books?"

"He believes I wish to be conversant with what is bandied about by the Polite World."

Wrapping her arms around her, for his words were suddenly as cool as the rain against the window, she said, "Do not be angry. I did not mean to invade your private chambers."

"I would not, I assure you, be angry if I found you in my *private* chambers." He turned to the desk to straighten some pages that had been blown about by the storm.

When she picked up a page from the floor and handed it to him, he took it without comment. Had he thought she was perusing his business papers as well as the bookshelf? Pain twisted in her center. She went to the door, wanting to escape this room before tears escaped her eyes.

"Emily?"

She should not look back. She should not let the heat of his eyes sear her like quicksilver flames. She should not let those eyes lure her into his arms with the unspoken promise of his kisses. She turned and was riveted by longing mixed with grief.

He crossed the room in a pair of steps, but did not grasp her hands as she had hoped . . . as she had feared. Holding her gaze, he whispered, "What is it?"

"You do not trust me."

He seized her arm as she whirled to leave. Bringing her back to face him, he asked, "Do you trust me?"

"I don't know what you mean."

"You know well what I mean."

She tried to swallow past the lump in her throat. She knew exactly what he meant, but, if he discovered the truths she had fought to keep secret, he surely would not welcome André—or Emily Talcott—to Wentworth Hall.

"Emily," he said in the same low, intense tone, "I told you I would not play cards with your father while on our visit to Wentworth Hall, but you watch me like a duenna guarding her charge, sure I will break that vow at the first opportunity."

She lowered her eyes before he could see her reaction. He must not guess that, of all she had tried to keep concealed, this mattered the least to her rebellious heart. "You are right, Damon. Old habits die hard."

"Old habits? I have made you no vows before."

She met his gaze squarely. "Others have broken them when Papa was insistent and gold was on the table."

"I am not like others."

She was certain of that as she was of nothing else. If she traveled the length and breadth of the world doing research for her books on gardens and exotic flora, she never would meet another man like Damon Wentworth. No other man could be a fusion of irritating arrogance and tender compassion. No other man could set her soul alight with his wit and her skin afire with his touch.

"Trust me, Emily," he whispered.

"I will try. Be patient."

"Patience? I suspect, as lief, I will be trying yours." He opened the door wider and smiled. "You are far from the sitting room where we planned to meet. Could it be you are lost?"

She met his bold grin with her own. "Just exploring, but, if you would be so kind as to point me toward the nearest staircase to the lower floors, I would be grateful."

"Grateful?" He brought her to him again. As she locked her fingers behind his nape, he murmured, "I ask again: how grateful?"

The best answer, she was sure, was none as she let her kiss speak for itself. This happiness must be fleeting, so she wanted to enjoy every bit while she could.

Chapter Fifteen

As Emily came down the wide oak stairs, she ran her hand along the bannister. She stopped in the door to admire the sitting room, for the chamber was as wondrous as the rooms of a royal palace. The ceiling might need a new coat of paint, and the stone floor was scratched and uneven, but her eyes were captured by a mural that covered three walls. The *trompe l'oeil* design suggested the room was set amid a glorious garden where rose vines were strung from fruit trees. Beneath every tree, bushes were laden with berries. Blackberries, blueberries, gooseberries, and raspberries twisted together in an invitation to gather a handful. Lattices outlined views of distant fields where animals grazed.

Even with a score of people in the room, it did not seem crowded. Emily was amazed to see Valeria and Mr. Simpkins amid the guests. She had not guessed they would be joining Damon here. Why had Valeria said nothing of this invitation?

Before Emily could speak to them and ease her curiosity,

Papa motioned for her to join him and Miriam. "Look at this glorious mural!" he said as she walked to them. *"This* is what we shall have some day."

"When you are victorious at the card table?"

His smile wavered at the bitterness she had not been able to silence. When Miriam chided her, Emily sighed and said, "Forgive me. I am fatigued after the day's long ride."

"If you had joined us in the carriage instead of riding cross-country like a hoyden," Papa reprimanded gently, "you would be more of a mind to converse tonight." He turned as footsteps approached.

Emily's spirits sank further when André appeared in the doorway. The man seemed incapable of simply walking into a room. He had to make an entrance as if he were taking a cue on stage. As well he should, she reminded herself. He was playing a rôle with every breath.

Miriam rushed to him, her pink silk skirts bouncing to reveal the openwork on her white stockings. "Do join us, André."

Stiffening, Emily saw a flash of disquiet in Papa's eyes before his smile returned. She was surprised. If Papa did not favor a friendship between Miriam and this fake marquis, Emily wished he would halt it.

"What a charming scene *en famille,*" André said, his gushing tone making every word seem even more insincere.

Or it might be nothing more than her ears hearing the truth, Emily decided. She took Miriam's hand. "Come with me. I want to give Valeria a scold for not telling me she was joining us here."

"Emily—"

"Do come."

When Miriam opened her mouth to protest, André kissed her lightly on the cheek. "Go, *ma chérie,* and greet your *amis.* That will give me and your *père* a chance to speak of subjects that would bring your feminine ears ennui."

Emily had not thought she could dislike the fake marquis more, but she had been wrong. How dare he act as if her sister had no more wit than a slowtop! Linking her arm through Miriam's, she tugged her sister across the room.

"Emily, you were most uncivil to André," Miriam chided.

"Me?" She shook her head. "If you wish to let him insult you, I should leave you to fry in your own grease."

"He didn't mean to be a sad vulgar. He is French."

"Which should make his manners more polished, not less."

"You look for fault in him in every way you can."

"It does not take much looking."

"Emily!"

"Emily!" cried Valeria at the same time. Rushing to them, her gown as ruddy as the sun at dawn, she hugged Emily and Miriam at the same time. "I am so glad to see you. I feared you had become lost in this draughty mausoleum." She gave a genteel shudder as she turned to include Mr. Simpkins in the conversation. "Who would have guessed Beelzebub's Paradise would look like this? Not a fitting place for a demon, is it?"

"That is no way to speak of our host," Mr. Simpkins said quietly.

Emily fought to hide her shock. She had never heard him disagree openly with Valeria. Seeing amazement on Miriam's face and a softening in her smile, Emily wondered if her sister might have perceived something in Graham Simpkins that others had missed.

"Mr. Simpkins," Emily asked, "will you and Valeria join Miriam and me in admiring the murals?"

"Delighted, I am sure." He bowed toward her and nearly upset himself on his nose. His fingers fumbled as he reached out.

Before he could touch Miriam's hand, if that, indeed, had been his intent, André grasped it. The *faux* marquis pressed it to his sleeve before flashing Mr. Simpkins a superior smile.

"Lady Fanning," he gushed, "it is ever a pleasure to see you. I should have guessed *ma chére* Miriam would rush to your side to share with you all the tidbits of luscious conversation we enjoyed en route to this austere place." His nose wrinkled to reveal his opinions of Wentworth Hall.

Emily said coolly, "Mr. Simpkins was about to escort us to the murals."

"He is," the marquis said, his eyes as cold as two unlit coals, "without question, welcome to join us in a tour of the *tableaux.*" He took a step away, pausing when Miriam did not follow like a well-trained pup. "Miriam, *ma chérie?*"

Emily held her breath as she watched her sister stare at Mr. Simpkins, who, for once, seemed to be returning her gaze. She resisted the yearning to put her hands on Mr. Simpkins's shoulders and give him a shove toward Miriam. Was the man half blind that he could not see how Miriam eyed him with longing? Mr. Simpkins need do no more than give Miriam the least hope that a relationship was possible, and her sister would toss aside the false poet like a child throwing away a broken stick.

When Mr. Simpkins mumbled something and turned to Valeria, Emily was certain she could hear her sister's heart shatter. Miriam said nothing as she went with André toward the far wall. Emily wanted to shake some sense into Graham Simpkins. Could he not see how much Miriam wanted his admiration?

She had no chance to put her thoughts into words or action, for Damon strode into the room. He was once again the well-dressed man who would draw every feminine eye in Town. His dark coat was without a spot of lint, and his silver breeches glittered in the light from the sconces on the wall. When she heard him whistling, she was astounded. She could not have imagined him being so light of spirit in Town.

"Where are the rest of our friends?" he asked to no one in particular.

From across the room, she heard Papa answer. "Mayhap they are gathering their thoughts before the challenge of the evening's entertainment begins."

When he saw Emily tense, Damon scowled. Dash it! Did Talcott think of nothing save his flats? The man still owed him a century or two from their last encounter at the card table.

His gaze returned to Emily. By Jove, he enjoyed the chance to admire her, even when she was as stiff as a corpse. He preferred her soft and willing in his arms. Looking past her, he saw a straggling, weak sunbeam glittering on the rain left by the swiftly moving storm. Twilight soon would descend on Wentworth Hall, but there still might be time to share with her the secret that drew him back to this tumbledown collection of stones whenever he could put business in London behind him.

As he walked toward her, drawn to her as surely as lightning was lured to the peaks of the house, he tossed over his shoulder, "Resting is not necessary, Talcott, for the entertainment here is simple and revolves around the sun's rising and setting." He folded Emily's fingers between his palms and smiled when they softened against him like a newly burst petal. "If you wish, my friends," he added, raising his voice, "lemonade is waiting you on the terrace before we enjoy an early dinner."

"Lemonade?" scoffed de la Cour.

Although tempted to teach the frog poet some manners with his bunch of fives, Damon said only, "I trust you will find the brandy there better suited to your taste, de la Cour."

His guests drifted toward the door leading to the terrace that had been rebuilt only the summer before, but he tightened his grip on Emily's hands as she turned to follow. She looked up at him with a question in her sapphire eyes.

"Wait a moment," he murmured. "If the rest of them are entertained, I think it is time for you to see my most precious secret here at Wentworth Hall."

A faint rosy glow brushed her cheeks. "Damon, I should remain with Miriam."

"Your sister has your father to watch over her, and we shall be thoroughly chaperoned as well, I assure you."

"Who?"

"Come, and you shall see."

For a moment, she hesitated, then she nodded. At her unspoken trust, which no one had offered him in longer than he could recall, something inside him leaped like a stag crossing the leas. He offered his arm, and she let him lead her to another door.

He wondered if she suspected how he would as lief sweep her into his arms and up the stairs, far from the others. Did she have any idea what power those exotic eyes had on him? Or how he was fascinated by the soft warmth of her whisper as she agreed to come with him? Surely she must know the magic spell just the touch of her fingers sent swirling about him, an enchantment that stole all thoughts but of her from his head. Thoughts of giving his fingers free license to roam about the slender curves that were emphasized so beguilingly by her simple gown. Thoughts of perusing her sweet body with the fervor of opening a long-awaited book, savoring each new revelation, sampling each pleasure. Thoughts of bringing her to the bedroom that belonged to the lord of Wentworth Hall, seeking every rapture and unleashing every ecstasy until her softness merged with him in the sweetest rhythms of love.

He silenced the groan as he forced the enticing, excruciating fantasy from his head. Emily Talcott would be aghast to discover the course of his thoughts. Or would she?

"Where are we going?" she asked quietly.

He noted the tremor in her voice. Mayhap her mind was enmeshed in images not so different from those plaguing him, although he had to own, if such thoughts were a plague, he wished never to recover.

"Patience," he replied to her as much as to himself. He

motioned to a serving lass who was waiting by the stairs. Taking the bonnet she held out, he handed it to Emily. "Your abigail parted with this reluctantly."

She smiled. "Kilmartin takes her duties very seriously."

"Something I suspect she learned from her mistress." When he saw her smile waver, he hurried to say, "A most admirable trait."

"You make it sound quite the opposite."

"How can you say that when you see what obligations I have saddled myself with?"

"This beautiful house?"

"You think it's beautiful?"

"Oh, yes!"

He could not doubt her sincerity as they walked out a side door and onto the broken stone of what once had been a fine walkway leading into the garden. The storm had washed away the day's heat and left raindrops glittering on the grass. "It is in need of much work."

"A work in progress is still a thing of beauty." She tied her bonnet in place, but tipped it so he could see past the lacy brim to her smile. "In fact, sometimes it is more beautiful, because one can imagine how it will become even more perfect."

"Like a half-remembered dream?"

Her eyes twinkled with merriment. "Damon, you have the devil's own way with words."

"As you do." He put his hand over hers on his arm as he noted how she tensed. Resisting the temptation to ask the question burning on his tongue, he said, "You have planted the seed of an idea in my mind, and I intend to let it grow into something lovely while I continue my work on Wentworth Hall."

"You do have a lot of work ahead of you."

Damon chuckled as he followed her gaze back toward the house which had been old centuries ago. The familiar, comfortable sensation of being just exactly where he should be filled him. The ancestors of Wentworths had held this land even before the Conquest, and some undefinable tether drew him back here again and again to infuse him with life. If not for his businesses in London . . .

If not for his businesses in London, he would not have had the chance to meet Emily and sample her lips. A craving tore through him like a whetted blade. He wanted to push aside the smothering mantle of respectability and taste those lips again. Right now, right here where anyone might see.

"M'lord?" called a cheerful voice.

Feeling anything but cheerful at the interruption, Damon forced a smile for the lanky man striding around the wall of hedge at the end of the path. No one would ever call Sanders handsome, for the man was ginger-hackled with freckles pocking his face. Not even a straw hat and a turned-up collar could lessen the scarlet left by his long hours in the sun. From the first hour of planting until winter lessened his time in the sun, Sanders looked like a snake peeling off its skin.

"I thought you'd be out to check our progress before this," Sanders continued in his gusty shout. He paused in mid-step and tipped the brim of his hat. "Sorry, miss. Didn't see you."

Damon smiled as his gardener glanced at him with a dozen questions flying out of his eyes like birds being flushed from the bushes. "Emily, this is Wentworth Hall's gardener, Sanders." He squeezed her hand before adding, "Sanders, Miss Emily Talcott from London."

"Lor'!" gasped the man.

Emily said, "It is a pleasure to make your acquaintance, Mr. Sanders."

"Just Sanders, miss. Don't go for titles here at Wentworth Hall, do we, m'lord?"

Biting her lip to keep from smiling at the man's contra-dictory words, she said, "Just Sanders it shall be."

"Sanders," Damon said, "we are ready to see what you have to show us."

"Aye, m'lord." He tipped his wide-brimmed hat to her again and walked back along the path. He paused only to throw a grin over his shoulder before disappearing within the shadows of a hedge.

"Come along." Damon tugged on her arm. "Sanders will be distressed if we delay."

She laughed. "Can I hope that this finally is the surprise you have teased me about?"

"You shall see it was worth your endearing curiosity."

When they came around the corner, Emily gasped. She heard Damon's low chuckle as she walked toward the bushes that had been hidden behind the hedge. She reached out to touch the outlines of a dragon that must be twice the length of a coach and four and nearly as tall. Beyond the reclining dragon, a collection of what might be chess pieces were growing in different shades of green. She could not keep from laughing when she saw what appeared to be Mother Goose's cow jumping over a box-wood moon.

"Do you like it?" Damon asked.

"It is incredible!" she whispered, afraid if she spoke louder the magic would vanish.

"It will be."

"It is now!" she insisted. When she saw his grin, she looked at the shrubs again. "Is this your work, Damon?"

"My ideas and Sanders's patient toil."

"I knew you loved plants, but this is remarkable."

He chuckled again as he sat on a low stone wall that was nearly lost beneath the hedge. Pushing aside a vagrant branch, he said, "I have been told I inherited all my worst habits from my father."

"All of them?"

He arched a brow in his most rakish expression. "Hard to believe there could be two men in one family who were seduced by Lady Luck at the card table and who terrorized the *grande dames* of the *ton* with their reputations, isn't it?''

"But you are not just Demon Wentworth."

"I knew you were more perceptive than the rest of the Polite World, Emily." He put his finger under her chin and brought her face toward him. "Don't blush. That name does not bother me."

"I'm not blushing."

"But you are."

"I don't blush."

"Then there must be another cause for that lovely rose in your cheeks."

She edged away. He must know well the reason her color was high. To be here with him in this glorious garden as the first stars began to pierce the navy-blue sky was the consummation of a dream she had barely dared to dream. So easily the words "I love you" could slip from her lips.

"I did get one virtue from my father," he continued.

"Yes?" She kept her voice even on that single word.

"He instilled a love of botany in me. Some of my earliest memories are of him sitting in his book-room as he catalogued the finds he brought back from America."

"America? He was in America?"

He smiled. Clasping his hands around his knee, he said, "Father sailed there on a Talcott ship. *The Talcott Treasure*, I believe."

"Yes, it must have been the *Treasure.*"

He gazed at the raw edges of the hedges that were being trained into topiary. "Father was a second son, so he had the luxury of exploring such distant lands before his older brother died and left him the obligations of Wentworth Hall."

"You could travel to America, if you wish." *You could travel with me,* she thought before she could squelch it.

"This garden is so tame compared to what waits there. Ofttimes, I consider it my misfortune to have been an only son. If I had been born second or beyond, I could have left Wentworth Hall to someone else and allowed myself to be tempted by the wanderlust that urges me to far horizons.''

"Some dreams must remain only dreams."

"Unfortunately so." He drew her to sit next to him. "What dream have you put on the shelf, Emily?"

"On the shelf?" She laughed. "Odd that you should choose that phrase."

"I meant no insult."

"Of course not!" she hastened to reassure him, astonished he would apologize when his words had not wounded her. Again she recalled how many times he had surprised her.

Searching her mind, she sought the dreams she had set aside when she assumed the management of her father's household. She was surprised, and more than a bit sad, when she discovered she could not recall any, save her own craving to travel. She feared she had lost the younger, more naïve Emily.

Damon's finger under her chin brought her face close to his. "If you wish to keep your dreams to yourself . . .''

"No, that is not why I hesitate." Coming to her feet, she walked toward the bush that would someday have the outline of a chess queen.

Sanders grinned at her from where he was snipping branches off a fruit tree that was nearly lost amid the berry bushes clinging to its trunk.

"My old dreams seem less important than what is happening right now," she said. "Mayhap it is because I have no time for them."

"You should always make time for dreaming."

She turned, for his words brushed the back of her neck. Looking up into his gray eyes, she whispered, "I can see how you have made your dream come true here."

"You do not sound surprised that I would have such a prosaic dream."

"I'm not." Boldly, she took his hands in hers and smiled.

"Once I would have been. Who would have guessed that Demon Wentworth was hiding such a life in the country and that he came to Town only to maintain an image which protected him from mamas with marriageable daughters?"

"That is not the only reason." When her forehead ruffled in puzzlement, he said, "If it were, I would never stray from here. However, my plans to restore this grand manor house to its former glory drain even the Wentworth fortune." His eyes sparkled as he bent so their gazes were even. "My dear friend Emily, you should have guessed by now that I go to London to deal with the business matters that a titled gentleman should not concern himself with."

"Not to play cards?"

"I would toss aside the flats without a second thought if I could stay here."

"Then why—?"

"Why do I sit at the board of green cloth and play the devil's books with what my foes call Satan's own luck?" His eyes became silvery slits. "I inherited *all* of my father's faults. I like winning, Emily, whether it is in a business deal or at the card table or here where Sanders is helping me wrest beauty from chaos." Standing straighter, he chuckled. "And think what your friend Valeria Fanning would say if I came to one of her soirées and discussed the balancing of account books or the cost of importing a marble carver from Italy to resurrect the friezes in the drawing room."

"I daresay she would find you quite boring."

"Or, more likely, she would waste no time in trying to provide me with a lady to oversee the task." He laughed and held out his arm. "I am grateful you have refrained from offering your opinions on my plans."

"They are *your* plans."

"Exactly." As he led her down chipped stairs toward a water garden that once must have been grand, he said, "If I had thought you would plague me with suggestions, I would never have asked you here."

Emily smiled and nodded, but something unsettled curled inside her. For once, Damon had not guessed the course of her thoughts, for she had so many ideas of how to enhance his gardens with the flowers she had read about in the book Damon had suggested to her in Mr. Homsby's shop. As for the interior of the house, she could imagine Axminster rugs in the foyer and repainting the fretwork along the stairs and . . . She silenced her thoughts. Damon was correct. It was his house, and he should be the one to determine how it was restored.

"Show me the rest," she said softly. "Do you have anything else as grand as the dragon?"

He laughed. "That is my favorite as well, but I warn you it is, in truth, a sea serpent which has crawled all the way from the shore to devour Wentworth Hall. Someday it may be large enough to do so."

As she walked by his side, listening to his enthusiasm, Emily wished this walk could go on forever, for she had never been happier.

Chapter Sixteen

Taking a sip of cocoa, Emily opened her satchel and set it in the middle of the huge tester bed. She shoved aside the ivory bed curtains as she searched the bag again. She was certain she had placed her notebook in here. Although the few scribbled poems would be no loss, she did not want someone to find it and discover the poems written in her hand.

"Your green book, Emily?" Kilmartin asked as she set out Emily's favorite yellow dress. "I have not seen it since you packed it at the inn."

"So I did put it in the bag then?"

"It was on the bed. I assumed you put it in your bag."

Emily frowned as she tried to remember if she had. The hour before they had left the inn had been frenzied. Papa had come to check on them, and Miriam had scurried in and out like a small creature preparing for the winter. Mayhap Miriam had picked it by mistake and put it in her bag.

She prayed not. Miriam could not read French, but her

sister was certain to guess what language the poems were written in and in whose hand.

"Kilmartin, will you check with Miriam?"

"Of course. I—" She rushed to the door as a knock sounded. With a smile, she stepped back and said, "Miss Emily, here is Miss Miriam right now."

"What have you done to this room?" gasped Miriam as she entered, looking like one of the pretty daisies in the fields with her blond hair in curls and her simple white gown.

Emily smiled wryly. The doors of the mahogany armoire were half open, and undergarments peeked out of the drawers. Both chairs were covered with clothes, and a vase of fresh flowers was almost hidden behind a tilting stack of books. The latter two items had been waiting for her when she returned from breakfast along with a note from Damon to enjoy them. She would have savored the scent of the rose blossoms and the books on topiary if she had not been bothered with her own misplaced book.

"I lost something," she answered.

"What? Your mind?"

She laughed, although her stomach cramped with dismay. "My green notebook. Could it be in among your things?"

"No." Miriam picked up a stocking and handed it to Kilmartin. "However, I suspect it could easily be here amid all this." As Emily turned to continue her search, Miriam said, "Will you sit a moment, Emily? I wish to talk to you."

"Of course." She sat on a red tufted chair, fighting the need to look for the book.

"I am worried about you." Miriam chose a chair facing her. "You seemed exhausted all evening."

"It was a long ride."

"Was it only that? I had thought you might be looking for any excuse to retire. Emily, I know you were eager to enable me to leave London for this short trip, but you need not suffer Lord Wentworth's attentions."

"I am not suffering them."

"You welcome them?"

"Do you welcome André's? Anyone who saw the two of you together might believe you are falling in love with him."

Miriam laughed, but the sound was dull as it echoed against the wide stone sills and the high ceiling. "Anyone? Graham Simpkins does not see. Or he does not care."

"Mr. Simpkins? But I thought—"

"Dear Emily," she said as she knelt next to Emily, "you may be the older, but you have no experience in matters of the heart. I have been in love, and I know what it is like. Splendid and appalling at the same time. I do not have those feelings for André."

"But I believe he hopes you might love him enough to buckle your life to his."

"Perhaps I will."

"Miriam!"

She set herself on her feet. "Don't fly up into the boughs! What does it matter whom I wed when I cannot have my beloved Mr. Simkins?" Covering her face with her hands, she moaned, "I love a man who cares nothing for me. André wishes to make me happy."

"But do you think of Mr. Simpkins when you are with André?"

Miriam's face lost all color. When she walked out of the bedroom, Emily did not follow. Instead, she gazed out the window at the gardens. She had to find a way to ease her sister's suffering, but, for the first time, Emily was unsure how to help.

No, she knew the solution. The time had come to speak the truth and damn the devil . . . and herself.

Damon checked the saddle on his horse before turning to watch his guests spill out the front door of Wentworth Hall. The village fathers of Wentworth Bridge could not have selected a better day to play out the old traditions. Even though the last of the curtain wall stood between him and the small village on the other side of the bridge that gave the village its name, he could hear lilting music. It would not end until midnight. By that time, several casks of good ale and a roasted ox would be consumed down to the bones thrown to the dogs. This day was as old as the Hall.

His gaze settled on the ebony hair sweeping along Emily's neck, refusing to be forced into curls. Recalling its silk against his fingers, he tossed the reins to a stableboy and walked to where she was standing beside her sister.

His smile became a frown when he heard Emily say in an intense tone, "Miriam, please! It will take but a moment for me to say what I must to you."

"I do not need to be chided for my foolishness again," her sister replied before rushing away.

"Is something amiss?" he asked quietly.

He might as well have shouted, for she started at his question. She glanced at him and away, but not before he noted the distress on her face.

She shrugged. "Just Miriam being as stubborn as I am."

He did not believe her nonchalant answer. "If you would prefer not to go to the village today—"

"No, no, I want to go." Her smile became more genuine. "I really do."

"I am glad." Taking her hand, he led her to the horse she had ridden to Wentworth Hall. "Ready to go?"

She hesitated.

"If you want to ride in the carriage with the others, Emily, you need only say so."

When she raised her chin, he could not guess if the motion were in defiance of him or her own thoughts. "I would be delighted to ride with you, Damon."

Those were the last words she spoke to him as they left Wentworth Hall. Behind them, the voices of his other guests were as joyous as the music growing louder as they approached the village. He paid neither the music nor the voices any mind. When he led the way over the arch of the stone bridge and into the village, he said as little as Emily. He might have tried to ease the silence with another woman, but Emily had spoken the truth. She was stubborn.

Swinging down from his horse, he greeted Mr. Frasier, who had been on the village council for as long as Damon could remember. The white-haired man wore a rumpled coat of a rusty black over his breeches that had musty odor.

"My lord," the elderly man said as he pumped Damon's hand, "I am so glad you could join us today. This ceremony has been held every year since Wentworth Hall was built, and I hate to think of us skipping a year."

"As I would." Not wanting the old man to see his smile at the words Frasier repeated every year, he turned to help Emily from the horse. A mistake, he realized, at the very moment he grasped her at the waist. Beneath his hands, her slender curves teased him to pull her closer. As he set her on the ground, he sought to hold her gaze, but it evaded him.

He sighed silently as he said, "Emily, allow me to present you to Mr. Frasier, the mayor of Wentworth Bridge. Mr. Frasier, Miss Emily Talcott."

Emily was shocked when Mr. Frasier shook her hand as earnestly as he had Damon's and said, "We are delighted Lord Wentworth has brought you to join our celebration."

"I have," Damon replied, "not wanted to inflict Wentworth Hall on any guests until it was in better condition."

"Thank goodness, you have proven a better master of that estate than your father." Mr. Frasier turned to Emily and smiled. "Lord Wentworth's father was a fine man, I assure you, but he had no mind for business and tradition. If not for Lord Wentworth here, I daresay this old ceremony would have died out."

Noting the detached expression Damon wore, Emily wondered which of the effusive Mr. Frasier's words had disturbed him. She could not ask, not when she had refused to share with him how distressed she was at Miriam's refusal to listen to the truth about the man who called himself Marquis de la Cour.

"But Miss Talcott cares nothing of that," Mr. Frasier went on, "do you, Miss Talcott?"

Emily smiled, not sure what else to do or say.

Damon came to her rescue by taking her hand and drawing it within his arm. "If you will excuse us, Frasier, I want Miss Talcott to see everything Wentworth Bridge has to offer."

"I suspect you do." Mr. Frasier laughed heartily.

She started after him as he went toward a whitewashed church that was set in the middle of the half dozen stone cottages that seemed to be the whole of the village.

"Pay no attention to Mr. Frasier," Damon said. "He enjoys a good jest."

"Apparently."

"Can I hope your answer means you are willing to call a truce about whatever I have done to upset you?"

"You?" She smiled sadly as she put her hand over his holding hers on his arm. "Forgive me, Damon. For once, you are not the one who has flurried my milk."

"And I suppose it is none of my bread-and-butter who put you into such a pelter?"

"Can we just forget it?" Her smile wavered as she looked past him to where her sister was giggling with the marquis. Beyond them, Mr. Simpkins was helping Valeria from an open gig. Blast that man! If he would just open his eyes and see the truth, Miriam would gladly set André aside.

"Can you?"

She shook her head. "I am not sure, but I can try."

His finger beneath her chin curved along her cheek in a clandestine caress. "I want you to enjoy this day."

Her heart fluttered like a newborn leaf in the wind. "I will try, Damon. I vow that to you."

"A vow you will keep?" He chuckled and tapped her nose.

"Like you, I always keep my vows no matter what."

"I know."

Before she could ask him to explain, Damon called to his other guests. Instantly they were surrouned by his friends, who were eager to discover every excitement waiting in this small village.

Swept along by the anticipation, Emily tried to do as she had promised. Damon's jesting and his friends soon pulled her out of the dismals. She would have a chance to speak alone with Miriam. The right time would come.

Emily decided the whole shire must be at the fair. As the setting sun began to lengthen the shadow of the church's spire, more and more people crowded onto the green. Music played a wild rhythm, and people danced in the road and on the grass. Food beckoned with delicious aromas. Sticky faces matched the stains left by butter and ale. Children raced underfoot, but no one chided them. This was a day for fun.

She wished she was having some. Wandering from table to brightly decorated table, she tried to stay close to her sister. André did not hide he was not pleased with her company, but she cared nothing for his opinions. Miriam seemed as delighted as one of the children with all the entertainments, clapping at the puppet show and cheering the races run by the village's lads.

André brightened when they passed Damon, who was speaking with Mr. Frasier. As if the mayor were of little import, the marquis pushed his way between Mr. Frasier and Damon.

"Are you going to spend the whole day with business, *mon ami?*" André demanded.

Emily wondered if only she noticed how Damon's back stiffened. His voice was even as he answered, "I just finished. I shall not be late, Mr. Frasier."

"Thank you, my lord," the old man said. He flashed the marquis a frown before walking away.

André laughed. "You English are as eccentric as I had been led to believe."

"That may be so, but I challange you to find a cook in all of France who can better Mrs. Wiggs's meat pies."

"Is that so?"

"If you don't believe me, I suggest you try one."

"A challange I must accept." He offered his arm to Miriam. *"Ma chérie?"*

When Emily started to follow them, Damon caught her hand, drawing her back. "Let me go."

He laughed quietly.

"I find nothing amusing about this."

"Odd, for I find it very amusing." He led her in the opposite direction. "Most of all, I find you amusing."

"What an appalling thing to say!"

"But the truth." He continued to smile. "I find things dull without you to enliven them with your ardor, which eases the cynicism that has become a deplorable habit with me."

Glancing back and seeing Papa join her sister and the marquis, much to André's dismay, if she could read his expression rightly, she relaxed. Mayhap Papa was not as oblivious to the situation as she had believed.

"You vowed to me," Damon said, drawing her attention back to him, "that you would have fun. How can you when you are shadowing de la Cour and your sister?"

"I was trying to have fun."

"I thought we were to be honest with each other."

Regret clogged in her throat. He had no idea how much she wanted to be honest. "Forgive me. I cannot help being uneasy about Miriam and that man."

"As well as you should be. 'Tis unlike you to let your sister act the blind buzzard with de la Cour." He scowled. "You should let her fry in her own grease."

"She is my sister, Damon."

He shook his head. "When are you going to stop worrying yourself near to sickness about your father and sister? You concern yourself so deeply with their lives that you have no life of your own."

"As you concern yourself unduly with mine."

"Not unduly, Emily." His fingers brushed her cheek with the tenderness that always unraveled her vexation with him. "I wanted you to have fun today, but I fear it is hopeless."

"I told you I would."

"A vow you will keep no matter what?"

She could not keep from smiling. "Point taken, Damon." She relaxed and took a deep breath of fresh air. "How can you bear to leave this for the stuffiness of Town? If I had a country house, I never would wander far from it."

"Don't you think even this becomes monotonous?"

"I cannot imagine that ever happening."

"Nor can I." His smile vanished as he gazed across the river at the walls of Wentworth Hall.

Emily bit her lip. So many things she was begining to understand about Damon, for his devotion to his ancestral home was the key to the many puzzles that made up the man who was working to rebuild a dream. Happiness spread like warm sunshine through her as she imagined sharing his dreams.

She lowered her eyes. Damon wanted no one to complicate his life. He had made that clear. She had too many entanglements in his life. She had no need for another, but her heart refused to listen. She yearned to be with him, to toss aside her past and make a future at his side and in his arms.

Impossible! taunted the voice of reason in her head. As she gazed at the warm tan of her skin, she recalled the shock in her mother's family's eyes when Papa had arranged to return to England after her mother's death.

"You cannot take the child with you," she could hear

her grandmother say as clearly as if the old woman stood beside her. "She will be ostracized."

"No one need know the truth." Papa had been confident of fortune always smiling on him. "I will speak of it to no one, and she is but a child. No one will heed her."

Grandmother shook her head, her sable hair falling forward into her troubled eyes. "But when she becomes of an age to marry, it cannot be kept a secret then. Charles, you know how parochial English society is. If they learned about me—"

"They shan't." He bent to look Emily directly in the eyes. "We will keep it a secret, won't we, Emily?"

She had been not much more than a baby, but she had understood that Grandmother was upset. She wanted Grandmother to smile as she did when she rocked Emily in her arms and sang the songs of the mountains and the trees and the spirits of the animals who lived among them.

"Yes, Papa," she had whispered, "I will keep it a secret."

And she had. Until she had met Damon, holding that secret within her heart had not been difficult. Now she wanted to open her heart to him, but she knew of no way to keep the secret from falling out.

"Emily?"

"Yes?"

He took her hand and placed a penny on it. Folding her fingers over it, he said, "Guard it well, Emily."

"A penny?"

"The quit rent on the bridge to Wentworth Hall. Since the first Wentworth took up residence here, the rent has been paid annually at this fair." He raised a brow and chuckled. "An archaic custom, but one that is enjoyed by everyone in shire. In fact, it's suggested that the name Wentworth is a tidying up of the name given to my family by the ancestors of the villagers here."

"What name was that?"

He grimaced. "Rent-worthy."

Laughing, she asked, "But why are you giving the penny to me?"

"Tradition states that it should be paid by the prettiest lady in the shire." Again he closed her fingers over the penny. "And that, without question, is you."

"You flatter me." She laughed and pressed the coin into his hand.

The church bell rang slowly. Damon smiled as he handed her the penny again. "If you fail to pay Mr. Frasier his one pence, we shall not be able to return to Wentworth Hall without swimming across the brook. The bridge will revert to the holding of the village fathers." His fingers closed over hers. "I can think of no one else I would trust with this important task."

"Trust?" she whispered.

"Will you do this for me, sweetheart?"

Sure he would hear her pulse thumping, she nodded. He gripped her arms and pressed his mouth over hers in a swift kiss that left her gasping for breath.

"Let us be done with my duties here," he whispered, "then I would like to show you another section of my gardens where the roses are the color of your luscious lips."

"I would like that."

"So would I." He burned succulent fire into her lips again before his tilted with a roguish grin. "This time without Sanders to watch over us like a protective mama."

She did not hesitate as she nodded again. Mayhap she was mad, but she wanted this moment of madness when she could forget about the secrets haunting her. She ached to surrender to passion.

Emily went with Damon to where Mr. Frasier stood by the thick stones of the arched bridge. The old man's eyes widened, then he grinned. Bowing his head toward them, he raised his hands. The crowd became silent.

"Greetings, Lord Wentworth," Mr. Frasier said, suddenly as somber as a judge sending a man to swing on a choker.

"Mr. Frasier." Damon's voice was equally grave.

Emily was amazed to discover that the sparkle of mischief in his eyes was nowhere to be found. Here was something Damon took as seriously as his garden. Comprehension was wondrous, for another facet of this man came clear for her. Damon might play the demon in London, but, here, he reveled in his life as the lord of Wentworth Hall and gladly assumed all its duties and obligations. He had been honest when he told her he would be happy to stay in the country all the time.

"Lord Wentworth, long before either of our great-great-great grandsires were born, this village has looked to Wentworth Hall and its lord for protection. In return, we have given our blood and our service."

"You have served well as the blood of this village was spilled alongside that of my family as we have defended this land from all who would have put us from it."

Mr. Frasier held out his hand. A man, who wore a drab coat that was almost identical to the mayor's, placed a parchment in it. When Mr. Frasier unrolled it, Emily was startled to see dark creases that bespoke the age of the parchment. She was not sure what Mr. Frasier read because it was, she guessed in Latin, but a few phrases were close enough to French to catch her ear.

Letting it roll closed, Mr. Frasier handed it back to his assistant. "You understand your obligations, my lord, as agreed to by the first lord who claimed this land when King Ethelred held England in dominion against the Norse threat?"

"I understand."

She admired Damon's lordly mien. For a moment, she could imagine him in the primitive tunic of his ancestors, a shield at his arm and a longbow in his hand. His hair would have drifted past his shoulders, and he would have not been constrained by the canons of propriety from stealing the heart of any woman who caught his fancy.

When he looked at her and slowly winked, she almost gasped aloud. To have him guess the course of her errant thoughts would be ... Would be what? Not humiliating or embarrassing. It would be dangerous for him to guess how he tempted her to be as brazen as a lass of ancient days.

Mr. Frasier cleared his throat, and Damon turned back to him. "In exchange for our fealty and the use of this bridge so that he might send a messenger to call us to arms, the lord of Wentworth Hall vows to pay a quit rent. Do you agree to this quit rent for yet another year, my lord?" His voice carried across the hushed rumble of anticipation from those watching.

"Yes, I agree to pay the quit rent, for Lord Wentworth holds his vows as dear as his life." He put his hand on Emily's arm and drew her forward to stand in front of Mr. Frasier. "Accept the pence for the quit rent from this lady."

At a sharp intake of breath, Emily wondered if everyone on the green had inhaled at once. Dear God, what had she done wrong? She wanted to be certain her hat was in place, that her skirt had not risen to reveal her stockings, that no crumb of the cake she had enjoyed earlier clung to her face.

Mr. Frasier smiled, startling her as his wrinkles rearranged themselves. "I will accept the quit rent from your lady, my lord." He held out his hand.

"Give it to him now," Damon whispered.

She handed Mr. Frasier the coin. He held it up for all to see. A cheer reverberated against the church. Beneath it, he said, "Thank you, Miss Talcott, and may you have every happiness in your future."

Startled by the old man's brazen wink, she glanced at Damon. His face was impassive, but she saw the twinkle

had returned to his eyes. "Wasn't that fun?" he asked
quietly.

"Yes."

"I told you that you would have fun at our celebration."

"And," Mr. Frasier interjected, "I suspect, for you, the
celebration has only just started." He chuckled.

"What —?"

Damon interrupted by saying, "Thank you, Frasier, for
another successful payment of the quit rent."

"My pleasure, my lord, as well as yours, I am certain."
Mr. Frasier smiled broadly and strode away with another
self-satisfied chuckle.

Emily tried once more to ask what the old man meant
with his cryptic words, but Damon took her hand and led
her to where the other guests were prattling about the
ceremony. As Miriam threw her arms around Emily and
asked a dozen questions about how her sister had enjoyed
being part of it, Emily glanced at Damon. His smile held
the promise of what they would share when they were
alone in the garden. Then she would get answers to her
questions and so very much more.

She could not wait.

Chapter Seventeen

When night came to claim the day, Emily was glad to ride back to Wentworth Hall. Too many questions plagued her, and the longing for that walk alone with Damon teased her.

Even the most boisterous of Damon's guests was subdued by the time they reached Wentworth Hall. Watching as they climbed out of the carriages and into the house as if each one wanted to be the first through the door, Emily smiled. She gave a yawning stableboy a sympathetic glance, but she was not tired. How could she think of sleeping when her dream of being in Damon's arms once more was about to come true?

She put her hands on Damon's shoulders as he helped her down. His fingers slipped up her back, holding her to him. Slowly, he lowered her until her toes touched the ground.

"It will cost you a kiss if you wish to be put down," he said softly, although no one could hear him but her. The others were in the house, and the stableboys were busy leading the horses into the stable.

"And if I wish to stay in your arms?"

He laughed as he put his arm beneath her knees and swept her up next to his chest. "I do like the way you think, my dear Miss Talcott."

"Do not get carried away in your rôle as the lord of this manor."

"I am interested only in carrying you away."

When his mouth found hers, she slipped her fingers up through his hair and answered his passion with her own. His lips brushed her cheek, her nose, her eyelids until she laughed with unfettered delight. The strong wall of his chest cradled her, freeing her to think only of this moment when everything was perfect.

"Damon!" came a shout from the house.

"By Jove," he muttered as he set her on her feet, "for the first time, I cannot wait to return to Town, so I need not worry about the duties of a host." Raising his voice, he called, "Have a new bottle of brandy opened."

When the man yelled back his thanks, Emily laughed. "You know your guests well, Damon."

"I know their thirsts well." He ran his finger along her lips, which were swollen from his kiss. "If only they respected my thirsts and my need to slake them as well." He curved his hand along her cheek. "Let me get them settled for the evening with a few bottles of French lace, and then we shall see to that walk I promised you."

"That sounds wonderful."

"I am glad you think so." He grazed her lips with a quick kiss before holding out his hand. As she slipped hers into it, he said, "Tell me. Did you keep your vow to have fun in the village?"

"Yes, but I have a question you have avoided answering."

"About the quit rent ceremony." He tapped the brim of her hat and chuckled. "Frasier is much the joker."

"He looks so serious, and he seemed to be hinting at something being unusual about me paying the rent."

"You are not of the shire."

"True."

"Old customs are held sacred here." A distant expression softened his eyes as he drew her hand into his arm again.

Emily laughed. "Mayhap André is correct. We English are eccentric."

"If he were correct about that, it proves the adage that everything can happen once."

When she was about to reply, Damon stopped by a gate leading to the kitchen garden. He reached under his coat and drew out a small packet. "I have been carrying this about all day, Emily, in the hopes that I would have a chance to give this to you when we were not surrounded by friends."

She took it and sat on the small wooden bench by the lighted gate, for her knees had turned to pudding as her heart threatened to sing. "May I open it now?"

"Of course. I hope you'll be pleased with what it holds." He smiled and put one foot on the bench. Resting his elbow on his knee, he leaned toward her. "As I am pleased to be with you, Emily."

She had been sure she could delight in no greater happiness than being in his arms. She had been wrong, for she was suffused with a gentle joy that urged her to put her fingers on his hand, which dropped from his knee. Her longing was not simply to be in his arms. It was to be with him when they laughed, when they kissed, when they traded heated words.

"Will you open it?" he prompted.

She unwrapped the packet and gasped as she lifted out a tiny square of cloth enclosed in a simple frame. Someone had stitched a view of Wentworth Hall, showcasing the gardens.

"My favorite elevation," he said with the soft huskiness she heard in his voice when he spoke of his home and the gardens he loved. "I hope it will be yours as well."

"It already is." She ran her fingertip along the even stitches. "Who did this?"

"My mother."

She saw grief in his eyes. "Damon, if this is your mother's work, I cannot—"

He pressed her hand between his. "My mother died when I was little more than a baby. Unlike you, I never had the chance to know my mother during the years of my childhood."

"My mother died when I was only three."

"I thought Mrs. Talcott died just a few years ago."

Brushing a vagrant strand back from his forehead, she whispered, "The second Mrs. Talcott. Miriam's mother, who Papa married shortly after we came home to London. It was my good fortune that she loved me as much as she did Miriam, so I did have a mother."

"You are, indeed, lucky." He sat beside her and rested her head on his shoulder. "And I will hear no more about you not accepting this."

She knew better than to start a brangle when he took that stubborn tone. "I shall look at this and remember walking in your incredible gardens."

As gently as she had stroked the needlework, his finger touched her cheek. She closed her eyes as warmth spread along her skin in a beguiling stream of pleasure. "I had hoped it would entice you to pay another call to Wentworth Hall."

"I wish I could."

"You can any time."

Standing, she held the picture to her breast as she gazed up at the house. "It is not easy to find time to leave Town."

"The Season, thank goodness, does not last forever." He set himself on his feet. "It simply seems that way."

"Until Miriam weds, I must be there for her."

"I would say she may soon make a match."

Horror stole all Emily's pleasure. Shaking her head, she

said, "Do not say that even in jest. I shall not have her married to that—that—"

"Frog poet?"

"Don't call him that!"

"Why?"

She faltered. She should tell him the truth. Damon would understand, wouldn't he? *Wouldn't he?* She did not dare risk finding out.

He seized her by the shoulders. "Emily, tell me why!"

"Release me!" She squirmed out of his grip and backed away.

When he opened his mouth, she whirled away. She paused and ran back to him. Pressing her lips to his, she fled before his arms could enfold her again. In his embrace, her heart beating with his, she knew she could no longer be false.

Thunder rumbled beyond the thick walls, but the night sky could be no more dreary than Emily's spirits. Sitting in the room with the mural of the sunswept garden, she tried to keep her sister involved in a meandering conversation with Valeria, so Miriam would stay away from the marquis.

"Why don't we retire?" she asked for what she feared was the tenth time.

"It is early yet," Valeria said, waving a bright gold fan in front of her hair that glittered with gems.

Emily smiled but took her sister's hands. "Why don't you come up to my bedchamber with me? We can talk."

"We can talk here." Miriam's eyes glowed as brilliantly as Valeria's jewels. "Besides, you will just badger me about that silly notebook."

"What silly notebook?" Valeria asked.

Miriam grimaced. "You know how Emily likes to write stuff down. She misplaced her book."

"A journal?"

Emily nodded, not willing to speak an out-and-outer.

"Am I in it?" Valeria smiled. "Of course, I must be. We do so much together." Jabbing Miriam with her elbow, she whispered just loud enough so Emily could hear, "Do you think Lord Wentworth had someone grab it?"

"Valeria!"

Her friend laughed. "Do not look so shocked, Emily. I hear the cant on the streets, too."

"But to suggest our host would—"

"Be interested in what you write?" Valeria's brows rose toward her bright hair. "I believe he is interested in everything you do or say or even write." She pointed her fan across the room. "Look! Here he comes now. Why don't you ask him if one of his staff has found it?"

"That is not necessary. I—"

"Lord Wentworth!" Again, Valeria interrupted. She waved her fan at him with all the subtlety, in Emily's opinion, of a cyprian.

He crossed the room, a flash of lightning glistening off his shoe buckles. "When I see this fair gathering, I wonder why the gentlemen have made themselves absent."

"You have been too generous," Valeria replied with a sniff, "with your servings of brandy. They seem to prefer its company to ours tonight."

"Nick-ninnies, the lot of them."

"True. Lord Wentworth, Emily was wondering if—"

"It is nothing," Emily hurried to say.

Valeria argued, "It *is* something. Emily brought a small book with her that seems to be missing."

Damon's eyes lost all hint of humor. "Are you suggesting someone in my house has purloined her book?"

Standing, Emily said, "Of course not. I misplaced it. Valeria, do not make such a to-do about this. I am sure I shall find it before I leave for home."

"If not," Damon said, "I shall arrange with Homsby to have it replaced."

Valeria rose and tapped him on the arm with her fan.

"Unlikely, for I doubt if Mr. Homsby would be interested in publishing Emily's journal."

"Journal?" He laughed. "No wonder you are so anxious to find it."

Miriam propped her elbow on her knee and rested her chin on her hand. "I don't know why you are in such a tizzy. The only ones who could read it are Papa and André. Neither of them would be interested."

"Only your father or de la Cour can read it?" A smile curled along his lips. "Are you saying it is in French?"

Valeria slipped her arm through Miriam's and brought her to her feet. "I do believe there was a bit of cake left from last night's supper. I just must have one more bite."

"Miriam," Emily implored, "stay and talk with us."

"I promised Valeria I would go with her," Miriam mumbled before she rushed away.

Chuckling, Damon said, "She has lost every intention of hiding her dislike for me. But, at least, you must own she is honest." His smile became predatory. "Will you be as honest when you enlighten me about this journal you keep in French?"

Emily wanted to groan aloud. "Why are you making so much of something so unimportant? You know I speak French. Heavens above, I read the marquis's poetry in French at Valeria's party. I can practice speaking with Papa, but the only way I can stay proficient in reading and writing it is to do so. I have been keeping these little notebooks for years."

"You are constantly a surprise, Emily," he said. "The more I come to know you, the more I suspect there is to know."

"I am not that complicated." She had to change the course of this conversation. "Oh, there is Papa. I must speak to him. Excuse me, Damon."

He caught her hand, but his gaze held her as surely. "I look forward to our walk in the garden. The moon should have set soon after midnight. Then we will be able to see the stars in the water garden's pool.''

"That is so late.''

"I would say it is about the perfect time. Meet me then, Emily.''

She was saved from having to reply when Papa called. Giving Damon a smile he could translate in any way he wanted, she hurried to where Papa was tapping his foot impatiently.

He wore a frown. When she asked him what was wrong, he answered, "I am bored beyond death, *ma chérie.* I had not guessed Wentworth would be such a puritan that he would not set up a single table for cards.''

"Surely you can find other things to do.''

"Such as?'' he asked.

"I don't know!'' Her eyes filled with hot tears as she wondered how he could be so selfish that he remained oblivious to the impending disaster if Miriam shared more than a flirtation with the *faux* marquis.

"Emily, that is no way to speak to your father.''

"Then I shall not speak with you.'' She saw his astonishment as she walked away from him for the first time in memory. She began to fear there was no haven anywhere for her bruised heart, save in the arms of the very man whose touch could betray it and her.

When Emily climbed the stairs nearest to her bedchamber, she had not expected to see André sitting by himself on a moon-lit balcony overlooking the front door. She noted the half-empty bottle of brandy by his side. If he had been drinking it alone, he could be altogethery by now.

He rose as she turned toward her door. "Good evening, Mademoiselle Talcott." He motioned to a chair next to his. "Do sit with me."

"It is late, and I told Damon—"

"Our host shall wait for his *rendez-vous* with you."

She flushed. "Sir, I don't know how things are done in France, but—"

"You know damn well how things are done in France."

"You are foxed! I bid you good evening."

He stepped in front of her and put his hand on the wall to keep her from slipping past him. His brown eyes pierced her as he said, "Not yet, Mademoiselle Talcott. It is time for the truth."

"Truth, *mon seigneur*?"

A sly smile settled on his lips as he sat and gestured for her to do the same. "I must again comment on your charming accent. I would guess it to be from what was once French Canada. But how can that be, I ask myself? How would a lovely Englishwoman come to be there?"

"My family's shipping line has sailed the Atlantic for several generations."

"Generations, exactly." He laughed as he grasped her hand. Although she tried to pull away, he tugged her down into the chair beside his. He ran his finger along her wrist, leaving disgust in its wake. "Once I began to pose questions to myself, mademoiselle, I found they led to many more."

"You are drunk!"

He kept her in her chair when she tried to rise, warning he was as strong as Damon. "Am I? Or is there, as it is said, *vérité dans le vin*? Truth within the wine, although I need not translate for you."

"You are babbling." Again she tried to stand.

His hand clamped hers to the arm of the chair. "You are trying to evade me, but I have seen the truth. Only a *fou* would not note your unique coloring, your raven-black hair and the warm, rich shade of your skin, and not ask other questions." When her fingers clenched by her side, he laughed. "However, being a gentleman, I would not ask you before your *bien-aimé*. I suspect you do not want Wentworth to know the truth."

"We all have things we wish to keep to ourselves."

"Once more, the truth. But you do not try to hide one thing." He smiled as he poured more brandy. Taking a deep drink, he said, "You do not wish to see me with your sister."

"That is true."

"Why?"

"I owe you no explanation." She shook off his hand and stood. "I bid you good evening, sir."

"Could it be," he asked as she walked past him, "that you do not believe me to be Marquis de la Cour?"

"What?" She widened her eyes as if shocked. "You aren't Marquis de la Cour? But Miriam believes—"

"You are wasting your protestations of innocence on the wrong man, mademoiselle. You know I cannot be Marquis de la Cour because . . ." He reached under his chair and drew out her missing notebook. "Because you are."

She gasped. "That is mine!"

"Exactly." He rose, holding out the notebook. "I am glad you are not denying it, Mademoiselle Talcott. I had my suspicions, but they were confirmed when I found your work."

She took the notebook. "Where did you get this? It was among my personal things."

"So it was." With the easy smile that had deceived her sister, he asked, "How have you kept the truth from Miriam?"

"How have *you?*" she returned.

"I have learned most people see only what they wish."

Emily swallowed roughly. "What I wish is no more of this conversation. Good evening."

To her back, he called, "If you denounce me, you damn yourself."

She turned. "You aren't going to tell anyone?"

"Why should I?" He lifted the bottle and splashed more brandy into his glass. "I like this *vie douce* I am living. I have newspapers eager for my comments and beautiful women swooning at my feet. Every door in London will open to me, and I am sure I would be granted an audience with the Prince Regent himself, if I wished." His smile vanished as he closed the distance between them. "And you shall continue to write your poems *d'amour,* so I might continue to enjoy this life."

"Just leave Miriam alone." She swallowed the tears burning in the back of her throat. "I will do what you want, if you will leave her alone."

"You shall do as I wish, and *I* shall do as I wish." He tilted the glass in a sardonic toast to her.

"If you do not leave her alone, I shall—"

"What? I need speak only one word in the right ear, and you and your family will be ruined. No amount of gold can buy back your sister's reputation."

She almost laughed aloud. If there had been any amount of gold, she would not have embarked on this path to begin with. Blast her father's love of gambling and her own lack of sense that had led her to this bumble-bath! Even if Papa agreed to stop gambling forever, she knew he owed money to Lord Lichton and to Damon. Damon! Would he help her?

When the fake marquis laughed in victory, Emily backed away from the balcony. First she must hide the book, making certain no one else could find it. Then she would go to Damon. She must share the truth with the only person she could trust. She prayed it was not too late to save her sister now that it was too late to save herself.

Moonlight splashed across the stairs as Emily descended to the first floor where she was to meet Damon. She could imagine ladies of long ago with their taffeta trains stroking each step. So much history this house had seen.

The foyer was empty, but Emily heard voices from the sitting room. Men's voices. Mayhap Damon would be there.

She heard laughter and the marquis's nasal accent. Blast it! She must be careful.

Deep voices must have covered the sound of her footsteps, for no one looked in her direction as she came to
the wide doorway. Emily's greeting vanished, unspoken,
as horror claimed her once more.

A small table was set in the center of the room. With
lamps surrounding it, the glow of moonlight had been
banished. A bottle stood in the middle of the table, and
a half dozen men sat around it. The shuffling of cards was
an undertone to the conversation. A single man sat alone
in a corner, holding a book close to his face. Her first
hope that it was Damon died when he lowered the book,
and she saw it was Graham Simpkins. Then where was
Damon?

The scene blistered through the hot tears filling her
eyes. Damon had given her his pledge he would not play
cards with her father during their visit here. Yet he sat
right in front of her at the table and laughed at something
Papa said. She heard the clink of coins.

Stepping back into the shadows, she pressed against the
wall and silenced her sob of betrayal. What a gawney she
had been to heed Demon Wentworth's pretty tales.

He cared as little for the truth as the marquis did. He
had broken his vow to her. Had he lied to her about his
love of gardening? Had that been only his way to lure her
into his seduction? She closed her eyes as she imagined
how easily he had persuaded her to offer him her lips. A
quiver rushed along her. She had been willing to give him
even more tonight.

To sell her very soul to the devil.

She ran back to the stairs. The echo of laughter chased
her, taunting her with too many shattered promises and
too many lies. She faltered as she touched the thickly
carved newel post and looked toward the window that
would reveal the garden which was awash with starlight.

No! She would not trust him again. Damon Wentworth
had proven he deserved his nickname, for only a demon's
spawn would entice her into believing his lies even as he

planned to break her heart. She would not give him the chance to hurt her again. Without another backward glance, she rushed up the stairs to collect her sister and Kilmartin. They would be on their way back to London before the next hour was rung by the tall-case clock on the landing.

Chapter Eighteen

Emily stared at her bedchamber wall. Hearing Kilmartin bustling in the dressing room, she wrapped her arms around her drawn-up knees. More than a fortnight had passed since she and Miriam had fled Wentworth Hall. Papa had returned to Town the day after them, saying little but that he had lost badly. Although she was curious about how Damon had reacted to her departure, Emily never asked. She knew she had been wrong to leave Wentworth Hall without an explanation, but Damon should have needed none.

She buried her face against her arms. The void in her life loomed large. So frequently, she had found herself thinking of an amusing story she would like to share with him. Then she realized she might never share anything with him but brown talk. Speaking of the weather and the latest prattle of the Polite World would be a cruel reminder of the hours they had spent discussing their love for books and gardening.

Her fingers froze as she set her brush onto the table. She would be welcome at a *conversazione* at Sir Joseph

Banks's house, but she must deny herself that pleasure. Going there, being among Damon's colleagues, and being ignored by him would be more than she could bear.

Emily rushed down the stairs at an unladylike pace and into her garden. Yet, even here she could find no peace. Every corner of the tiny space held the memory of Damon's laugh and his eyes glowing with delight as he admired her roses and her.

"Miss Emily, a gentleman calling for you," Johnson announced from the doorway.

"Lord Wentworth?" she asked, turning on the bench.

"A *gentleman*, Miss Emily."

She swallowed her fury at the butler's insult. No reason to suffer angry whims when Johnson was repeating only what every gabble-grinder in Town had.

"I shall be with him in a moment, Johnson," she said quietly. "Please have him wait in the parlor."

He scurried away, and, with a sigh, she set herself on her feet. Shutting herself off from life would solve nothing. When she entered the foyer, an unwelcome sight awaited her.

"Good day, Lord Lichton," she said, hoping distaste did not fill her words.

"Good day, Miss Talcott." He kept his hat away from Johnson who was trying to take it.

The butler backed away when Emily motioned for him to leave.

She was curious why the earl had refused Johnson's invitation to wait in the parlor, but she asked, "May I know the reason for your call, my lord?"

"You should know by this time, Miss Talcott." He reached beneath his gray coat and removed a small wallet. Taking out a slip of paper, he handed it to her.

Despair clogged her throat when she read Papa's meticulous handwriting. *Owed to Lord Lichton, £300.* Beneath it was his signature and last night's date. Three hundred pounds! This would impoverish them.

"I do not have this much money in the house," she said.

"I shall wait."

"Here? Now?" she choked.

"Charles owes me the money. I need it to pay obligations of my own."

"I shall have the money sent to your house, my lord."

For a moment, she thought he would refuse, but he nodded. "Very well. I shall expect it by day's end."

Emily blinked as the door closed loudly behind the earl. Looking down at the slip of paper, she crumpled it into a ball. She had been a cabbage-head. No matter how she had tried to save her family, her father's *affaire d'amour* with the card table had defeated her. She had tried her best, but it was not good enough. Everything had exploded in her face. The false marquis had arranged with Homsby to take a share of her money. Miriam was throwing her heart away on a man who was bamboozling her. Papa had not altered his ways.

And Damon had betrayed her heart.

She bit her lip as she fought not to release the sob aching in her chest. In her memory's ear, she could hear Damon chastening her for thinking of her family's happiness before her own. He had called her a fool, and she was, for she had lost every bit of happiness.

No longer. She climbed the stairs and knocked on her father's door.

"Emily!" he gasped as he opened the door. He was wearing his dressing gown. With a smile, he motioned for her to sit.

She shook her head. "Papa, I must speak to you of a desperate matter."

"Desperate?"

She held out Lord Lichton's note. Papa's smile disappeared.

"Papa, I cannot pay your debts any longer."

He shoved the note into the pocket of his robe. "Do not worry your head. I shall even my debts to Lichton."

"But there is no money."

"I know."

Emily stared at him. "You know? I thought—"

"That you had cloaked the truth from your father?" He put his hand on the black marble mantel. "I wanted you to hide the truth, Emily, for I never wanted to face the fact that, without your stepmother, I could not manage the family's business. It has been easier to play the gamester, so much easier that I agreed to go to Wentworth Hall even though I feared for you at the hands of its lord." He sighed. "I took that risk, because I dared to believe Dame Fortune would turn my way at the card tables there."

"You need have no concerns about Lord Wentworth and me," she said coolly, even though the words pierced her like a dagger. "I can take care of myself."

"That I know." Turning, he picked up a book from a table. "Did you think I had no idea of the truth?"

"The truth?"

"Of your success as an author."

Emily stared at him in disbelief. "How . . . ?"

"The turn of a phrase betrayed you." He smiled. "How proud your mother would have been of you, *ma chérie!*"

Tears blinded her. "I knew of no other way to—"

"To pay for your father's weakness at the card table." He held out the book to her.

She accepted it, discovering it was the first she had published. Holding it close to her chest, she bit her bottom lip to keep it from trembling.

"Ma chérie," he said, "you are so like your mother. Beautiful and loving and as headstrong as a bear."

Emily whispered, "But if you knew the truth, how can you watch Miriam with that impostor?"

"Between your efforts and mine, Miriam has never been alone with him." He rubbed his chin. "Emily, you should have denounced him from the beginning." When she started to explain, he waved her to silence. "Go tell your sister the truth."

"What if she refuses to listen? She would not let me say a word during our trip back to London." She took his hands. "Papa, come with me. She will heed you."

He shook his head. "I can't."

"But, Papa—"

"No, *ma chérie*. I can't. Not now." Taking the slip of paper out of his pocket, he stared at it. He sat heavily in his chair.

Emily stared at him. Papa was a weak man, who avoided his pain and his family's by living a fast life at the card table. He would not change, no matter how much she wished him to. She put her arms around his shoulders and gave him a hug before leaving to do what she should have done weeks ago.

She rapped on the door to Miriam's bedchamber. When she heard her sister's hurried steps inside, she called, "Miriam?"

"A moment."

When the door opened, she entered her sister's cluttered room. She was astounded, for Miriam usually kept her clothes within her dressing room.

"I was looking for a special dress to wear." Miriam's laugh was strained. "I fear I made quite a mess."

Sitting on one corner of the bed, Emily said, "Papa and I are worried about you. About you and André."

"Do not speak to me of André. You know nothing of him."

"I know that you should have nothing to do with him."

"Because he is French?"

"Certainly not!"

"Because he is a poet?" Miriam scowled. "I find your jealousy uncommonly petty."

"Jealousy?" Standing, Emily laughed. "How could I be jealous of *him*?"

Miriam's eyes became storm dark. "I have seen you

scribbling in your journal, and I know you struggle to write poetry. That André has succeeded in getting his glorious poetry published infuriates you, doesn't it?"

"Of course not. Miriam, you must listen to me."

She clamped her hands over her ears. "I shall listen to no more."

"You must. Damon has told me—"

"And you believe anything he tells you? After he lied to you at Wentworth Hall?" Miriam ran to the door. "Who is the greater fool, Emily? You or me?"

Emily had no chance to retort as Miriam whirled out of the room. Not that it mattered, for Emily had no answer.

Emily pushed open the door to Mr. Homsby's bookshop. When she saw Jaspar, his assistant, dusting the bookshelves, she smiled. This was just what she had hoped for.

"Good morning, Jaspar," she said, smiling.

His eyes lit up as if fireworks had exploded within them. "Miss Talcott!" He sidled up to her, reaching past her to put the dustcloth on the counter.

"Is Mr. Homsby in?"

"He is busy."

She struggled to keep her smile from wavering as she leaned back just enough so the ribbons on her gown brushed his arm. "I am glad."

His eyes widened as he boldly ran his finger along her arm. She tried not to flinch. Everything might depend on this. If Miriam would not heed her and Papa refused to help, Emily knew only one person who might convince her sister to listen to reason. Not Mr. Homsby, for he would gladly lie in church to keep the marquis's books selling.

"Jaspar," she murmured, holding his gaze with hers, "I am in terrible trouble. I am not sure what I shall do." She pulled a handkerchief from her bodice and wiped a feigned tear from her eyes. "I hope I can turn to you."

"Me?" His gaze rose from her bodice to meet hers.

"I would be ever so grateful." She put her fingers over his on her arm. "Ever so grateful."

He gulped, his Adam's apple bobbing wildly. "What can I do, Miss—"

"Emily," she whispered.

He grinned, but she sensed his nervousness. She must be careful not to overmaster him. "What can I do, Emily?"

"I am afraid events have conspired against me." She dabbed her eyes again. "I must speak with my publisher without delay."

"Mr. Homsby would not like that."

"Nor would he like a swarm of solicitors descending on this shop like a plague of locusts. Oh, dear, Jaspar. I know of nothing else I can do. If my silliness has ruined me, I could live with that. But to ruin my dear Mr. Homsby." She gasped, pressing her fingers to her lips. "And you! If he is forced to close, what will you do?"

"Close?" He stepped back and wrung his hands. "I need to warn Mr. Homsby."

She caught his sleeve. "Why worry him? I have no doubts that I can put an end to this without risking this shop, but I must speak with my publisher."

"Miss—Emily—I—"

"Just give me the address." She pulled a slip of paper from her reticule and handed it to him. When he hesitated, she added, "Employment is so hard to find now that the war is over and all the soldiers are home."

Jaspar gulped so loudly she feared Mr. Homsby would hear, but he bent to scribble on the page. Thrusting it at her, he rushed back to his work, clearly wanting to appear industrious if Mr. Homsby had any inkling of the possible trouble ahead.

Emily smiled. All might not be lost, after all. As she closed the door behind her, her smile faltered. She might be able to help her family, but she could not heal her breaking heart. Not alone.

* * *

Hearing church bells ring through Old Park Lane, Emily looked out the carriage window. They were slowing before a house whose number matched the one on the slip of paper in her hand.

The building had a simple façade like the others along the narrow street off Piccadilly. If she had not held the address in her hand, she would have guessed it to be a family residence.

When Simon handed her down, the coachee wore a troubled expression that matched the disquiet bubbling inside her. She said nothing. This task was hers alone.

A small brass plaque by the door had been recently polished, for she could see streaks on it. That slight imperfection in the elegant building with its marble sills and Flemish brickwork gave her the courage to reach for the knocker.

The door opened to reveal a shadowed interior and the dour face of a porter. The man, who wore a sedate coat of blue over gray breeches, bowed his head and motioned for her to enter.

She held out her *carte des visites*. "Please inform—" She hesitated, then said, "The author of Marquis de la Cour's poems wishes to see her publisher."

The man's pristinely gloved hand accepted her card. He glanced from it to her. Still without speaking, he turned to climb the stairs.

Emily tightened her hold on her bag as she looked around the foyer. The parquet floor was nearly hidden beneath the bright red and gold of an Oriental rug connecting a trio of potted ferns. Several doors led from the foyer, but all were closed, their mahogany panels refusing to give a hint to what waited behind them. The space was not stuffy, so she guessed they were not often shut. By the curve of the wrought-iron-and-mahogany banister, a tall-case clock ticked, making the only sound other than her furious heartbeat.

Seeing a glass, she edged toward it. Her recalcitrant locks were slipping from her sedate bun. How she wished, just this once, her hair would stay in a wreath of curls as Miriam's did! Adjusting her bonnet, she pushed the loose strands beneath it. Yellow ribbons crisscrossed her bodice and matched the ruffle at the hem of her skirt. A narrow band of ribbon accented her short, puffed sleeves. She looked her best and knew, with a sigh, that her appearance might be of the least concern when she was calling, uninvited, on the publisher of Marquis de la Cour's poetry.

She turned when she heard footsteps on the stairs. A young man with thinning brown hair came toward her. Holding out her hand, she said, "I am Emily Talcott. I want to thank you—"

The man's soft laugh interrupted her. "I am Finch, the secretary, Miss Talcott. If you will follow me, I would be glad to take you in."

"Thank you." She laced her fingers through the strings of her reticule, wondering how she could be such a blind buzzard.

Emily followed Finch up the stairs and along a long corridor. As on the ground floor, all the doors were closed. He paused before one halfway toward the rear. He opened it and smiled as he motioned for her to enter. Taking a deep breath, she did.

The room was not large. Books lined one wall behind the glass and walnut doors of a massive bookcase. Across from it, a tall window offered a view of the street, but its sounds were muffled amid the thick rafters tracing a geometric pattern in the high ceiling.

Finch crossed the chamber to a leather chair set in the shadows. He bent toward the chair, and she struggled to breathe. She must make every effort to appear her best before her publisher.

A man came to his feet and faced her. When he stepped out of the shadows, the sunshine caught blue fire in his black hair.

"Damon!" she gasped.

Chapter Nineteen

"Emily, this is a pleasure." Damon smiled as he came forward to take her hands. Lifting one to his lips, he chuckled. "Or do you prefer I address you as Marquis de la Cour during this call?"

"You are not surprised!"

"No." He gave her a roguish grin. "But you are."

"How did you know?"

He went to a sideboard and poured two glasses of wine. Offering her one, he said, "Finch, thank you."

The secretary nodded. "Of course, my lord." He left, closing the door behind him.

Too much was now so clear. Damon's secretive smile when he spoke of the poems, his comments about business in town, his ease in Homsby's shop, all the books in his office at Wentworth Hall.

"Is publishing books one of your business projects?" she asked.

"Old Gooseberry Press has become one of my favorites."

"Why that name?"

He chuckled. "You must be astonished. Otherwise, I

suspect your quick wit would give you the answer." Sipping his wine, he smiled. "You saw the tangle of gooseberry bushes at Wentworth Hall."

"And old gooseberry is another name for a devil."

"Very good, Emily."

She smiled, then realized her delight at seeing him again was letting her entice her into forgiving him. Turning away, she fought her longing to beg him to explain why he had broken his promise to her.

Damon led her to a leather settee. "Sit, Emily, before shock sends you toppling onto your face. When you left Wentworth Hall in such a hurry, I was sure you had discovered the small part I have played in the saga of our frog poet."

"That is not why I left." She held the glass tightly, for she did not trust her trembling fingers. "You forgot your vow to me."

"Vow? Not to play cards with your father? I recalled it every minute while you and your family were my guests."

"I saw you and Papa at the card table."

Laughing, he plucked the wineglass from her fingers and caught her hands in his. "Emily, I never broke my pledge to you. I vowed not to play cards with your father. I said nothing about sitting at the card table while he and my other guests played."

She stared at him.

"You never saw cards in my hands, did you?" he asked. "You could not, for I did not touch the flats."

She leaned her forehead against their clasped hands. Joy erupted within her. "I should have listened to my heart that told me you would not betray me."

"Your heart?" he asked softly. "Dare I believe to hope it speaks to you of me often?"

When he tipped her hand over and pressed his mouth to her palm, thoughts of the past disappeared within the enchantment of his touch. He raised his head, and she saw enticing fires in his eyes.

"I was not surprised," he whispered, "when you shared your suspicions with me that our frog poet was an impostor. Even then, I had my suspicions about you."

"But why?"

"I saw you flinch each time the marquis's name was mentioned. Yet I could not doubt your delight in the book your sister brought to you. My curiosity led me to spend more time with you. When I glimpsed the fervor you tried to hide, I found I wanted to learn more of it."

"Even though I wrote drivel?"

He smiled as his arm slipped around her waist. "Do you expect me to disavow my opinions on that?"

"Yet you brought a copy of the last book for a gift." She hesitated, then knew she must speak the truth when she was in his arms. "For whom?"

He laughed. "Frasier has long admired the marquis's work. Do you think the good mayor has changed his mind after meeting our impostor?"

"So you never will like my poetry?"

"I fear you cannot ask so much from me. I would as lief ask something of you."

"What?"

"This." His smile was warm against her mouth as his lips found hers.

Her dreams of being in his arms were eclipsed by this intoxicating ecstasy. As he sprinkled spark-hot kisses across her cheeks, his arm tightened around her, pulling her against the hard breadth of his chest. He was a puzzle she would be delighted to spend a lifetime solving.

Emily stiffened. She was cockle-brained to be bewitched by a love that could not be hers.

Damon frowned. "If you do not wish to kiss me, Emily, you need only say so."

She tried to wish away the tears filling her eyes. "It's just . . ." She could not speak the appalling truth he had not discerned. Instead, she quickly she told him the reason she had come to speak to her publisher. "I fear Miriam will do something foolish. You must come with me to Hanover Square. Once Miriam listens to you, she must own she has been bamblusterated."

"She will give little credence to anything I say," he said with obvious regret, "for she abhors me."

"But she must listen!" she said, startling herself as much as she did him. She gripped Damon's hands. "She must!"

Emily was not pleased to see a familiar carriage in front of her house. As Valeria came down the steps, Damon chuckled.

"She looks like a living fashion-plate," he said, "and has about as much substance."

"Valeria is my friend."

"Really? How odd!"

"We have been bosom-bows for years."

"I own to being amazed, for I daresay I have never heard her speak of anything but her *modiste* and the latest fashions." As the footman opened the door, Damon added, "Doesn't that bore you?"

As Emily stepped from the carriage, she said, "Valeria, do join us for a glass of lemonade."

Valeria shook her head, bouncing her white tulle bonnet. "I came to see Miriam, but she refused to see me." She glanced with curiosity at Damon, but said, "She has never failed to receive me before."

"She is distressed. We had a brangle earlier."

"Is it serious?"

She shuddered. "Miriam refuses to listen to me."

"Speak sense to her before it is too late."

Emily had no chance to ask Valeria what she meant, because Valeria hurried to her carriage. Exchanging a baffled look with Damon, Emily went to the door.

"I stand corrected," he said as she opened it. "Lady Fanning does concern herself with things other than fashion."

She did not answer. Sending Johnson for her sister, Emily invited Damon into the sitting room. She motioned for him to sit, but he remained on his feet as she paced the room from the garden window to the hall door.

"Give the man a chance to delivery the message," Damon said with another low chuckle.

"I am sorry." She realized she was wringing her hands. "I want Miriam to see her folly."

"Folly is the right name for André de la Cour."

"I wish you would not call him that."

"He has given us no other name yet, Emily. If you would offer me some brandy, I would be most grateful to accept."

"I see one thing has not changed. You disdain the ways of the Polite World."

"Why should I when you have offered me some of that blasted brandy every time I have called and I have yet to accept as much as a dram?"

She went to the sideboard. Lifting the top from the brandy, she poured a serving. "Miriam may not come. She took offense with everything I said earlier." She looked up at him as she sat. "Damon, she was so hurt by Mr. Simpkins's attention to Valeria. Now she is determined to prove she cared nothing for him by being seen with the talk of the *ton*. I fear I shall break her heart anew."

He perched on the arm of the chair and brushed his hand against her icy cheek. "Emily, you have come to see how dangerous lies can be. If you wish, I'll tell her the truth."

She shook her head. "No, I shall tell her. It is my duty as her sister."

"Duty." His lips tightened. "You should occasionally think of something else."

"But not today. I—"

When Damon looked past her, she saw Johnson stood in the doorway. He held out a slip of paper. "Miss Miriam asked that you read this before she saw you next."

She thanked him and opened the slip of paper.

Emily, she read,

I can no longer endure your antipathy toward André. He swears he loves me. He knows my heart longs to belong to another, but he accepts that. Is that what love is, Emily? Accepting fault and loving still? André asked me to marry him while we were at Wentworth Hall. I know I shall find no other who wants me as André does. When next we meet, sister, I shall be Marquise de la Cour.

Wish me happiness, Emily. We will call upon our return to Town.

Your loving sister,

"Miriam," she whispered.

Damon swore viciously. "The girl is mad!" He pulled the page from her hand and reread it.

Emily wrapped her arms around herself, wishing she could do the same to her sister. But Miriam was, by this time, far from Hanover Square on her way to marry an impostor. After all her efforts to protect her sister, Miriam was ruining her reputation by eloping with a rogue.

"How long since you last saw her?" Damon asked as he balled the letter and tossed it onto the hearth.

"I last spoke to her about two hours ago." She sighed. "I should have guessed something was afoot when everything she owned was spread about her room. She must have been packing to leave."

"Good!" He strode down the stairs. She followed and paused as he reached for his hat. "They cannot have gotten far in two hours." His broad hands caressed her shoulders as he kissed her swiftly. "I shall stop them."

"I am going with you."

"They must be headed for Scotland. That is the only place they can marry so quickly."

"But to where in Scotland?"

"De la Cour knows the way to Wentworth Hall. I suspect they will head north in that direction. Emily, the trip is not an easy one."

She smiled. "I know, Damon, but Miriam is my sister. I have failed her by not persuading her to see de la Cour's deception. I shall not fail her again."

The small village on the far side of the Scottish border was peaceful in the early-evening twilight. A few houses clung to the side of a tarn that had become ebony with the night. In the distance, a cow lowed, and the rattle of the sheep bells played a vesper.

A carriage slowed as it approached a farm boy driving a gaggle of geese toward the water. A gap-toothed grin lightened his face as he pointed along the road toward a cottage set apart from the others in the shadow of the tiny church. He caught the coin tossed to him.

Damon handed Emily and Kilmartin out in front of the stone cottage with its pair of windows glowing brightly onto the porch that slanted to one side. Emily's knees wobbled beneath her. They had been riding hard since leaving London. When his arm encircled her waist, she was glad for his offer of solace.

"Thank you," she murmured, but pushed herself out of his arms that invited her to linger. "Look! That phaeton cannot belong in this village."

He strode past her and peered into the stylish carriage which was filthy, warning it had traveled far. Coming back, he said, "No one in it."

"Could it be the one André rented?"

"We shall know soon enough. Let's go."

As she hurried up onto the small porch, Emily prayed they had reached the end of their journey in time. They had stopped in other villages along the border with no luck. From the window by the door, a light sprayed into the deepening shadows.

Damon rapped loudly. Wringing her hands, Emily found herself wondering if Johnson had delivered her message to Papa. She did not want Papa to fear for the disappearance of both of his daughters.

The door opened. A bulky woman with a dusty apron peered out. Her broad face was lit with a smile while she shoved strands of black hair back beneath her kerchief.

"Be quiet with ye now," she said in a rich, lowland brogue. "The master's marrying."

"Who?" asked Emily.

"Those who come asking."

Damon cursed under his breath and pushed past the woman. The plump woman called after him, then gasped as Emily followed him into the room, which was crowded with pieces of mismatched furniture around a harpsichord. It was empty.

"They aren't here!" she gasped. "Damon, we have to find them."

He put his hands on her shoulders. "I know. If—"

A shout came from behind a door nearly hidden by the harpsichord. Something crashed and broke. Damon ran, tearing open the door. Emily followed and gasped.

Three people stood by a stone hearth that took up the whole back wall. One man was lying on the floor, clutching his nose, in the midst of shards of a vase. A balding man, who was dressed all in black, was speaking to the man who stood over the downed man.

Emily ignored the men as she cried, "Miriam!"

Miriam whirled. "Emily! What are you doing here?"

"It appears we are not the only ones interested in halting this marriage." Damon chuckled as he folded his arms over his chest.

Emily had not thought she could be any more astonished, but when the man, who had clearly knocked the other down, turned, she stared at Graham Simpkins. And the man on the floor was André!

Mr. Simpkins stamped across the room and stuck his nose almost in Damon's face. "If you think to keep *me* from stopping this travesty, Wentworth, you shall see—"

"No," Damon said, laughing, *"you* shall see, Simpkins, if you put on your barnacles."

"There is no need for those hideous things."

"Put aside your vanity for a moment. It has nearly cost you Miss Talcott's affection."

Emily exchanged an astonished glance with her sister as, mumbling, Mr. Simpkins reached under his coat and drew out a pair of glasses. He set them on the very end of his nose, then pushed them up with irritation.

"Hate the things," he muttered, "but I am as blind as an owl at noon without them."

Miriam gasped, "Then you were not always ignoring me when you walked past me?"

He rushed to her and seized her hands. "My dear, Miss Talcott, I had no idea you were looking at *me* until Valeria told me I was a complete block."

"Valeria!" She sniffed, yanking her hands out of his. *"My* eyes work perfectly well. I see how you stay close to her, hoping for her attention, no doubt."

"Miss Talcott!" He caught her fingers again. "Miriam, if I may, please heed me. I stay near Valeria because I can always be certain who she is."

"I don't understand."

Emily was tempted to echo the words, but Damon's laugh halted her. He walked across the room and jerked André to his feet.

Ignoring the fake marquis's complaints, Damon said, "It is simple. Lady Fanning always wears bright colors to complement her bright hair. Even without his barnacles, Simpkins could not fail to guess who the glorious peacock was among the swans."

"Enough of this!" shouted André, grabbing a handkerchief from the man in the black coat and dabbing at his bloody nose. "You are interrupting our wedding. Come here, Miriam."

Emily put her hand on her sister's arm. "You don't want to marry him, do you?"

Her lips tightened. "If you have come to try to talk me out of marrying André—"

"I came to talk him out of marrying *you,* for it is clear you will not listen to me."

André laughed, but she saw his apprehension as he looked past her to Damon. He quailed, but declared, "I can think of nothing you might say, Mademoiselle Talcott, to convince me not to marry *ma chérie.*"

She opened her bag and poured out a half dozen coins. "Look at the dowry my sister has."

He scowled. "What sort of hoaxing is this? That is no more than a guinea!"

"That and a bit of gully-fluff in my pocket are the only things left of the fortune my father inherited. What he did not spendthrift, he gambled away." Looking at her sister's colorless face, she knew she must not falter. "My father led our family's shipping company into ruin." When the false marquis opened his mouth to protest, she said, "I have spoken the truth. Will you?"

"What truth?" asked Miriam, tears glistening in her eyes.

"Ask this man his name. It cannot be Marquis de la Cour, for that person, if the marquis can be deemed a person, is me."

Mr. Simpkins gasped, "Can this be true?"

Emily nodded. "I started writing the poetry because I needed money to save our family from destitution. To protect the ones I love from their own folly. Too late I have learned they must, as Damon has put it so inelegantly, fry in their own grease. I shall not pay Papa's debts any longer, and, Miriam, if you wish to wed this man, I shall do nothing to halt you now that you know the truth."

"You wrote the poems, Emily?" Miriam choked, her eyes wide. *"You* are Marquis de la Cour?"

Damon said as he slid his arm around Emily's shoulders, "You should be proud of your sister for ignoring the prestige that could have been hers. She withheld the truth, for she feared it would injure you."

Miriam turned to André. "Who are you?" she asked in a broken voice.

He did not answer for the length of two heartbeats, then said, "Andrew Montebank."

"At last you have spoken the truth." Damon laughed. "It would have been better if you had not tried to pretend you were familiar with that café in the Loire, for it does not exist."

"You were baiting me?"

"And you swallowed the hook completely. You were bold to try such a charade."

"Like everyone else," he retorted, "I believed the fabulous Marquis de la Cour to be French. How was I to guess he—*she* would be English?"

"You should have been wiser to stay on a Covent Garden stage than to try for a grander rôle."

Montebank flinched, then bowed his head. "My compliments, my lord, on your obviously excellent source of information."

"I called upon old friends and reminded them of old obligations," he said with the secretive smile he wore each time he hinted at his duties during the war. "In the past fortnight, they have uncovered much about your past, Montebank." Turning to Emily, he gave her a warmer smile. "That task occupied me completely, so I could give no time to other matters, such as discovering why you left Wentworth Hall so abruptly."

She entwined her fingers with his, wishing she could apologize once more for her doubts. He had done more than he had promised to protect her father and her sister and *her* from foolishness.

Damon continued, "There surely must be a law against impersonating another for personal gain."

Montebank blanched. "My lord—"

"For the sake of Miss Talcott's reputation, I suggest you vanish. Otherwise, I shall see that you get the punishment at Tyburn you so rightly deserve."

Montebank looked at Miriam, then fled.

When her sister began to weep, Emily started to go to her. Damon halted her. She glanced at him, and he shook his head, motioning toward Mr. Simpkins.

Emily smiled when Mr. Simpkins gently drew her sister's fingers down from her face. Damon put his arm around Emily's shoulders, and she leaned her head against his shoulder as she had wanted to for so long.

Mr. Simpkins enfolded Miriam's fingers between his palms. "Miss Talcott—Miriam," he said softly, "when Valeria told me that you were in love with Marquis de la Cour, I feared I would never be happy again, for my heart sank into the deepest pit. I rushed to your house to ask you to reconsider."

Miriam blinked back tears, but raised her chin. "Why have you spoken to me so seldom?"

"I own to both vanity and shyness. Miriam, I did not dare to speak with one as lovely and dainty as you. I found it easier to speak with my old friend while I pined to ask you to stand up with me."

As quietly, she said, "I thought you loathed me."

"Believe me, my dearest Miriam, when I tell you that my feelings are quite the opposite." He dropped to one knee and took her hand. "Will you consider becoming my wife? I vow I shall endeavor to make you happy every day of our lives."

"Yes." Miriam's chin rose again as she walked with Mr. Simpkins into the outer room. "But not here. In Town with a big wedding so all our friends might come."

Emily rolled her eyes.

Damon's chuckle warned he had not missed her reaction. "Such a wedding is not cheap."

"I will explain that to her once we are back in Town."

"Are you in a big hurry to return to London? I thought we might stop at Wentworth Hall for a few days."

She smiled. "An excellent idea. That will give us some time to come up with a way to explain all this."

"And time for a honeymoon."

"Yes, and—" She gasped as she saw his broadening smile. "A honeymoon? Whose?"

"Ours."

"You want to marry me?"

He pulled her to him, ignoring the chuckle from the bald-headed man in black who still stood by the hearth. Kissing her fiercely, he murmured, "Tell me you will marry me, Emily."

"No, I cannot," she choked as she pulled away.

"Why not?" He pointed to the man who was watching them with a smile. "We need only to speak our vows before this gentleman. Or do you wish a grand wedding, too?"

"It is not that."

"Then what is it?" All humor left his voice. "I thought you loved me as I love you, Emily."

Pain seared her. "I am not what you think."

"I think you are lovely and loving and spirited and intriguing. I know you write silly poetry as Marquis de la Cour. Is there more I should know before you share my name and my life?"

When Emily looked past him, the bald man closed his book and left them alone. Damon scowled and took a step toward the door to recall the man. She put her hand on his arm. "Do not cause a scene, Damon. No matter what you do, I shall not marry you."

"I deserve, at least, an explanation." When she started to speak, he added, "An honest explanation."

"I will not marry you because I love you."

He laughed gently and took her hands in his. "But marrying is what people in love do. Is that not what you write in your poems? 'Be my love and spend every day with me/Be my love and share every drop of moonlight with me/Be my love and let eternity flow around us, unseen and untouched by time.' " He grimaced. "I hate that poem more than any of the others, which may be why I cannot get it dislodged from my mind." He brushed her lips with his. "Nor can I dislodge you from my mind and heart, but that is because I love you."

"Damon—"

"The truth, Emily. No more hiding behind a frog poet."

"The truth," she whispered. "As you know, my father, like yours, spent time in America. There he married."

"So you have told me. That explains nothing."

She swallowed her tears as he tipped her chin up. She could not avoid his gaze or the truth. "My mother was what they call a *métis,* for her father was French and her mother an Ojibwa. An Indian."

"Yet your father wed her," Damon said softly as his finger slipped along her cheek.

"He loved her with a heart that cared nothing for anything but the love within it."

"As I love you."

She started to smile, then turned away. "Damon, this is not America. I saw what happened when we lived in Boston. What was accepted there reluctantly would be reviled here. You could ruin your family by making me a part of it."

Gently he took her by the shoulders and brought her to face him. "So, because of this, you have given up your life while you oversaw your father's house and launched your sister? Is that the real reason you began writing your drivel about a love you were sure you never would have for yourself?"

"Mayhap."

"My dearest Emily, do you think *I* care about the whims of the Polite World?" His hands encircled her face as he whispered, "I ask you this again, my love. Marry me."

"Damon, I—"

He claimed her lips as he pulled her to him. When he stripped her breath from her with his fevered kiss, her heart's demand to belong to him resounded through her. He lifted his mouth from hers only far enough so he could say, "Marry me. Let us show the *ton* that we care nothing for their opinions."

"Yes," she whispered, unable to fight both him and her heart. "If you want me as your wife, I want to be your wife."

Emily stood by the window and looked at the topiary garden of Wentworth Hall, which was redesigned by the moonlight. As she rested her hands on her chin and propped her elbows on the deep sill, she could see the glories that Damon had spoken of. Someday they would be reality, but, for now, her imagination brought the dream to life.

Warm lips teased the back of her neck, and she was spun into Damon's arms. His cravat had been tossed along with his collar onto the dresser by the high bed in the chamber belonging to the master and mistress of Wentworth Hall.

"Welcome home, Lady Wentworth," he whispered.

"I cannot believe we are married." She clasped her hands behind his nape. "I thought we never could be more than friends."

"We can still be friends. The dearest of friends." He laughed as he bent to tease the pulse at the curve of her throat. "I suppose you think I should have gotten down on one knee to propose as prettily as Simpkins did."

"I never would expect the usual from you."

He drew her to the larger window which overlooked the bridge leading to the village. Flinging it open, he said, "You should know that no one there will be surprised to learn that the viscount has taken a wife."

"No?"

He put a penny in her hand and smiled. "I was not quite honest with you, my love."

"Really? That is no surprise."

He laughed. "I failed to tell you tradition states the viscount's wife should pay the quit rent on the bridge to Wentworth Hall."

Emily gasped, "Even then you wished to marry me?"

"I have wanted you as mine from the moment I first saw you lamenting about your father's condition in your foyer."

With a sigh, she said, "There still is the problem of Papa."

" 'Tis no problem." Cupping her elbows, he drew her into the warmth of his arms. "Emily, I can promise you that your publisher hopes you will pen more of your poems in the years to come. Your royalties can pay your father's gambling debts while my profits shall help with the completion of the topiary garden and restoration here at Wentworth Hall."

Laughing, she asked, "Is *that* why you married me, my lord? So you could share in the profits of my talent?"

"Talent!" He snorted gracelessly. "That drivel? The maidenly dreams of a young woman who has never savored the ecstasy of love?" His smile returned as he whispered, "Dear wife, I believe, after tonight, your poetry is due for a change of style."

AUTHOR'S NOTE

I hope you enjoyed this story. Look for it to continue in *A Convenient Arrangement*, which will be available in early 1999. Lady Valeria Fanning finds herself and her orphaned nephew destitute and dependent upon the new Lord Moorsea, whose estate is in desolate Exmoor. Lord Moorsea, also known as Lorenzo Wolfe of *A Phantom Affair*, is looking for a quiet life so he can write his poetry and study history. When these two meet, sparks must fly as Lorenzo seeks a convenient arrangement to marry off Valeria before he loses his own heart—and his tranquil life—to her.

I enjoy hearing from my readers. Please write me c/o Zebra Books, and a self-addressed stamped envelope is appreciated.

WATCH FOR THESE REGENCY ROMANCES